Another Good Killing

Stephen Puleston

ABOUT THE AUTHOR

Stephen Puleston was born and educated in Anglesey, North Wales. He graduated in theology before training as a lawyer. Speechless is his first novel in the Inspector Marco series

www.stephenpuleston.co.uk
Facebook:stephenpulestoncrimewriter

OTHER NOVELS

Inspector Marco Novels

Prequel Novella– Ebook only
Dead Smart
Novels
Speechless
Another Good Killing
Somebody Told Me

Inspector Drake Mysteries

Prequel Novella– Ebook only
Devil's Kitchen
Novels
Brass in Pocket
Worse than Dead
Against the Tide

ISBN-13: 978-1532813306
ISBN-10: 1532813309

In memory of my mother
Gwenno Puleston

Chapter 1

An Aston Martin DB9 is as good a place to die as any. Maybe better.

I peered into the car and noticed a plastic envelope attached to a lanyard draped over the driver's head. Printed in large font on a sheet of paper inside it were the words GREEDY BASTARD. The man wore a dark suit with a subtle check pattern, was clean-shaven, his hair neatly trimmed. Instinct made me press two fingers into his neck and feel for a pulse but from his limp head and the dark red stain on his white shirt I knew he was dead.

I scanned the inside of the car, the sumptuous seats, and the dashboard with the sat-nav screen flickering above the Bang & Olufsen sound system that looked like something from a *Star Trek* film. I wondered if there was any identification in the man's jacket but rifling through it without latex gloves would be risky. I knew that the crime scene investigators were only minutes away.

Level 7A of the Royal Bell car park had more luxury cars than I had ever seen together in one place. A deep blue Series 6 BMW was parked on one side of the Aston and a Lexus 4x4 filled the wide slot on the other. I stepped back towards Lydia Flint who had her mobile pressed to her ear, dictating the car registration number to central operations. She finished the call and put her mobile back into a pocket.

'I told them it was urgent,' she said.

I nodded.

We had arrived at the car park only minutes after I had taken the call. Two uniformed officers were waiting by the entrance; the older of the two had given me a frightened look as I'd barked instructions for him to secure a perimeter around the building.

Car parks always seem cold unwelcoming places and a chill wind scoured my cheeks as I looked over the centre of Cardiff. Then I heard a bump and the squeal of tyres as a Scientific Support Vehicle reached us, drawing to a halt behind the Aston Martin. In the distance I heard an ambulance approaching too. I stood up and saw Alvine Dix emerge from the passenger side. She was a tall woman with an awkward gait; she walked like a boxer preparing for a fight.

'Might have guessed it would be you, John.'

'Good morning, Alvine.'

'I hope you haven't contaminated the crime scene.'

'I hope so too.'

She gave me a brief intense stare then walked over towards the driver's side door and peered in.

'We'll need to establish a perimeter.'

'I want to see the lanyard around his neck.'

She glared at me. 'It'll take as long as it will take. You know that.'

I sighed. I hated it when Alvine was this obstructive. 'And I need an ID. The least you can do is to take a look in his pockets.'

She gave me an exasperated look and moved back towards the Scientific Support Vehicle. An unfamiliar crime scene investigator was standing nearby holding a white one-piece suit for Alvine.

'This is Tracy Jones,' Alvine said as she struggled into the protective clothing.

I smiled at Tracy. She smiled back; it was a difficult smile to ignore. She had thick wavy hair that brushed the collar of the CSI outfit and eyebrows that crowned two delicate, almost playful, eyes.

'John Marco,' I said, holding out a hand.

'Just be careful Tracy. Looks can be deceiving, Detective Inspector John Marco may look Italian but his father is from Aberdare.'

'Nothing wrong with that. I was brought up in Pontypridd,' Tracy said, glancing first at Alvine and then over at me. I smiled again.

'Let's get to work,' Alvine said, fastening her zip.

After a few minutes, Alvine emerged with a wallet and some personal identification that she dropped into an evidence pouch.

'Once you've got a name, don't touch anything else.' There was more aggression in her voice than she needed.

I snapped on a pair of latex gloves and rifled through a thin black leather wallet. Inside were an AMEX platinum card in the name of Matthew Dolman, two Visa cards in the same name and a neatly folded receipt from the restaurant of the Vale of Glamorgan Racquets Club alongside five twenty-pound notes.

Next to me Lydia's mobile rang and I heard her responding in monosyllabic terms to the caller as she jotted down the details of the car owner.

I replaced everything and secured the evidence pouch.

'A Matthew Dolman owns the car,' Lydia said.

'He's our man. His wallet is full of credit cards.' I turned to Alvine. 'We're going to talk to the staff at the entrance. Let me have a report as soon as.'

She pouted and said nothing. Then I glanced at Tracy who smiled.

We retraced our steps back to the stairwell.

The call to attend the suspicious death had spared Lydia and I all but the first half an hour of a carefully constructed PowerPoint presentation from Detective

Inspector Hobbs on organised crime and the football hooligans of Cardiff. After ten minutes, Hobbs' patronising manner annoyed me. But then Dave Hobbs invariably irritated me and I knew the feeling was mutual. He had small piggy eyes that disappeared to almost nothing when he squinted and he'd given me an angry look when I'd excused myself. He was probably thinking that I was sloping off without good reason and calculating how he could complain about me.

Lydia's recent promotion to sergeant and her natural enthusiasm had resulted in some carefully measured comments expressing her disappointment as we left the meeting along with an inquiry as to whether she would be included in the post-briefing circulars.

She had a lot to learn.

At the bottom of the stairwell, we found a uniformed officer fielding questions from the driver of a Mercedes saloon who was waving his hands and ranting that he was already late for a meeting and that he had nowhere else to park. I stepped over to the driver's window, flashed my warrant card and leant down.

The driver had small black eyes and a large double chin.

'This is a crime scene, sir. You must find another place to park.'

His chin dropped slightly and then he scowled before closing the car window.

Both uniformed officers I had seen earlier were busy directing traffic as the ambulance arrived. It was pointless now having paramedics attend; an undertaker would have sufficed. I walked over to the entrance booth. Lydia was talking to two men in navy uniforms with the words Royal Bell stitched into the fabric of their jackets. Images from the various levels of the car park flickered on the two screens on a desk.

'Who found the body?' I said.

One of the men nodded. 'There was a problem with the CCTV. So I went to investigate.' He hesitated. 'It was terrible seeing him like that.'

I turned to look at both men. 'Do you know Matthew Dolman?'

They exchanged a serious glance. The older man replied. 'He's ... was ... I mean, the managing director of the National Bank of Wales.'

Chapter 2

Before we left the Royal Bell car park and headed for the bank's offices in the commercial centre of the city the attendants had confirmed in deferential tones that both of Dolman's sons worked with him. I raised a hand when they launched into a detailed description of the Ferrari and Range Rover each Dolman brother owned. The wind whipped around the pavements as we strode through the streets, and Lydia had to raise her voice as a bus pulled to a halt behind me, its engine chugging nosily.

'Is Alvine always like that?' she asked.

'Like what?'

'Tetchy. Do you two not get on?'

Lydia managed a puzzled look. I had become accustomed to Alvine so I expected her to be grumpy.

'No, she's always like that. We should get someone to call and speak to his wife.' I replied, changing the subject as I fumbled for my mobile. I called family liaison and explained the situation before confirming Dolman's home address.

The bank was a six-storey building with healthy-looking trees in manicured borders outside two large glass doors. The morning sunshine glistened from the enormous glass windows above. It occupied one side of a small square to the south of the railway tracks that dissected the city. I noticed the name plaques of lawyers and accountants adorning the facades of the other buildings. Ever since more powers and responsibilities had been transferred to the Welsh government from London, companies like the NBW had flourished.

I pushed open the door and marched up to reception, producing my warrant card. 'I'd like to see one of Mr Matthew Dolman's sons please.'

The receptionist had make-up an inch thick that made her look like a Russian doll. Her lips barely moved when she spoke. 'Do you have an appointment?'

There was an implication that unless I could answer in the affirmative there wasn't a hope in hell of my request being successful.

'It's urgent.'

She blinked and picked up the telephone.

A couple of minutes later a glamorous woman with tall heels and a sharp suit glided out of the lift door and gave me a look that said *I am-sure-we-can-sort-this-out.*

'I'm Mary Fox. Troy Dolman's personal assistant. Can I help?'

'Detective Inspector John Marco and Detective Sergeant Lydia Flint. Is Mr Dolman in the building? Only I understand that he and his brother have both arrived at work.'

'Neither Troy nor Rex Dolman are available. They are *very* busy.'

'So am I. I need to see them. Now.'

She sighed, raised her eyebrows. 'I'll see what I can do.'

Fox looked surprised when we followed her towards the lift. On the sixth floor, we stepped out onto a luxury carpet. Fox strode over to a large oak door that had the NBW logo prominently displayed. She punched in a security code and we followed her in. She stopped alongside two large leather chesterfields, opened her mouth before realising that inviting us to sit down was pointless. We walked through an open-plan office set out along a tall glass window, and in an office at the end I could see a group huddled around a table. A man with a shaven head looked up, narrowed his eyes, and frowned. Fox pushed open the door and I heard her say something about the police wanting to speak to them.

Apart from the two men that I guessed were the Dolman brothers, the others gathered their papers and left. The crisp sweet smell of freshly cut roses filled the air. Breaking bad news never got easier no matter how often I had to do it.

'This is Detective Inspector Drake and Sergeant Flint,' Fox said before introducing both Dolman brothers.

She left and pulled the door closed behind her. It thudded smoothly into place.

'What's all this about?' Troy Dolman stared.

I tried to guess his age. A square jaw and broad shoulders made it difficult. He must have been a little over six feet and two or three inches taller than his brother standing next to him who was my height. Troy had a classic film star appearance and I settled on early forties and supposed that his brother was younger. Rex had the build of a man who ate an apple for breakfast, an orange for lunch, and a salad for dinner. In contrast to his brother his face was gaunt, his eyes sunken.

'I have some bad news. I think you might need to sit down.'

Troy's frown deepened, but Rex sat and leant over the desk.

'I'm afraid your father was killed this morning.'

There was a brief silence and both men stared at me. Troy Dolman sat down heavily. 'Jesus Christ. There must be a mistake. I spoke to him last night. He ...'

'How did this happen?' Rex ran a hand across his neatly trimmed hair.

'We had a report of a disturbance at the Royal Bell car park. His body was found in an Aston Martin.'

'I don't believe it,' Troy mumbled.

Rex started chewing on a nail. 'Does our mother

know?'

'Someone's trying to contact her at the moment.'

'She'll be at home. We'll have to go to her.'

'We'll need to speak to all the family in due course and speak to your staff. Did your father have any enemies?'

Both men exchanged a glance.

'A few months ago we had hate mail ...' Rex said.

Troy cut across him. 'He thought it was nothing.'

'Did you keep the letters?'

'The originals were given to the police.'

Lydia turned to Troy. 'What sort of letters were they?'

'A lot of comments about greedy bankers.' He shrugged and waved a hand in the air as though he were swatting a fly. 'How we were the parasites of modern society.'

I thought about the words on the lanyard as I glanced at Lydia who nodded an acknowledgement of their significance now that we knew of the hate mail. I looked over at Troy.

'What happened when you reported this?'

'An officer came to investigate.'

'Who was that?'

'Just a moment.' He reached for his smartphone on the table and scrolled through the numbers. 'Inspector Hobbs.'

Chapter 3

Queen Street police station had been included in every modernisation package I could remember. But the old building had been lost in the reorganisation that followed the creation of the Wales Police Service. We threaded our way through the old corridors and narrow staircases to the second-floor Incident Room. Lydia dropped her bag onto a desk and shrugged off her jacket, hanging it on a stand nearby.

I strode over to my office which felt humid; no fancy air conditioning here, so I heaved open one of the old casement windows. The radiator behind me gurgled so I gave it a gentle tap which did the trick, temporarily at least.

I sat down and noticed Lydia standing by my door. 'There was something odd about the Dolman brothers,' she said, and I noticed that despite the mugginess she had the ability to look fresh at any time of the day. Her long auburn hair had a glossy, newly washed appearance that skirted one side of her face. She had a smooth curve to her upper lip with a perfect little 'v' in the middle. Flicking back her hair exposed all of her face and I could see more clearly her dark intense eyes. It had only been a few months since she had replaced Boyd Pierce after his transfer to a specialist unit in the economic crime department, and like Boyd she had a keenness for doing things correctly. I suddenly realised that I hadn't spent enough time getting to know her.

'They showed little emotion.' I replied as I booted up my computer.

Lydia nodded in agreement.

'Maybe all the family are like that. All upper-class detachment and too repressed to show their real emotions.' I glanced at the clock on the monitor. 'I'll need to speak to

Dave Hobbs. He'll have finished that seminar by now.'

'I'll dig around into Matthew Dolman and the National Bank of Wales.' She turned and left.

The next few hours were spent in a blur of activity. I briefed a team of uniformed officers to get the preliminary work undertaken near the Royal Bell car park. They had to interview anybody who might have seen anything, suspicious or otherwise, that morning. There were offices to visit and staff names to collect. And Lydia built a database of all the CCTV cameras in the middle of Cardiff.

The office manager got exasperated when I told her we needed a board in the Incident Room within an hour but she was as good as her word when two civilians hauled one in, sweating and cursing as they manhandled it through the doors.

The first few hours after a murder are always crucial to any inquiry. But Alvine Dix in forensics seemed oblivious to the demands of modern policing priorities. I had taken Lydia with me to witness for herself Alvine's cantankerousness. She had glared at me and even grimaced at Lydia but in truth, my demand for results this quickly was unfair. Alvine had made it quite clear that I would have to wait.

My email inbox was choked with circulars and reminders but I left most of them unread and at the end of the afternoon I headed out to see Superintendent Cornock.

He had one of the better offices, spacious and airy and he had been a fixture at Queen Street for years. I knocked on his office door. There was a muffled shout, which I took as an invitation to enter. In one corner, Cornock drizzled dried food over the surface of an aquarium. It let out a faint humming sound and a trickle of bubbles broke the surface. Every time I visited his office I was convinced he had added a new miniature structure for the amusement of his tropical fish.

'Sit down.' Cornock nodded towards one of the visitor chairs.

Cornock's skin looked ashen, as though his diet was seriously deficient of some important vitamin. He had an old-fashioned short back-and-sides and recently he had substituted his usual white shirt for a discreet powder-blue version. He settled back into his chair and gave me one of his probing looks. 'I've already had ACC James on the telephone warning me in advance that his wife pays for an annual parking permit at the Royal Bell. She works as an accountant in one of the big firms in the city. What can you tell me?'

'Matthew Dolman was killed this morning. I had to leave the seminar run by Dave Hobbs. Shame really, I was looking forward to hearing the latest about the gangs associated with Cardiff City football club.'

Cornock gave me a quizzical look as though he wasn't certain if I was joking.

'Dolman was the managing director of the National Bank of Wales,' I continued.

Cornock nodded. 'Dolman was a very important individual. An establishment figure in 'post devolution' Wales, so just keep that in mind.'

I wanted to say something smart about Dolman's life being no less valuable than a steel worker from Port Talbot or a worker from one of the call centres that had opened in Cardiff. I could see that there would be interference in the investigation and that if I was really unlucky there would be politicians poking their noses into the case too.

'And we broke the news to both his sons – Troy and Rex.'

'How did they react?'

'They were shocked, but also cool. Lydia Flint thinks there's something odd going on.'

'Woman's intuition?'

'She's right, sir. It was all very business-like somehow.'

'What do you expect? They're bankers.'

'Apparently he'd been receiving death threats. Three letters in the past few months, telling him that the recession was all the fault of the bankers, that they were all greedy bastards and that poverty could be eradicated if their bonuses were taxed heavily.'

'And presumably they ignored them.'

I shook my head slowly. 'Far from it. They made a complaint. Apparently Detective Inspector Dave Hobbs went to see them.'

Cornock sat back in his chair and tapped his fingers on a pile of papers on his desk. 'Can you imagine the fallout if we have done nothing about this. You had better send me the details and copies of all the letters. I'll talk to Dave Hobbs.'

'There's more, sir.'

Cornock raised his head and peered over at me.

'There was note clipped to a lanyard left around Dolman's neck. It had "Greedy Bastards" written on it.'

Cornock started turning an expensive silver ballpoint through his fingers. 'Can you imagine the telephone calls I will get tomorrow? There will be politicians and press screaming for information. Tell the family not to talk to anybody until we've worked out a strategy. And I want an embargo on any details about these notes being released.'

'Yes, sir.'

'Have you seen his widow?'

'Were going there now.'

'Bring me up to date first thing in the morning.'

I stood up and turned to leave.

'And how are *things*, John?'

I knew what he meant to ask. He wanted to know if I was still on the wagon. He wanted to know if I could be trusted. 'Only after that incident with your cousin you'll appreciate that I need you to be in control.'

Jeremy Marco was a first cousin who had challenged me about some family business in the middle of my last investigation when things hadn't been going well. It had ended up in an unseemly brawl that Cornock had smoothed over. He had wanted reassurance then that I wasn't back on the booze. And he was after the same reassurance now.

'I haven't touched a drop for years.'

Cornock nodded. 'And how is the family?'

'Fine, thank you, sir.'

I hesitated; we looked each other in the eye. He was my superior officer and one day I would ask about his family. About his daughter that had become a drug addict and a wife who was a recluse. Perhaps Cornock was waiting for me to ask. But I thought the better of it and I gave him a brief nod and left.

Back in the Incident Room Lydia was staring at her monitor.

'The CCTV from the car park has come through, sir. It will take hours. We'll need extra resources.'

I nodded my agreement and then looked at a picture of Matthew Dolman pinned to the middle of the board. 'Where did you get this photograph?'

'A Google search. He's got a really high profile.'

Now I understood Cornock's comments.

'Let's see Mrs Dolman,' I said.

I found the sat-nav in the glove compartment and punched in the postcode for Dolman's home. The screen flickered into life with the quickest route to Penarth, a town that was one of the wealthier suburbs of the city. Twenty minutes later we were driving up Windsor Street, passing the railway station towards the centre of town and then left towards the expensive, detached houses with fantastic views over Cardiff Bay. The Dolman residence had heavy electronic gates. There was an intercom system so Lydia jumped out, spoke briefly into the microphone and we waited until the gates swung open. The wheels of my car made a soft crunching sound as we crossed the fine gravel and parked behind a Range Rover Sport. Next to it was a Range Rover Evoque with a personalised registration plate – 752 BD. In fact, all the cars parked in the enormous driveway had personalised number plates and they all ended in the letter D.

Standing by the back door was Rex Dolman. A family liaison officer I recognised stood alongside him. 'Good evening, sir.'

I nodded. Rex gave me a brief, bony handshake. 'My mother is in the sitting room.'

He led us through the kitchen; it was spotless, no extraneous equipment cluttering the work surfaces. The hallway was long enough to house a tenpin bowling alley and at the end, I heard muffled conversations.

Heavy floor-to-ceiling curtains hung either side of enormous bay windows. From the open fireplace the sweet smell of burning wood filled the room. The barest remnants of a sunset still gave the room a magnificent view over Cardiff Bay. Brenda Dolman didn't get up when her son introduced me. Her face was heavily lined and I could still see the faint streaks of mascara under her eyelids. She clutched a cut-glass tumbler that had a thick piece of sliced lemon floating on top of a clear liquid. I guessed it wasn't lemonade from the faraway look in her eyes. She reached over and found a cigarette in the pack of Camel Blue sitting on the coffee table alongside a heavy glass ashtray.

'This is Charlotte,' Rex Dolman said, turning a hand towards the woman sitting on the sofa opposite his mother. Charlotte had a long sculpted face of perfect proportions, with lips an immaculate glossy red. She had thin well-kept blonde hair drawn back into a ponytail and the most flawless make-up I had ever seen. She uncrossed her legs and stepped over towards me with the grace of a racehorse captured in slow motion.

'Charlotte Parkinson,' she said, giving me a brief smile before returning to the sofa.

At the other end sat Troy Dolman who gave me a curt nod. Rex pointed to the empty sofas. It came as a surprise when he sat down next to Charlotte and she placed a reassuring hand on his knee. I had seen some oddly matched couples in the past and I thought to myself that it takes all kinds.

'Please accept my condolences, Mrs Dolman,' I started.

She looked at me blankly before sipping her drink.

'What time did your husband leave home this morning?'

'The usual time.' Her voice had been sandpapered by too many cigarettes.

'And what time was that?'

'About eight-thirty.'

'Did he tell you where he was going?'

She frowned. 'He was going into work. Like he does every morning.'

I calculated how long the journey to the Royal Bell car park might take: twenty-five minutes, maybe more depending on the traffic.

'The attendant of the car park says he arrived about nine-thirty. Did he go somewhere after leaving home and before arriving at work?'

Brenda Dolman gave a disinterested shrug. 'We live independent lives, Inspector,' she drawled.

I stared over at her. Her husband had been killed that morning and apart from the tell-tale signs of some tears earlier that day she appeared unaffected by his death. Everything about her and her sons made me wary and I could hear Cornock's advice telling me to be careful. 'Did he say whether he was meeting anyone?'

'No.'

'Was he going to the Vale of Glamorgan Racquets Club?'

She let out an impatient sigh. 'Not that I know.'

I glanced over at Rex and Charlotte, sitting, hands threaded together, and then over at Troy, wondering if he had a trophy girlfriend or wife. The whole family felt distant, dysfunctional and I knew that it would be hard work getting anything that might help the inquiry.

Lydia cleared her throat and made her first contribution. 'Do you know of anyone who might want to kill your husband?'

It was a standard question. The sort of thing we always have to ask, never expecting an answer that would identify the killer.

'It must have been something to do with that fucking bank.'

I stared at Mrs Dolman expecting neither the outburst nor the strong language. I sensed Lydia equally taken aback. And I noticed Rex moving uncomfortably and then Troy cleared his throat but before he could say anything I turned to her. 'Where were you this morning?'

'Here of course. All morning.' She leant forward and stubbed out her cigarette.

I hesitated, allowing the silence to fill the enormous gap between their lives and ours. And the fact that everything about them, their lack of eye contact and disinterested body language made me feel they had no interest in finding the killer. Eventually I said, 'I'll need to go through all his personal effects.'

She got up and led us into the hallway and then through to another large room almost as big as my apartment where one wall was lined with books. She was shorter than she appeared and older somehow. A computer with two monitors stood on top of a large glass-topped desk. It had a sterile professional feel. I pondered whether either of Dolman's sons had been sorting through his papers before we arrived. Lydia flicked through the contents of a filing cabinet.

'Everything is in alphabetical order,' she said. 'All neat and tidy.'

The computer sprang into life in seconds. I scanned the contents of Dolman's desktop. It didn't take me long to realise that the important parts of Matthew Dolman's life were in the National Bank of Wales.

'A forensic team will have to look at this computer,' I said.

'And these,' Lydia said, holding up various data sticks.

I switched off the computer and went back to the sitting room where Brenda Dolman was pulling deeply on another cigarette. Smoke tickled my nostrils and awakened all the usual desires, but I knew that I'd already had my five for the day. Smoking any more would break the promise I had made to my mother that I was doing my best to stop.

'I'll need to see his bedroom,' I said.

Brenda Dolman rolled her eyes. 'Follow me.'

At the top of the staircase we turned left down the landing; discreet downlighters and table lamps bathed the light cream carpet, the woodwork looked recently painted and fresh flowers stood in a glass vase on an oak sideboard.

She stopped by a door. 'This is Matthew's bedroom. We've slept apart for some time.' She avoided eye contact and turned her head, reaching a hand to her cheek, brushing away a tear that never came.

Half an hour later Lydia and I returned to the sitting room, no wiser for having sifted through expensive shirts, designer suits and highly polished brogues.

'A forensic team will call to remove the computer,' I said. 'And we may need to interview you again Mrs Dolman. And if you're contacted by the press you should say nothing.'

She gave me another tired look and sat back in her chair. Rex showed us to the back door again and we left through the electronic gates.

'She was a cold-hearted bitch,' Lydia said without a trace of emotion. 'When my boyfriend's father died his mother just cried all the time.'

'Bankers. What do you expect?'

'Some emotion would have been normal.'

'I've never seen so little reaction from a woman who's just lost her husband.'

I started the engine and we left Penarth but the image of Mrs Dolman drawing on her cigarette stayed in my mind. I headed back for the centre of Cardiff. Streetlights shrouded the road a dirty white colour and soon I drew up outside the Queen Street car park. I watched Lydia as she unlocked her Fiesta and then I turned back and headed towards the Bay. Most of the parking spots had been taken which meant a long walk to the entrance of my apartment building. Inside, I threw my keys onto the kitchen worktop, poured a glass of water and then slumped onto the sofa before flicking through the channels. Within five minutes I was fast asleep.

Chapter 4

A thunderstorm woke me with a start, rain hammering against my bedroom window. I stared at the clock; there was another twenty minutes until the alarm would go off. I threw back the duvet and sat on the edge of the bed. A light flickering on the bedside telephone warned me there was a message. I pressed play. My mother's accent sounded more Italian when it played over the loudspeaker. More than half a lifetime living in the valleys of South Wales had not completely eradicated the soft rhythms of her Tuscan accent.

She wanted to meet for lunch today. She made her trip into Cardiff sound a coincidence but an invitation to meet her usually meant she wanted something. I made a mental note to call her back after breakfast. I trundled through into the kitchen, flicking on the Gaggia coffee machine before walking through into the bathroom. My apartment felt small after the Dolman house. The bathroom was tiny, the bedrooms cramped and not even one of their sofas would have fitted inside my sitting room.

After a shower, I got dressed. I gave the dark brown moleskin trousers hanging in the wardrobe a cursory glance before deciding that a visit to the National Bank of Wales justified a suit. Not my best, but the sombre navy one that had recently been dry-cleaned. I found a clean white shirt and a dark tie with discreet blue stripes.

After a hurried breakfast, I stood by the mirror in the hallway and adjusted my tie. I looked like an estate agent or maybe a lawyer, definitely not a banker judging by the expensive clothes I had seen the day before.

As I drove past the old tinplate works along Central Link, passing the Bute East Dock on my left, I kept thinking about the Dolman family. What did they think about ordinary people, those who could not afford to live behind electronic gates or buy new cars that cost three times the average salary? Now they would have the Wales Police Service crawling over their lives, shining an inquisitive light into every hidden corner.

I parked next to Lydia's Ford Fiesta and strode towards the rear entrance of Queen Street before punching in the security code. An antiseptic smell drifted through the stairwell and after I pushed open the door on the second floor the odour of furniture polish hung in the air. Lydia looked over at me.

'Good morning,' I said. 'You're in early.'

'I wanted to make progress with the CCTV footage.'

After booting up my computer I read the post mortem report. There were comments referring to a long thin blade piercing the aorta, making it clear that death would have been instantaneous. The killer struck twice, as though he were making certain. I picked up the telephone handset and dialled the pathologist's number.

'Thanks for the report, Paddy,' I said.

'Interesting case,' he replied. 'The killer stabbed twice. It would have taken a lot of precision to pierce the aorta and the left ventricle cleanly. It suggests that the killer either knew exactly where to strike or he got lucky.'

'What do you mean "lucky"?'

'The only way to guarantee that death would have been more or less instantaneous is to pierce the aorta or heart and then remove the knife or dagger. Or, in this case, probably a stiletto. And I don't mean the heel of a shoe. Otherwise piercing the heart doesn't guarantee a quick death and if somebody had found him it's conceivable that he could have been saved. I haven't seen a knife wound like this for ... well, I can't remember. Did you find the murder weapon?'

'No.'

'You probably won't. Unless he kills again.'

'What do you mean?' My throat contracted a fraction.

'It felt like a good killing. As though the killer knew exactly what to do to make certain Dolman would die.'

'And why does that make you think he will kill again?'

'Just a gut feeling.'

'And how is that supposed to help me?'

'I'm just the pathologist. You're the detective.'

'Thanks a lot, Paddy.'

I reread Paddy's report and then I Googled 'stiletto'. It had been developed in the fifteenth century as a secondary weapon for knights to finish off a stricken or severely wounded opponent. But there hadn't been any signs of physical combat inside the Aston Martin.

Lydia's voice broke my concentration. 'You need to see this, boss.'

I stepped out of my office and walked over to her desk. She had been trawling through the CCTV coverage from the car park.

'There's something odd going on.' She clicked her mouse. 'There are cameras on every floor. Each level has a number and a letter, 1A and 1B and so on to the top. The only reason they have the letters is that both levels with the same number are accessed from the same stairwell.'

'So that makes sixteen levels altogether.'

'That's right. And sixteen cameras. Each camera is supposed to record one complete level.'

'But ...?'

She clicked again. 'There is a separate camera at the entrance where the cars pass the attendant. It was nine thirty-six when Dolman arrived.' The image of his Aston

Martin filled the screen as it slowed to negotiate the entrance. 'We have Dolman on the CCTV camera for every floor until 6B. The coverage for floor 7A and 7B was disrupted at 9.28.'

'So the killer knew he was arriving.'

'Looks that way, sir.'

'We need to establish who was in the car park that morning. You'd better search through all the CCTV coverage and then talk to that attendant again.'

Lydia was already scribbling on her notepad.

'Make a list of every car that came into the car park from seven am. Do we have a list of the people who pay for parking?'

Lydia nodded.

'Then cross-reference their names against the people who parked that morning. I'm going to Dolman's office.'

Smart new office blocks sat alongside buildings saved from demolition by listed building orders. Railway tracks quartered the city, and the Victorian prison dominated an enormous area in the middle, a few hundred metres from one of the biggest shopping malls outside London.

I passed a bored-looking man shivering by a small mobile truck selling various electronic cigarettes and it occurred to me that I might try them; it might even persuade my mother that I was serious about quitting. But it just made me reach for the cigarettes in my pocket. The seller curled up his mouth, giving me a disinterested look and I reached for my lighter and then my mobile. My mother answered after two rings – obviously waiting for my call.

'I'm shopping,' she said, pre-empting my question

about her trip to Cardiff. 'Where can we meet for lunch?'

'I don't know that I'll have time.'

'Just for a sandwich? Half an hour.'

'I'll text you later.'

'I'm looking forward to seeing you.'

A few minutes later, I reached the National Bank of Wales. The receptionist gave me a wary look and picked up the telephone immediately. She pointed to the lift. 'Can you make your way to the sixth floor, Inspector?'

Mary Fox greeted me as the doors slid open. 'Good morning, Inspector. This way.'

Matthew Dolman's corner office overlooked a square with a small garden and a water feature. Rex Dolman was already sitting by a large conference table, Charlotte by his side. Sparkling Waterford crystal glasses sat alongside two bottles of Ty Nant water on a small tray.

'Is your brother going to be joining us?' I asked.

'He's in the middle of an important meeting.'

More important than my inquiry into his father's death?

Another member of staff appeared with a cafetière of fresh coffee. I opened my notebook as Charlotte leant over, asking how I liked my coffee before passing over a china cup and saucer.

'Can I just get clear,' I said, waving a hand rather limply towards Charlotte. 'How are you related to Matthew Dolman?'

'Of course, Inspector,' she said. 'We weren't properly introduced last night.' She passed over a business card. It made her a senior associate at one of the premier law firms in the city.

'Charlotte and I are engaged,' Rex announced as though it were the first time he had shared the information with anybody. 'And she does a lot of work for the bank.'

I glanced at Charlotte who was giving Rex a dewy-eyed look. I turned back to him. 'I need to know exactly what your father was working on.'

'Of course. There were many very sensitive commercial transactions. I've put together this list.' He pushed over an A4 sheet of paper. I scanned the various names and contact details.

'Are there any particular transactions that hadn't been successful?'

'The bank often works for clients where deals don't come to fruition. There can be a variety of reasons for that. Sometimes the customer pulls out; sometimes the customer isn't paying enough. But I doubt that anyone on that list would want to kill my father. Banking is very boring, Inspector.'

I sipped the coffee; it tasted expensive, probably reserved for the sixth-floor staff, and much better than the instant at Queen Street.

'There was one deal a year or so ago,' Rex said, averting his eyes. 'An engineering company we supported at the start of the recession found it difficult to follow our survival strategy so we had to appoint administrators.'

'The owner, a man called Stanway, took it badly. He couldn't come to terms with his business failure.' Charlotte had the sort of polished accent that lawyers must spend hours practising – not a hint of a Cardiff accent or any part of Wales come to that. 'Since then he's been engaged on a long campaign to discredit the bank.'

'What do you mean?'

'He started this website which repeated libellous comments about Matthew. Naturally, the bank had to protect its reputation and after a court order the website was taken down. Then there were letters and articles in the newspaper. And he commenced proceedings against the bank for negligence. Not merely on one occasion but several.'

'I'll need his details,' I said.

'I've highlighted them.' Charlotte pointed to the list.

I looked down at the sheet and noticed the yellow lines surrounding a section of text.

'I'll need to see your father's office, go through his personal effects.'

Before I finished the coffee, I saw Troy Dolman marching across the open-plan office. He opened the door and strode in. He adopted a wide-open stance and put his hands on his hips. 'I didn't want to mention any of this last night in front of my mother but it's about time the Wales Police Service got off its arse and did something about finding the person who was sending those threats to my father. I want to know what you're *doing* about it.'

'We'll be investigating every possible avenue of inquiry.'

'That's just not *good* enough, Inspector.'

'We're waiting for the results of the forensic analysis of the note found in his car. Then we'll compare the results to—'

He raised his voice. 'Sounds like bullshit.'

'A colleague of mine investigated those letters—'

'And what did he do about them?' Troy Dolman stepped towards me.

I should have been concerned that any inactivity by Dave Hobbs might have a detrimental effect on his career but a part of me secretly hoped he had allowed the letters to languish at the bottom of a pile.

'I don't have that information.'

'Unless I get some satisfactory response I shall go straight to the chief constable.' Dolman gave his brother and Charlotte a brief nod and stormed out. I stood up as

Rex hurried to follow his brother. I watched Charlotte picking up her papers before leaving the room. She reached out a hand in one smooth movement. 'I can go through the Stanway file with you if that would be helpful.'

'Thanks.'

Rex Dolman returned with a member of staff that I had seen crying yesterday. 'This is Ann Roberts,' Rex said. 'She worked for my father. She can help you.' And with that Rex turned and left. Ann Roberts had little make-up, flat sensible shoes and even though she couldn't have been thirty, wore the sort of clothes my mother might choose.

Ann threaded her fingers together and placed them on her lap. Her short straight hair made her round face more matronly – she probably knitted and went on walking holidays to Northumberland.

'Did Matthew Dolman have a diary?'

'He kept everything on the computer.' She tipped her head towards the desk.

'Do you know of anyone with a grudge against him?'

'There were the letters.'

'Was he worried about them?'

'Not particularly. He didn't take them seriously.'

'Did you?'

She nodded briefly, fidgeting with a gold watch on her wrist. 'I told him to be careful.'

'Rex and Charlotte have mentioned a Mr Stanway who had a grudge against the bank.'

Ann nodded. Then she glanced over her shoulder. 'This is confidential isn't it? I ... it's just that ...'

'What?'

'It's nothing.'

I leant forward, hoping for eye contact. 'Is it something important?'

She hesitated. 'No, nothing.' She got up. 'I'll find you

his diary.'

She walked over to Dolman's desk and sat down. She stared at the screen; her hands skimmed over the keyboard. I gazed over and saw that she had regained her earlier composure but I still wondered what she wasn't telling me. Seconds later a printer hummed on the cupboard behind me. She strode over and scooped up the various printed sheets that she thrust in my direction. I read the entries. I would need time to cross-reference all the various appointments to Dolman's clients but what struck me was the regular appearance of the Vale of Glamorgan Racquets Club.

'Was Matthew Dolman a regular squash player?' I said.

'Not really. He played "real tennis".'

She must have seen the puzzled look on my face.

'I don't know much about it. It's like tennis and squash but played inside.'

I nodded.

It was lunchtime when I had finished working through all the paperwork Ann kept producing. I waited for two civilians from operational support to collect Dolman's computer and then as I headed for the lift my mobile bleeped with a text from my mother.

Chapter 5

The redevelopment of the old Brewery quarter in the middle of Cardiff had resulted in several Italian coffee shops opening. And my mother had visited each one until she was certain which one offered the best coffee, panini and Parma ham. She gave me a warm smile when I walked over to her table near a window. Hair shorter than I remembered and the occasional silvery streak evidenced a recent trip to the hairdresser. She cupped my face with both hands and kissed me twice.

'You look tired, John.'

'Mamma.' I tried to get an exasperated tone.

'You're not eating enough. You must have a proper lunch.'

I had given up explaining to my mother the pressures of working as a police officer, as she had ignored all my previous attempts. I reached over and picked up the plastic menu card. We exchanged small talk until a waiter appeared by the table.

She ordered a panini with Parma ham, mortadella cheese and rocket. She was particular about her order of Americano – it had to have two shots of espresso and water just off the boil. The waiter gave a knowing nod before looking over at me.

'I'll have the same panini. And a double espresso.'

I replaced the menu in the plastic holder behind the condiment set. I could sense my mother getting ready to say something.

'Have you spoken to Dean recently?'

It was a softening-up question. She knew I didn't have regular my contact with my son.

'It's been a month, maybe six weeks,' I said casually.

She raised her eyebrows.

'How's Dad?' It had the desired effect, however temporary, of distracting her from discussing Dean. My father was working too much as well. He was arriving home late, she barely saw him.

The waiter arrived with our sandwiches.

'Your father and I are thinking about going to the caravan in Tenby over Easter.'

The bread had been lightly toasted, the cheese soft and the ham succulent.

'I want you to bring Dean over for the weekend.' My mother started eating but she kept her eye contact direct. 'We haven't seen him for such a long time.'

'When is Easter?'

'In six weeks' time. It gives you enough time to speak to Jackie and make the arrangements.'

'She's probably booked a holiday.'

'It will be good for you to spend time together. The campsite has just opened a swimming pool.'

I nodded. It had been a year since my parents had purchased a static caravan on one of the sites near Tenby. The decision had been justified by my father's reluctance to take holidays from his ice cream business. My mother's increasingly irate complaints that he needed to have time off or he would be in an early grave had led to various brochures appearing with details of the caravans available.

My mother was eating her way through the panini and I stared over at her, pondering if she had already spoken with Jackie. It had been three years since she moved to Basingstoke after she got married to an accountant. My mother had always liked Jackie; at least she had always said so.

'It might give you an opportunity to spend quality time with each other after what happened at the party.' She dabbed a napkin to her mouth; I noticed a small bead of olive oil on her lips. She stared over at me, waiting for my reaction. I had apologised to my cousin, Jeremy, but the possibility that my behaviour might deteriorate hung over me. I raised my hands in the air. 'You're right. But I'm not going to lose my temper like that in front of Dean again.'

My mother nodded slowly, picking up the remaining half of her sandwich. 'I want you to build a relationship with your son.' There was steeliness in her voice that she quickly tempered. 'It's important for Dean's sake.'

Since Jackie had moved away I had made little effort to keep up contact with my son. Pressure of work and the punishing hours made regular contact awkward or so I convinced myself whenever I felt guilty. I finished my lunch, pushing the plate to one side.

'I'll talk to Jackie.' I managed an exasperated tone that earned me a sharp look. 'What are the dates again?' I said, tapping the calendar on my smartphone.

'It is Easter, John. *Everyone* knows the dates.'

I took her comments just as they were intended – as a reprimand. Then the coffee arrived and I turned my finger around the small espresso cup. My mother emptied a sachet of sugar into her Americano and gave me a smile that said she was pleased to have had her own way.

I peered at the piles of paperwork on my desk. Although I had only spent forty minutes having lunch with my mother, it felt longer. I would call Jackie tonight, I promised myself and then got back to work.

I punched in the words 'bankers' bonuses' and followed a trail of entries about the level of pay in the banking sector. There were learned articles on various websites about the impact that bailing out the banks had had on the finances of various economies. With the financial services sector forming a huge part of the United Kingdom economy there were many disgruntled comments about the pressure from the EU to curb bankers' bonuses. Under a heading Greedy Bankers I read that 2,700 bankers earned an average of £1.6 million in 2013. I hesitated, surprised at the mind-boggling sums involved. Another search told me it was sixty times more than the average salary in the UK. Maybe this newspaper headline had inspired the author of the note hanging around Dolman's neck. There were plenty of other websites and I spent another hour learning all about the Robin Hood tax, named after the outlaw in English folklore that stole from the rich to give to the poor and designed to punish the banks and provide monies for public services. There was even a cheeky video with some famous actors that brought a smile to my face.

I typed the name Matthew Dolman into the search bar on Google just as Lydia appeared in the doorway of my office. 'Do you want a coffee?'

'Thanks.'

I got up, put my hands to the small of my back and stretched. I didn't have the make-up for an office job. Staring at a computer all day was not my idea of policing. Lydia returned with two mugs and plonked one down on my desk

'Any luck with that CCTV?' I said.

'It will take hours.' She slurped her coffee.

'I've done a preliminary search against Matthew Dolman.' I glanced over at my monitor. 'He's got a really high profile in the banking world. He is a fervent believer in the value of the financial services sector to the economy.'

'So he's not going to vote for an independent Wales then?'

I drank some coffee. It was bitter and too strong.

'Interestingly, he supports devolution.'

'There's one particular programme where he appears in a discussion about the banking sector. There was one of those anti-capitalist protesters taking part. Dolman treated him like a piece of dirt, demolished every argument that he had. Made the man look a complete idiot.'

'Are you suggesting …?'

Lydia shrugged.

'Send me the links.'

She left my room and moments later, I clicked onto the video showing Dolman in a studio defending the banking sector. Dolman was wearing a dark navy suit and a pale blue tie, the sort favoured by politicians. Jamie Henson was introduced as a spokesperson from the Wales Against Poverty action group. He looked uncomfortable in his ill-fitting sweater and unkempt beard. A sharp-suited financial journalist completed the line-up; he had a confident swagger, even sitting down. Dolman goaded Henson remorselessly as the discussion developed. The presenter tried to sound neutral but struggled to keep Henson from shouting and when he accused other members of the panel of being banking sympathisers because they didn't agree with him there was an embarrassing silence and averted glances before the programme finished.

I froze the screen and stared at Henson wondering what exactly he hoped to achieve. I turned my attention to Dolman's diary and his papers, thinking vaguely that I had had enough of sitting behind my desk for one day. There were regular appointments at the Racquets Club but no details of who might be his playing partner. I rang Ann Roberts again and she gave me a list of names.

'Alan Turner was one of his regular partners,' she said.

I fumbled through the papers and found the contact

telephone number. A silky voice at the management consultancy he ran told me that Mr Turner was at the Racquets Club. It was time to see for myself what a 'real tennis' court looked like.

'Lydia,' I shouted before hearing her chair moving in the Incident Room. 'Something we need to do.'

Chapter 6

A mile outside Cowbridge a small sign on the entrance of a lane announced the location of the Vale of Glamorgan Racquets Club. I slowed the car and indicated before turning left up the drive lined with silver birch and well-kept shrubbery. The tarmac in the car park looked newly laid and thick white lines marked the edge of each delineated parking space. Lydia was still reading the various sheets of Dolman's diary as I finally parked my Ford Mondeo alongside a gleaming Series 6 BMW.

The main building nearby had grand columns either side of the main entrance door and Georgian windows that looked recently painted. A brass plaque shone by the front door that opened effortlessly.

My brogues clattered on the wooden flooring as I stepped towards a door, slightly ajar, with a sign saying 'members only'. I peered into a large room filled with chesterfield sofas. Down the hallway, I heard voices and we walked down a corridor lined this time with old maps in heavy frames. Beyond a door, that had 'secretary' printed in black letters, a radio played some classical music so I pushed it open, Lydia following close behind me.

A man sitting by a desk gazed at us over the top of reading glasses. 'How can I help?'

I held out my warrant card. 'Detective Inspector Marco and Detective Sergeant Flint. I'm looking for Mr Alan Turner.'

He stared at the card and then me before giving Lydia the same treatment. Then he switched off the radio.

'I'm the club steward Philip Rees. I think Mr Turner is on court. Please come with me.'

He led us through into a corridor lined with windows. It was cooler than the rest of the building and through the glass we could see two men in white shorts and matching tennis shirts: both ignored us.

'This is the spectators' gallery,' Rees said. 'The game is almost finished. I'll leave a message for Mr Turner.'

He left us and we stepped towards the glass. There was a clattering sound as the ball crashed against the roof.

'I thought tennis was what they played at Wimbledon,' Lydia said.

'Apparently that is lawn tennis. Whereas this is the 'game of Kings'. I did a Wikipedia search before leaving Queen Street.'

Lydia nodded. 'Looks a bit like squash.'

'For posh people.'

We watched them for another ten minutes until the players gathered their equipment and left through a doorway at the far end. Behind us there was a board explaining the basic rules of real tennis. I started to read but the complexities soon confused me. One of the men we had seen playing strolled into the gallery, still in his sports clothes, a bead of perspiration on his forehead.

'Inspector Marco, good afternoon. Alan Turner.' He held out a hand. He had a brisk forceful handshake. He had intense brown eyes that clear rimless glasses did nothing to hide. A small paunch strained at the waist of his shorts but otherwise he looked fit and young for a man who must have been in his sixties.

'This is Detective Sergeant Lydia Flint,' I said.

He repeated his handshake and then said abruptly, 'Follow me.'

He led us into a small room lined with more ageing chesterfields. Moments later Rees entered with a jug of water and three glasses on a tray. Turner pointed towards the sofas.

'I understand you knew Matthew Dolman,' I said.

Turner nodded, enthusiastically. 'He was a good friend of mine. His murder is shocking. Awful.'

Turner filled three glasses and took a long swig before sitting down.

'Can you think of anyone who would want to kill him?'

'I know he had received death threats in the past few months. But he had pretty much ignored them.'

He finished half of his glass as Lydia reached for hers.

'You played tennis with him every week,' Lydia said, peering at the printed pages of Dolman's diary.

'We played every Tuesday after work.'

'He's got a diary entry here for Friday lunchtime. It says VRC. And it looks to be every Friday for the past few months.'

Turner managed a brief conspiratorial smile. 'That was Deborah.'

'Is that one of the players?' I said.

Turner snorted. 'You might say that. But it wasn't on the tennis or squash courts here. She was his mistress.'

'Mistress?' Lydia said. 'That's a bit old-fashioned isn't it?'

Lydia was right and it made me realise that in the world of banking and serious money things were different.

'Girlfriend then,' Turner shrugged. 'He saw her most Fridays.'

'Why put down that he was playing tennis?' I said.

'I don't know. Appearances I suppose.'

'But he and his wife lived separate lives anyway.' Lydia raised her voice.

I reached over for the remaining glass of water. 'I understand you worked with him on various transactions.'

Turner managed a long slow drink of water. 'We did

a lot of work together. Are you thinking his death is linked to recent deals?' His tone was slow, measured, quite different from the earlier exchanges.

'What were the recent deals you were working on?' I said.

I could see Turner thinking, calculating what exactly I knew about Dolman's business. Was he thinking he could lie?

'There was a case involving Stanway Engineering that the bank had to put into receivership. But I can't think that anybody involved would want to see Matthew dead.'

'And what exactly do you do Mr Turner?' Lydia asked.

Turner sat back in his chair and crossed one foot over the opposite knee. He drew a finger over his forehead before tugging at his nose. 'I help make things happen.'

'He helps make things happen,' Lydia said, curling up her lip.

Sitting in my office the radiator behind me imitated my stomach after a hot Indian curry. Rattling the thermostat made little difference and it kept on gurgling.

'He was a dinosaur.' Lydia continued as I sat back in my chair.

'At least we know that Matthew Dolman played away from home.'

'I *hate* footballing metaphors.'

Perhaps it was not the best choice of words I decided. I ran my fingers over Turner's business card on which he had written Deborah Bowen's contact details. This time I recognised the name. She was a journalist with the *Western Mail*, the only newspaper that claimed to have an exclusively Welsh viewpoint.

'And did you see the way Turner was calculating his

answers?'

Before I had time to reply, I saw Dave Hobbs standing by the door of my office. He was wearing one of his grey suits. I was convinced that he had several, each reflecting a subtle shade of his greyness. He had one of those light blue shirts that could look inexpensive but probably cost a fortune, and a dark navy tie.

Lydia noticed him too. 'Good evening, Inspector.'

'I'm sure you're in the middle of an important conversation,' Hobbs said.

'Come in, Dave,' I said, trying the casual approach. 'I'm sorry I missed the rest of your seminar. Perhaps you can send me an executive summary. I can work out the rest.'

Hobbs twitched his lips. Then he looked down at Lydia. 'Inspector Marco and I need to have a word.'

'Of course,' she said getting up.

For a short man Dave Hobbs looked a lot taller sitting down. Perhaps he had short legs; I hadn't really noticed. He stuck out his jaw and rolled his head around a couple of times.

'I hear you're investigating the Matthew Dolman murder.'

'We'll have it wrapped up pretty quickly. Did you meet him?'

Hobbs narrowed his eyes and I saw him draw his tongue over his thin lips.

'There was nothing to those death threats.'

'Really?' I tried to sound nonchalant.

'I passed them through the usual channels of course. Forensics drew a blank. And Superintendent Pearson didn't want me to follow it up. He told me that it wasn't an adequate use of police resources.'

Now I knew why Hobbs was sitting in the visitor's

chair in my room. Guessing that I would seize the opportunity to criticise him for some inactivity about the death threats, he had come to gloat. It looked like yet another day whereby Dave Hobbs could seem Teflon-coated and all the shit we faced as police officers would just glide off him.

Behind him, I heard the telephone ring on Lydia's desk.

'Can you send me a full report?' I said through gritted teeth, knowing it was the sort of bureaucratic reply Dave Hobbs would enjoy.

A moment later, I heard Lydia's raised voice. 'Jesus Christ.'

And then her shout. 'You need to see this, sir.'

I kicked back the chair and it banged against the radiator. Hobbs was in front of me as we strode out into the Incident Room and gathered over Lydia.

'Operational support sent me this link to a video on the internet.'

She double-clicked on the link and the words *Bankers – Greedy Bastards* filled the screen. I stared down as the title disappeared and the screen filled with two people who started a rant about the price the bankers had to pay for the pain that society had endured. The voices were disguised; it was even difficult to tell their gender.

'When was this posted?' I said.

'Don't know, boss.'

'We need to find out. Now.'

Hobbs said something quietly under his breath. I looked over at him – he was chewing his lip. 'This changes everything,' he said.

'This is going to create so much crap ...' But before I could continue the mobile in my pocket rang. I recognised Superintendent Cornock's number.

'Have you seen the internet?'

'Yes, sir.'

'Get over here.'

Chapter 7

I tapped the door to Superintendent Cornock's office and deliberately pushed it open without waiting for an invitation. Cornock was fiddling with the power cable of a laptop on the conference table.

'Sit down, John.' He waved a hand to one of the chairs.

Then he clicked the laptop into life and the screen filled with the same image that I had seen moments earlier. We watched in silence the initial announcement that all bankers were greedy bastards and that the reluctance of politicians to put things right meant that something had to be done.

The arguments sounded so plausible. They had all the statistics about the number of people who had lost their jobs because of the banking crisis, the number of people made homeless, the public services cut to meet the cost of the bank bailouts, and the impact the subsequent recession had had on the health service. And everything could be directly blamed on the greed of bankers. Some electronic device had been used to filter the voices of both narrators. I strained to identify whether they were male or female.

'We need to find these people,' Cornock said. 'We have had the press on the telephone already.'

Cornock switched off the laptop images.

'I have made arrangements for you to be briefed by special branch.' He drummed the fingers of his right hand on the table.

'When?'

The superintendent looked at his watch. 'In half an hour.'

The urgency in his voice meant the senior officers of Southern Division of the Wales Police Service were taking this seriously.

'I'll also need to see the full report about the previous death threats that Matthew Dolman received.'

Cornock gave me a dull look. 'There was a full forensics examination of those letters.'

'Was there anything positive?'

'Nothing.'

'How did Matthew Dolman react?'

'At the time he wanted to ignore them. Didn't believe they posed a threat.' Cornock closed the cover of the laptop. 'There will be a press conference sometime tomorrow. Keep me informed, John.'

I pulled the door closed behind me and retraced my steps to my office. Lydia was still at her desk but she gave me a worried look and darted a glance towards my door. My mobile bleeped as a message arrived: a reminder from my mother to call Jackie and, irritated by her interference, I kicked open the door of my room.

Both visitor chairs were occupied.

'Good afternoon, John. Sergeant David Pack and Constable Jo Francis. You're expecting us.'

I out-ranked both of them and their informality rankled.

'You're going to share intelligence about these anti-capitalist groups?'

'We've got a specialised team looking at the video at the moment.' Pack did all the talking. The constable by his side just nodded occasionally.

'I was told you might have some useful intelligence.'

Pack rolled his eyes. 'We know of two groups of agitators in South Wales. We wouldn't have put any of them into the category of being capable of murder.'

'Does one of them include Jamie Henson who appeared on the same television programme as Dolman?'

Pack nodded slowly. 'He is known to us.'

Pack leant over my desk and pushed a folder towards me. 'There are some contact names of known protesters. Others of interest and left-wing nutcases.'

Pack and the constable stood up. 'Thanks for your time, John. Please keep us informed of any developments.'

'And I'm sure you'll do likewise.'

'Of course.'

Pack at least managed a degree of sincerity in his handshake. I watched as they smiled at Lydia before marching out of the Incident Room. Moments later, she stood in the doorway. 'I take it they were special branch.'

I nodded and pushed up the sleeve of my shirt before reading the time – it was almost eight pm. The second full day of the murder inquiry had passed too quickly. 'I didn't think you'd still be here.'

'They arrived just as I was preparing to leave. Did they have anything helpful?'

I nodded towards the folder on my desk. 'Some background on extremists.'

'Do you want me to get started?'

'Tomorrow.'

Lydia's face brightened. We walked down to the car park together. When I was still drinking, an invitation for her to join me in the pub would have been second nature – relaxing after work. But all too soon I'd have drunk enough to blot out work completely. The smell of the spices from the takeaways and restaurants filtered through the air as I walked over to my car. There was cumin and coriander and if I was working a nightshift the noise from the open windows would fill the air with the smell of frying food, all typical of Cardiff city centre.

I pressed the remote but nothing happened. I squeezed a second time, again no response. Cursing that the battery must have died I opened the car manually. It was a short journey to my apartment block and soon enough I was fiddling with the key for my front door. I thought about my mother's message and realised that I really did not want her calling tomorrow. I had to scramble through a drawer for my address book before finding Jackie's landline number. It rang out three times before I heard her voice.

'Hello, John.' She sounded tentative.

'I was wondering ...'

'Yes?'

'My parents have bought a caravan in Tenby. They've arranged to spend a week there at Easter. I was hoping that Dean might come with us.'

I was expecting a liturgy of questions designed to maximise my guilt and her criticism of the frequency of my contact with Dean.

'When is that?' The simplicity of her reply surprised me.

'In six weeks.' I gave her the dates. There was silence at the end of the phone. 'Are you and ...' Then a blank spot hit me when I realised I couldn't remember the name of her husband. 'As a family, I mean, are you going away?'

'We don't have any plans. What do you suggest?'

It made a welcome change to have a telephone conversation that was constructive and helpful. 'I can come and collect Dean and then bring him home after the bank holiday. The campsite has got a new swimming pool apparently,' I added, hoping it would be persuasive enough for her to agree.

'It should be all right. Let me think about it. I'll talk to Dean tomorrow.'

She rang off and I stood in the kitchen thinking that

she didn't sound like the competent no-nonsense Jackie that I was accustomed to. We had split up after one evening when I had arrived home in the early hours after visiting various bars in the city. Unable to stand straight I vomited all over the hallway and then over the bathroom. I didn't believe her at first the following morning but then she showed me the photographs. I had crossed a red line, one that she had drawn in our relationship before and that I had ignored. Later that week she moved out with Dean.

Suddenly I felt hungry and I opened the fridge door and stared in. I knew that the shelves were empty – perhaps I was hoping for some miracle. The remains of a lettuce, a block of extra mature cheese, some tomatoes and a tub of caramelised onion chutney would not make a decent meal. The freezer section had a lasagne and a tub of ice cream. Once I'd reheated the lasagne I scraped it onto a plate and spooned some of the chutney alongside it. The late-night news replayed the video we'd seen earlier today in full. I looked on almost mesmerised as I listened to the alternating monologues from the two individuals again, trying to discern some accent or meaning or clue. What would Mrs Dolman make of this? Either or both of these men — there could have been a woman involved, of course, it was impossible to tell — were probably responsible for the death of her husband. But her reaction had been muted. And then I recalled the almost unreal scene in the house with her sons and Charlotte as though we were talking about some recently deceased distant relative.

The lasagne was cool by the time the news broadcast finished and I switched channels, finding a version of *Top Gear* where they tested an Aston Martin DB9. Jeremy Clarkson sat in the driver's side of the stationary vehicle playing with the satellite navigation dashboard like a teenager with a new toy. By ten-thirty my eyelids ached and I yawned. I left the dirty plate on the coffee table, switched off the television and went to bed.

Chapter 8

I was back in Queen Street before eight the following morning carrying various daily newspapers and a bag with a jumbo sausage roll and a milky coffee. It wasn't healthy eating, but I was starving and looking at the dried-up remains of the lasagne from the night before as I left the flat persuaded me that I needed comfort food. I spread out the papers on my desk and then tore open the bag. I had just taken a mouthful when Lydia appeared at the door. I scanned the headline – 'Terrorists Taunt Police'.

'I thought Italians liked good food and decent coffee.'

'There's a time and place for that. And it's not this morning.'

'Where do you want me to start, boss?'

'Arrest the killer, then torture him, or her, for a confession.'

I ate more of the sausage roll.

'Very funny.'

She was right – we needed to prioritise. And with every move likely to be scrutinised I had to make certain there were no mistakes.

'Did you see the TV news last night?' Lydia said. 'It was wall-to-wall coverage of that YouTube clip.'

I nodded. 'You should read what they're saying about the WPS.' I nodded at the paper in front of me.

'A politician in London wants the Met to be called in.'

'Then it'll be the FBI and god knows what. Let's build a complete picture of Matthew Dolman. I want to know everything about his life. Get started on Stanway and his engineering company. I'll look at the background of the extremists that special branch told us about.'

I finished the last of the coffee, dropped the plastic beaker into the empty sausage roll bag and threw them both into a bin by my feet. I turned on my computer as Lydia returned to the Incident Room. Telephones rang and the hustle and bustle of the city centre police station filtered through the air like damp mist.

I picked up the special branch file on Jamie Henson. Born in Merthyr Tydfil he had excelled at school, winning various scholarships and a place at university in Cardiff. I read that Henson had been 'radicalised' by a Marxist academic and that after graduating he had dropped out, taking menial tasks while spending time with left-wing and anti-capitalist causes. He had founded the Wales Against Poverty group that had a website and a newsletter with photographs of its members campaigning. There was a section reporting a discussion with one of his university tutors that described him as 'very bright'. But committed enough to murder?

I turned to the rest of the individuals in the file. After Henson the report identified Neil Cleaver, a computer science graduate who had met Henson at university, as the most influential group member. His family and background was much like Henson's so they had a lot in common. There were others involved too and I read the profiles of a dozen more people.

I printed off a sheet with the words 'Wales Against Poverty' printed in large bold letters and then stepped out into the Incident Room where I pinned it to the board underneath the photograph of Matthew Dolman. Behind me, I heard the hum of a printer as it came to life. A moment later Lydia stepped over and pinned a sheet with the name Stanway Engineering printed on it to the board. I stood back and stared over at the names.

'It's going to take hours to go through all the papers

on the Stanway file.' Lydia folded her arms and sighed.

I stopped by a row of boxes near Lydia's desk. I lifted the top of each box in turn and saw the files relating to George Stanway. I remembered Charlotte Parkinson's comments and realised that with typical lawyerly understatement there was an enormous amount of work that needed to be done. It was going to be a long day.

Once I was back in my office, I called the *Western Mail* newspaper and got the confirmation I needed that Deborah Bowen was working so I grabbed my coat and left.

'I'm going to see Bowen. Let's meet for lunch.'

'Where?' Lydia asked, a trepidatious tone to her voice.

'Your choice,' I said.

'Crumbs in the Morgan Arcade,' she said, smiling.

I nodded, already thinking about the second of my five-a-day habit.

I buttoned up my jacket against the brisk wind that blew down Queen Street as I walked towards the castle. Halfway along I passed a busker with long hair and a bushy beard who was playing a decent version of the Beatles song 'Hey Jude'. I slowed for a moment and hummed along. I fished my cigarettes out of my pocket and fired my lighter. The smoke filled my lungs and I picked up my pace before I reached the crossroads with High Street and turned left down towards St Mary Street.

It had made a change when the city council limited traffic in the middle of town to buses and taxis. Less congestion made the middle of Cardiff feel cleaner somehow. A few minutes later, I was passing the old Howells shop before reaching the offices of the only daily newspaper published in Wales. The politicians in the Welsh

Assembly in the Bay had been generating a lot of publicity recently about the lack of Welsh-focused news. Apparently, the public didn't know what they did in the Assembly and the politicians blamed the BBC in London for broadcasting news programmes about the health service and the education policies in England but never anything exclusively about Wales. I found the paper's office and I shared the lift to the third floor with a group of young journalists with smart accents and excited voices. The receptionist gave me a disinterested look when I flashed my warrant card and asked for Deborah Bowen. She spoke into a telephone and I heard her ask if Debbie was available.

Behind her was a glass wall that allowed me to watch the journalists tapping away in front of large monitors. Then a young girl with very dark hair and striking black make-up appeared.

'Please follow me.'

I did as I was told and she led me to an office with a tall glass door that she rapped politely with her knuckles. She pushed it open after hearing a muffled sound.

'Detective Inspector Marco,' I said, holding up my warrant card.

Deborah Bowen had deep bags under sad eyes.

'I'm investigating the death of Matthew Dolman.'

She stared down at the chaotic piles of papers on her desk. Two empty coffee mugs stood at one corner alongside a large box of tissues. Her jacket was crumpled in a heap on a small table, her handbag visible underneath.

'Of course,' she said.

'I'm sure you know why I am here.'

She raised her head. She narrowed her puffy eyes. 'You've discovered that Matthew Dolman and I had a regular liaison. And you think I might help with your investigation.' She fiddled with her hands. 'It's just terrible.

Awful. Have you found the killer yet?' She balanced both elbows on the desk and leant over towards me.

'It's far too early in the investigation. What can you tell me about your relationship with Matthew Dolman?'

The telephone rang on her desk and it startled her. Then she moved her arms and some of the papers fell onto the floor; she stopped and drew a hand over her mouth.

'He was a good man. And I loved him and he loved me and this is so very difficult.'

I hesitated. 'In the past few months he had received death threats in the post. Did he mention those?'

'Yes. But …'

'Did he say he was frightened of anybody? Or whether anyone had threatened him?'

She raised her hands in the air in exasperation. Then she blinked away tears.

'Look, I can't do this now.' She stood up. 'I'm going home.'

'I may need to speak to you again.'

She ignored me, shrugging on her coat before grabbing her bag and walking past me out of her office.

At least there had been emotion. What part did Bowen really play in Dolman's life? I scanned the room feeling uncomfortable, knowing that I should leave, but an instinct suggested that I should just shift through her papers. It was mad of course and I dismissed the notion but I knew Bowen could tell me a lot more about the real Matthew Dolman.

Crumbs restaurant occupied a corner slot and condensation ran down the inside of the large window. Lydia sat at a table talking to a young girl who must have taken hours to prepare her hair into the two-layered bun on top of her head. I walked over and sat down.

'What can I get you to eat?' The young girl said to both of us.

I turned my head and scanned the board behind the counter realising that everything was vegetarian. My gaze settled on the aubergine chilli. I heard Lydia ordering a medium salad bowl with her usual selection. I gave the waitress my order and she left.

'How did you get on with Deborah Bowen?'

'She was really cut up. Could hardly speak.'

Lydia nodded, and then frowned.

'I'll need to see her again.'

As we waited Lydia told me about George Stanway and the campaign that he was running against the National Bank of Wales. There had been several newspaper articles that were one-sided, all favouring Stanway's interpretation of the events. Although his first two cases against the bank had fizzled out, the current legal action might get further than a preliminary assessment.

'Stanway is very determined,' Lydia said.

Her salad arrived in a round wooden bowl. I noticed the Opera magazine on the table.

Another girl appeared with my chilli and a glass of water. 'Enjoy,' she said, giving me a brief smile.

'Do you like opera?'

Lydia poked the coleslaw in her bowl with a fork.

'I saw *Nabucco* once in Verona.'

She stopped and looked up at me. 'In the Arena? In Verona?'

'Years ago. Two women sitting behind me got angry when I shouted Bravo instead of Brava.'

'I've always wanted to go the Arena.' Lydia dabbed at the coleslaw again. 'Do you speak Italian?'

My first mouthful of aubergine chilli was surprisingly

meat-like. Perhaps there was more to this vegetarian cooking than I thought.

'A little. My mother's family is from Lucca and she came to live here when she married my father.'

'I love Italy.' She had stopped eating now and gazed at the cover of the magazine. 'I had a boyfriend who was a musician at university and he got me interested. One summer we went to Verona but we couldn't get tickets.'

I realised as she talked how little I knew about her. 'Where did you go to university?'

'Bangor.' She must have seen the surprise on my face. 'I studied Environmental Conservation. I wanted to change the world then.'

'So why join the police?'

'A friend of mine did and my then boyfriend … the musician, dared me one night after we'd argued. He said I could never hack it and that I'd get thrown out within a year.'

'And your boyfriend?'

'The musician? He went to work on the Isle of Wight.'

'And you're still a big opera fan?'

She nodded. 'I've wanted to go to the Arena in Verona for years.'

'I was very young when I went there.' Trying to excuse my lack of enthusiasm for my night at the opera wasn't going to lessen Lydia's envy. I stared at the bowl in front of me. 'Are you a vegetarian?'

'More or less.'

'What does that mean?'

'No red meat. Although I occasionally eat chicken and fish.'

We finished our meal and headed up the arcade to the Hayes and then back to Queen Street. Lydia frowned and stepped away from me as I fired my third cigarette of the day.

'So when are we going to see Deborah Bowen again, boss?'

'We'll call her before the end of the week.'

'She'll probably have a lot to tell us about Matthew Dolman.'

Lydia was right. We weren't getting much help from the Dolman family so far.

She continued. 'I wonder if the family know about Deborah?'

'We'll find out soon enough.' I glanced over at Lydia. She had one of her inscrutable looks. 'We'll need to go and talk to Jamie Henson and his mates before that.'

Lydia nodded her acknowledgement as we reached Queen Street police station.

'I'm going to talk to forensics,' I said as I punched in the security code into the keypad by the entrance. 'When I'm back I want an update on the work the uniformed lads have been doing.'

Chapter 9

The forensics department was crowded into a series of rooms in the basement of Queen Street. There was a vague smell of antiseptic and bleach as I entered and walked through to Alvine's office. But it was empty so I wandered towards the main crime scene laboratory.

Tracy sat on a stool, her left leg draped languidly to one side. She was wearing a navy dress that hung on her slim figure. She gave me a warm smile and then stood up, reaching out her hand. Tracy's skin felt smooth and there were no rings on either hand.

'We weren't properly introduced,' I said. 'Detective Inspector John Marco.'

'Tracy Jones.' Her smile puckered her cheeks.

'How long have you been working with Alvine?'

'Only a couple of weeks. I was based in one of the CSI departments in Swansea before that.'

'How are you enjoying it?'

I heard the sound of movement in the office space outside. There was a moment of opportunity that I did not want Alvine to ruin.

'Just finding my feet. You know how it is, a fresh face in the department. And I've just moved into a new flat.'

I heard Alvine's voice somewhere behind me. No time like the present.

'Perhaps I can tell you all about Alvine and the intricacies of Queen Street sometime?'

She smiled again. 'Thanks.'

I found my mobile. I had just finished entering Tracy's number when the door crashed open and Alvine swept in. She gave me a suspicious look and then stared at my handset. She narrowed her eyes. 'You didn't tell me you were here, Marco?'

'Were you responsible for the tests on the letters that Matthew Dolman had received before his death?'

Alvine nodded. 'Dave Hobbs was in charge of that investigation. They were printed on a standard laser printer using paper easily available in the local supermarket. The only difference was the smell. The letter that was hanging around Matthew Dolman's neck seemed perfumed but there wasn't any chemical trace. I wondered whether there was something in the car or on Dolman's clothes. So I checked with the pathologist but he found nothing.'

'All I could smell in the car was leather.'

But I hadn't opened the plastic envelope with the message from the killer so I had to rely on Alvine. 'Without evidence from forensics there's not much I can do. Any fingerprints in the car?'

'Dolman's and three other sets. Some of them are partials.'

Progress, of sorts.

Alvine continued. 'I'm waiting the results of any match.'

'No sign of a struggle?'

'The inside of the car was spotless.'

'I'll need a full report,' I said, thinking about how Cornock might react. Announcing to the world that afternoon that the Wales Police Service had made progress would be uppermost in his mind. I made to leave.

'What did you make of the news this morning?' Alvine said.

'I saw that video last night. Superintendent Cornock reckons it's anti-capitalist extremists.'

'There must be lots of those around.'

'Anything on the data stick recovered from Dolman's place?'

'Nothing. It was empty.'

I stepped towards the door but Alvine hadn't finished. 'The pathologist's report was interesting. Dolman was killed with a stiletto-type knife. It is quite a feminine weapon. Small, easy to carry and rather elegant.'

'The killer would have needed a lot of force to pierce his breastplate though.'

'Still doesn't rule out a woman.'

As I opened the door, I turned back and looked at Alvine. 'Let me know if you turn up anything else.'

Tracy frowned, avoiding eye contact. I left, taking the stairs back to my office.

Special branch always struck me as an awkward mixture of police officers and spooks. They worked in the ether somehow, gathering intelligence, influencing senior officers and coordinating work with the intelligence services. They never got their hands dirty, apart from making the occasional arrest. I spent the rest of the afternoon reading the file they had left me about the anti-capitalist groups. There were two active in South Wales. I knew about Jamie Henson so now I focused on the second group based in Newport. Paul Youlden was the ringleader and a section about his personality described him as 'aggressive', 'belligerent' with a borderline personality disorder. A career in the army had been cut short by an altercation with an officer. One of the members of his group was a Greg Jones and a summary told me he was a graduate, considered too naive to be dangerous. Jamie Henson's name appeared with alarming frequency amid the spider's web of interconnecting members. I checked against the Police National Computer for the names of the prominent activists and found previous convictions for drug offences and assaults and affray. The reports classified the activists into various groups, some active and others marked 'dangerous' or 'volatile'.

By the middle of the afternoon I heard the door of the Incident Room crash open and then raised voices as officers from operational support came in. I left the reports on my desk and filed through hoping that the preliminary grind of police work had produced some nugget of evidence or a fresh lead.

I stood in front of the board, Dolman's image staring down behind me.

'Let's have an update on your progress.'

It did not take long for me to be disappointed.

It was going to take days to build a complete picture of everyone who was working in the offices near the car park and even longer to get statements from them all. There were offices belonging to lawyers and accountants and financial services companies and call centres. None of the customers of the Royal Bell car park had seen anything unusual that morning. I knew that a long investigation was the last thing that senior management would want.

'Somebody must have seen something,' I said.

Lydia replied on their behalf. 'We need more resources really.'

Resources. It was always about money in the modern world of policing. In any inquiry the bean counters from the finance department would send me memos warning me about my budget and that I had to be careful with the use of *valuable resources*.

I nodded, thinking about the look on Cornock's face if I asked for more manpower.

Once we were finished I got back to my desk and noticed the email from Alvine confirming that the prints found in the car had no match. They probably belonged to the Dolman family. I didn't think a killer would be careless enough to leave fingerprints.

It was early evening when a shout from Lydia reminded me about the press conference so I walked through to the Incident Room and switched on the television.

I turned to Lydia. 'Was there a smell in his car?'

'What do you mean?'

'Alvine Dix is convinced there was perfume on the note on the lanyard but she couldn't find a trace.'

'I didn't smell anything,' she replied, making me feel rather pleased that it confirmed what I remembered.

I sat in a chair next to Lydia's desk and stared at the board – Matthew Dolman's face peered down at us.

'How are you getting on with Stanway?' I said.

'We'll need to go see him.'

I nodded. 'First thing in the morning.' I checked my watch and then adjusted the sound on the television.

We watched as Assistant Chief Constable Neary read the official press release. She had a confident measured tone and even I believed that Dolman's murderer would soon be safely apprehended. The PR department had arranged in advance for Neary to pick out favoured journalists to ask the right questions. She flicked a finger towards one of the local hacks and gave him a brief nod commending the intelligence of his question. She gave him an equally intelligent reply before moving on to journalists from the London broadsheets.

Cornock sounded dynamic as he fielded questions about the video, by then seen in over forty countries.

'Have the participants claimed responsibility for killing Matthew Dolman?' A voice asked.

Cornock said. 'We have had no contact from the group that made this video.'

'Or it could all be just a massive publicity stunt,' I

said.

Lydia ignored me.

'Where will the investigation go from here?' It was a woman's voice.

We listened as ACC Neary made another diplomatic reply. The press conference ended as they always do with the press dissatisfied but the senior officers of the WPS pleased that they had managed the event successfully. In the end, it changed nothing and I doubted that Cornock's appeal for witnesses would prove fruitful.

I got back to work knowing that with no forensics and no immediate suspect we had to concentrate on digging into Dolman's life and the National Bank of Wales. Somebody wanted him dead and seeing Stanway the following morning was a good place to start.

Chapter 10

Lydia took the A470 out of Cardiff and indicated for the junction for the Rhondda valleys. In Porth she indicated right and followed the signs for Ynyshir and Ferndale. We passed terraces closely packed together and side streets filled with small cars, lined with dusty pavements. Only one of the many chapels we passed was a place of worship and it had big banners outside advertising the Pentecostal church that had taken it over. The rest had been converted into shops selling second-hand furniture or were lying empty and forgotten.

After stopping at a pedestrian crossing the sat-nav told Lydia to take a left turn. And then a right and after five minutes she pulled in and parked the car near the pavement. 'Stanway lives at number forty-five.' She nodded towards the opposite side of the street. 'I spoke to the sergeant at the local station just in case there was some intelligence. But he knows nothing about him, although his son has been involved in quite a few scrapes.'

We left the car and walked over the road. I pressed the doorbell and a set of chimes rang through the house. A short man with a large barrel chest opened the door.

'George Stanway?' I pushed my warrant card at him. 'I'm Detective Inspector John Marco and this is Detective Sergeant Flint.'

Stanway had a thick growth of stubble and hair cropped close to his scalp. After showing us in, he sat down on one of the ancient chairs and stared at us, almost defying us to sit down. The three-piece suite would have been fashionable thirty years ago and the springs creaked as we sank onto the cushions.

'We are investigating the death of Matthew Dolman.'

Stanway said nothing.

'How well did you know him?'

'How long have you got?'

'Where were you on the morning he was killed?' I tried the direct approach.

'I was probably in bed. I work late, delivering pizzas.' He spat out the last few words.

'The National Bank of Wales has given us a lot of information about your vendetta against Matthew Dolman.'

'And that gives me a motive to murder him?'

'You'd better tell us your side of things.'

'When everything was going well Dolman was all over me. Couldn't do enough. I had weekends in London with other businessmen that used the bank including that Malcolm Frost who killed himself.'

'Who?'

'His company was in the running for some big government contract but he lost out and the business went under. At the time Dolman took us to all the best restaurants – the bank paid for everything. Or should I say – we did.'

'So what happened?'

'I lost everything because of Dolman. It was after one contract went sour. I missed one regular instalment on my business loans. Then the bank sent in consultants that I had to pay for to make a complete assessment of my business. That is really what started things off. After that they reduced the overdraft facility, wanted me to make huge increased payments on the bank loans. Until everything went tits-up.'

Stanway straightened his sitting position and then leant over towards me.

'The bank called in the receivers. Initially that slimeball said it was just to get the company through a difficult period. But he had it all mapped out. One of his other customers, obviously a better one than me, had been set up to buy the business. They bought it from the bank at a knockdown price and surprise, surprise, the bank provided finance for the new business. I can never prove it but I am convinced that Dolman got a massive backhander for getting everything organised. How do you think he affords that Aston Martin and the house in Penarth that looks like something out of Las Vegas. I hate all these fucking bankers and Dolman is top of the list.'

'The bank says you refused to listen to their advice.'

'That's bullshit too. They wanted me to do things that were unsuitable. Even the management consultants I had to pay for thought some of the suggestions they'd made were crazy. There is even talk of them floating the new company on the stock market. And you can guess who will benefit. It wouldn't surprise me if Dolman had a deal to own some of the shares.'

I looked around the lounge. Although it was clean, the furniture was old and tatty. A faded print hung above an ancient television. 'Is it you and your wife who live here?'

'We rent this place. My wife works part-time in the council offices down in Ponty.'

Lydia made her first contribution. 'We'll need a detailed account of your movements for the hours before Matthew Dolman was killed.'

Stanway shrugged. 'You can talk to my boss in the pizza delivery business. He can tell you I was working late. I didn't get back here until gone one in the morning. I slept until mid-morning. My wife can vouch for that.'

Lydia scribbled down a contact telephone number for Stanway's employers.

'We'll need to speak to your wife,' I said.

Stanway shrugged again. 'Whatever.'

'Do you and your wife have any children?'

'What have they got to do with anything?'

'They must have been affected by what happened to you.'

Stanway moved to the edge of seat. 'So your twisted copper's mind thinks they would kill somebody. You're fucking mad.'

'Don't leave the country without telling us,' I said, getting as much venom into my reply as possible. I thrust one of my business cards towards Stanway, more out of habit than any real expectation he might call me.

The front door slammed shut behind us. We walked back to the car.

'What did you make of him, boss?'

I reached the car and leant on the roof, briefly glancing over the road at Stanway's home. 'He's got a good motive to kill Dolman. But does being bitter and twisted make him capable of murder?'

Lydia nodded. 'Back to Queen Street?'

'I've got a detour first.'

Chapter 11

I could have given Lydia directions to drive north to the top of the Rhondda Fach Valley and then down through Aberdare to the address in Mountain Ash. But I knew that if anybody had seen me drive through Aberdare my mother would have known within minutes and there would have been complaints that I didn't call to see her, didn't want to keep in touch and that I really had to understand that family was important. So we went the wrong way round, back down to Pontypridd and then rejoining the A470. We turned left at Abercynon and I told Lydia to take the minor road that threaded its way through the villages on the valley floor. It was a reminder of my childhood travelling through Ynysboeth and Penrhiwceiber until we reached Mountain Ash.

I directed Lydia down Clarence Street, ignoring the perplexed look on her face. My first serious girlfriend had lived in one of the houses, and I can remember the fumbling of clothes, lips and tongues intertwined and my initial embarrassment at having come too quickly being vanquished by performing a second time. At the end Lydia had to double back to the main road and then down towards the river and the railway tracks until we found the building mentioned in the special branch intelligence report.

Two small motorcycles were parked outside and a bicycle was chained to some railings. She parked next to an old Ford Fiesta. The place looked empty, barren.

'Are you sure we've got the right place?' Lydia asked.

The Corporation Street Working Men's Club was an old building with a flat roof and rotting wooden windows. The letters on a sign outside had faded badly but I could make out the words 'Members Only'. I yanked open the door. The smell of stale beer assaulted my nostrils, awakening old memories best forgotten. Since the smoking ban in pubs and clubs most licensed premises were much cleaner, but these premises were clearly an exception. The carpet in the hallway was threadbare. I heard the sound of a radio and pushed open the glass doors into the bar area.

'We're closed, mate,' a voice said from the far end of the room. 'Are you from the council?'

'WPS.' The man stopped cleaning the tabletops and looked over at me. 'Is Jamie Henson here?'

'He'll be upstairs.' He jerked his head towards the doorway at the far end of the room.

Beyond it was another small hallway and an un-carpeted staircase. At the top there was a strong smell of urine and I noticed the door to a toilet wide open. I pushed open the first door in front of us and stepped into a large room. It felt damp and un-used; heavy dust sheets covered a snooker table. We left and walked down the hallway towards another door.

Inside two men were huddled over computer screens. A single electric fan heater took the edge off the chill in the room. I held up my warrant card. Lydia did the same.

'I'm looking for Jamie Henson,' I said, peering at the two men and trying to recognise the face that I had seen from the programme with Matthew Dolman.

'What do you want?' The older of the two men stood up. I recognised Henson now. In the television documentary he was wearing small dark glasses and a ponytail tied behind his head. Now his hair was loose over his shoulders.

'We are investigating the death of Matthew Dolman.'

Henson folded his arms, glaring at me severely. 'And

you think I had something to do with that?'

I scanned the room. A laser printer sat on one table. The monitors were the old bulky sort and the computers on the floor by the tables buzzed loudly.

'What exactly do you do here?' I said.

'It's none of your business.' Henson stepped towards me.

'You took part in the discussion programme with Matthew Dolman. And he made you look a right prick. That must have annoyed you.'

'Is that a question?'

I moved further into the room around Henson. 'Your website makes it clear how much you loath the bankers.'

'People like you who work for the state can't possibly understand. The bankers lined their pockets, then when they fucked up, the country had to bail them out. But not before thousands of people lost their jobs, their homes and thousands condemned to low-paid employment.'

'So did Matthew Dolman deserve to die?'

The question hung in the air for a moment. I could see that Henson wanted to agree.

'I'll need the names of everyone in your group, and details of all the subscribers to your website.'

The second man stood up abruptly. He was shorter than Henson with a round face and small dark eyes. 'Unless you've got a warrant then *nothing* is leaving this room.'

I paused and then looked over and recognised Neil Cleaver from the mugshots in the special branch file. 'Now, look Neil.' Using his first name had the desired result of catching him off guard. A brief frightened look crossed his face. 'With your previous convictions I would suggest that cooperation would be best.' I tried to make my voice sounded reasonable.

I sat in one of the office chairs, pretending to make myself comfortable. I looked up at Henson. 'Where were you on Monday morning between nine and ten am?'

'Am I under arrest?'

I was sorely tempted. It would mean I could take all the computer equipment back to Queen Street for the attention of Alvine Dix and her team.

'Do you know anything about the YouTube video that was posted online after Dolman's death?'

'Of course I don't. That has nothing to do with Neil or me. We just run a group that wants to bring to the attention of the public the inequalities in our society. Did you know that the United Kingdom is one of the least equal countries in the world? So much wealth is concentrated in the hands of a tiny minority. And the rest of us have to put up with being harassed by the state.'

'Have you seen the video?'

Henson nodded.

'Do you agree with it?'

Henson was clever enough to see my next question. 'I agree with everything they have said about how we need to tax the bankers. But I'd never kill anybody.'

'Do you know who prepared the video?'

'Do you think I would honestly tell you if I knew?'

'It would be the right thing to do.'

'You must be fucking mad if you think I'm going to cooperate with a detective inspector from the Wales Police Service.'

I stood up, shrugged and walked over towards one of the printers. In a large frame hanging on the wall was a poster with the words – *if you tolerate this your children will be next* underneath the image of a man staring into the distance.

'It's from the Spanish Civil War,' Henson said,

looking at the print. 'It is a lesson to us all that we have to stand up for what is right. Draw a line in the sand and stand up to evil in society.'

I picked up a leaflet from the printer. It advertised the date of a public meeting in Pontypridd.

'Maybe I'll come along,' I said, holding the leaflet.

Henson shrugged; Cleaver just looked at me blankly.

Back in the car, I found an evidence pouch and carefully placed the leaflet inside.

'You had no basis to remove that paper as part of the inquiry. That will *never* be admissible evidence, sir,' Lydia said. 'You've acquired it unlawfully.'

I closed the pouch, ignoring what Lydia had said but knowing that she was right; an instinct had made me scoop up the printed sheet. Even if the printer produced the note around Dolman's neck I'd have to find a reason for a search warrant. I started the engine.

'I've never seen that poster before,' Lydia said. 'But I've heard the song.'

'Song?'

'"If You Tolerate This Your Children Will Be Next" was a hit for the Manic Street Preachers a few years ago.'

'Really? I prefer Elvis myself.'

Chapter 12

'I hope it wasn't too inconvenient for you to come here. I couldn't face going to work today.'

Deborah Bowen had called first thing that morning apologising for her rudeness when we first met and suggesting we visit her at home. She was curled up on a sofa in the sitting room of the sprawling old farmhouse in one of the villages in the Vale of Glamorgan outside the city that had well-maintained pavements, prominent speed bumps and a fancy public house.

I stared over at Deborah. The puffiness under her eyes had gone up but she still looked pale.

'My doctor gave me something to sleep last night.'

The same woman who opened the door to us when we arrived came in with a tray and an expensive-looking cafetière with three mugs.

'I know this is difficult but we need to ask you some questions. Any piece of information might help find his killer.'

She blinked.

'Did Matthew mention the death threats he'd received?'

'He laughed them off to start with but then sometimes I could tell he was worried. But there's something I have to show you.'

She reached into the buff folder lying on the table and handed me the plastic envelopes inside.

'These were delivered here when I was at work.'

I stared at the text. The font was the same size as that on the message on the lanyard on Dolman's body and those on the messages sent to the bank. 'When?' I read the first message – *Bankers will pay for their injustices* – and then handed the sheet to Lydia.

'The most recent arrived last week and there was one the week before.'

I knew I was raising my voice. 'Did you report this to the police?' I read the second message, the menace in the words was clear – *Bankers will pay*.

'Matthew didn't want to. He didn't take them seriously.'

Lydia butted in. 'How did Matthew react? Was he worried? Did he take any precautions?'

Deborah gave her a quizzical look.

'Did he have any idea who might be responsible? Jamie Henson, perhaps, who took part in the television debate with him?' I added.

She shook her head. 'I don't think so, he never mentioned Henson by name.'

There was the sound of footsteps on the staircase and then a child's voice. The door opened and a boy walked in. Deborah smiled at him. 'Charlie, I've got to talk to these two important people. You go to the kitchen. Ask your grandmother to make you some breakfast.'

He glanced at Lydia and I and then left. Deborah got up and closed the door behind him. 'He doesn't know how to react. He knows I'm upset.'

'How long had you been having a relationship with Matthew Dolman?'

Deborah poured the coffee and pushed our drinks towards us.

'He was going to leave his wife.' She sat back, curled her fingers around a mug. 'He was wonderful with Charlie.'

'Was he Charlie's father?'

Deborah nodded. 'After Charlie was born he tried to patch it up with his wife. But things never worked out. We drifted along until recently when he made a final decision to leave her.'

'If there were problems in his marriage why didn't he split from his wife sooner?'

'Things had been tough at the bank. The recession had caused them problems. But things were improving.'

Deborah did not seem the sort of person who would have willingly acquiesced in the role of old-fashioned mistress, hidden away.

'Was there anything else going on?'

'Something wasn't right at the bank although he never told me the details. But there was this trust fund that owned some of the shares. I never knew the details ... But his wife controlled the trust.'

Deborah reached for her coffee, avoiding eye contact.

Lydia replaced her mug on the tray and sat on the edge of her chair looking over at Deborah. 'How much time did you spend together?'

'Fridays, I always saw him on a Friday. We might have a take away and watch a film or something.'

Lydia puckered her brow.

'And we had holidays together. He had just bought this flat in Nice on the Riviera. We had two wonderful holidays there. It was as if we were a real family. He was fantastic with Charlie, taking him swimming, teaching him a bit of French.'

I stared over at Deborah. She stopped, swallowed hard, and reached a hand to brush away a tear. 'Did he ever mention any problems at work, other than what you've just told us?'

She pursed her lips, shook her head. 'He didn't mention anything.'

'There was a business called Stanway Engineering. Did he ever mention them?'

She looked blank. 'I've never heard of them.'

After another half an hour it was obvious that Deborah had little further she could add. 'We won't take up any more of your time.'

Deborah got up and walked with us to the front door. 'Inspector. Matthew was a good man. And he loved Charlie.'

'Of course.'

Standing in the doorway her skin looked drawn and she pulled her arms around her body against the cold morning air.

I watched the green fields and well-maintained hedgerows of the Vale as Lydia drove back to the centre of Cardiff. Deborah had responded positively to Lydia's sympathetic tone. It made me realise that she achieved more than I could have done on my own. I recalled a briefing about body language and how important it could be to make a witness feel at ease. My usual approach of asking direct questions and expecting direct replies wasn't always recommended.

'What did you make of Deborah Bowen?' Lydia had stopped by some traffic lights on the outskirts of Cardiff.

'She looked better than when I first saw her.'

Lydia drove off once the lights had turned to green. 'I am surprised that as an intelligent woman with her own career she tolerated such a second-hand relationship with Dolman. She must have loved him very much.'

The simplicity of her remark was striking. Deborah had tolerated a relationship because she loved Dolman and now he was dead. The father of her child would not be around ever again. And I wondered what Dean would think when I wasn't around anymore.

Lydia continued. 'Some people make relationships too complicated. At least he saw his son regularly which is more than a lot of fathers manage.'

I wondered how much she knew of my circumstances. And how little in reality I had seen Dean. 'Have you got any family?'

She glanced at me. She looked rather puzzled as though I should really know if she had any children. We had reached the Culverhouse Cross roundabout and she slowed as she negotiated the junction and the various traffic lights.

'No kids if that's what you mean. And you, boss?'

'Dean lives with his mother in Basingstoke.'

An awkward silence followed. I wanted to add something profound but all I could think of was my mother's last comments about me seeing Dean more often.

'How old is he?' Lydia asked.

'Eight.' I could sense Lydia wanting to ask me how often I saw him. I could feel the reproach in her silence. The imminent Easter weekend would be the opportunity I needed to feel more like a real father. She accelerated away down the slip road into the A4232 link road from the M4 into the city. We sped along towards the Grangetown Link, the short elevated section, before we reached the city itself. Passing the junction with Penarth, I realised that this was the same route that Dolman had taken on the morning of his death. It must have been a journey that he had taken dozens, maybe hundreds of times, and if the killer had been following him, Dolman would have been oblivious to any car trailing behind.

'We'll need to get these letters to forensics as soon as possible,' Lydia said.

I nodded. 'First though let's go and check out Stanway's employer.'

Our progress through the city traffic was painfully slow. Every traffic light seemed to turn red as we approached, every pedestrian crossing had a stream of mothers with buggies and elderly people taking their time to cross the road. Eventually we drew up alongside the pavement near the *Pizza House*. Three small vans were parked further up the road with the takeaway's logo covering every available square inch of the bodywork.

I got out of the car and a thick warm doughy smell filled the air. We walked over towards the main entrance and, stepping inside, the pungency and sweetness of oregano assaulted my nostrils. The telephone rang incessantly and a small girl wearing an apron with the restaurant's name printed in bold red letters jotted down the orders. There was a long counter along one side and at the back I noticed a few tables. This wasn't a place of fine Italian dining. One girl behind the counter was grating mozzarella, another chopping various vegetables. I leant over the counter and flashed my warrant card. 'I need to see your boss.'

She carried on slicing red peppers barely taking her gaze away from the chopping board and then she nodded towards the rear of restaurant. 'Back there. In the office.'

I glanced over at the girls hard at work: it was probably minimum wage contracts, maybe even the zero hour contracts the politicians love to debate. Hot air hit us as we passed the enormous pizza ovens. I rapped my knuckles on the office door. I didn't wait for an invitation, we just barged in.

I was expecting a swarthy Italian-looking man but the woman sitting by the desk had shocking red hair. She drew heavily on a cigarette and didn't seem at all surprised that strangers had appeared in her office.

She squinted at my warrant card but didn't bother with Lydia's.

'Detective Inspector Marco,' I said.

'How can I help?' The voice was thick and gravelly.

Her accent would have been completely at home in the Rhondda valleys.

'We are investigating the murder of Matthew Dolman.'

'Who?'

'It's been all over the newspapers.'

'Don't read the papers, love.'

'And on the television.'

She shrugged.

'One of the people linked to the enquiry is George Stanway. I understand that he works for you.'

'That's right.' She glanced at a board on the wall by her desk. It had names along the top and dates printed down the left-hand side. 'He's not working today.'

'Was George Stanway working on Monday morning, between eight and ten?'

'He normally does the pizzas in the evening. Works late at night. We have somebody else in the morning that does the breakfasts.'

'Well then, tell me, was he working that Sunday evening?'

She stood up and ran a finger across the board from last Sunday along the columns of names. 'He was working all right. He likes doing the Sunday night because it's so busy.'

'When did he finish?'

She turned towards me, a narrow plume of smoke crawling up her face. She dragged on the cigarette. 'Can't say love, between one and two I'd guess. You know how it is if things get busy. I can check from his time logs if you want.'

I glanced at my watch knowing we had wasted enough time. Lydia thrust her card towards the woman. 'Please check your records and give me a ring once you can confirm the time he finished working.' She even gave her a brief smile.

We left the Pizza House and retraced our steps to the car.

'I'll go and see Mrs Stanway,' Lydia said before jumping into the car. I followed and as she pulled out into the traffic, my mobile buzzed into life. I recognised the voice of the receptionist in Queen Street. 'There's some fancy lawyer in reception wanting to see you.'

Chapter 13

Charlotte Parkinson had already organised neat piles of papers on the table in one of the interview rooms near reception before I arrived. She gave me a professional smile and held out a hand. I had no recollection of arranging a time for the meeting although I could recall an understanding that Charlotte would explain to me the intricacies of the legal case Stanway was pursuing against the National Bank of Wales.

'Thank you for seeing me,' Charlotte said.

I nodded.

'My secretary rang earlier and she was told that you might be back this afternoon. It's just that next week is rather busy for me. I'll be travelling to London on Sunday and then flying to Geneva on business.'

'Of course.'

I nodded at the papers on the table before her. 'Perhaps you'd like to explain the Stanway case to me more detail.'

'I can leave you with these copies.' She patted a slim-fingered hand on one of the larger piles. 'George Stanway has commenced proceedings against the bank using different reasons. One of the first that he tried was a claim for breach of contract. He tried to allege that the National Bank of Wales had an agreement with him that they would support the business through thick and thin. The case wasn't particularly well argued and the bank was able to get the case dismissed. However, that wasn't the end of matters.'

'There's always a but.'

She smiled.

'He tried four other legal cases before I became involved. Once I started working for the bank we adopted a more *active* approach to dealing with Stanway.'

Charlotte spent an hour running through the executive summary she produced of the individual cases that Stanway had commenced against the bank. Sections highlighted in yellow demonstrated the vitriolic and aggressive language he had used in emails and letters. Most of the terminology left me cold. But Stanway was on a one-man mission to seek revenge against the National Bank of Wales and Matthew Dolman. But would it make him a killer?

'I explained before that the final straw for the bank was when Stanway libelled Matthew Dolman on his website.'

'So what happened then?'

Charlotte sat back and gave me a resigned look as though I shouldn't have to ask. 'Stanway started proceedings again, this time for negligence.'

'How far did he get?'

'The claim is ongoing. We think he's got someone helping him. Probably a struck-off lawyer, doing it for a few pennies.'

'So what is he claiming?'

She sighed. 'Millions, in damages I mean. And he has applied for disclosure of a lot of the bank's documentation and internal files.'

'Could that be embarrassing?'

She shook her head. 'Of course not. And Stanway knows that full well. Our guess is that he is hoping we'll try and do a deal. Pay him something to go away quietly.'

'Is that likely?'

'Of course not.'

I reached over and flicked through the first few pages. If her assessment of Stanway's attitude was correct he certainly had a motive to kill Dolman.

'If I can help in any other way then please contact me.' Charlotte got up and gathered the various papers that she had used into a neat folder and dropped them into a leather briefcase. She glided out of the interview and I watched her leave Queen Street wondering what on earth she saw in Rex Dolman.

I had little time to think of an answer as my mobile bleeped with a message. *Something important. Contact me AD.*

I found Alvine waiting in her lab. Tucked under my arm was the folder that Deborah had given me with the threatening messages she had received.

Alvine stood, arms folded, staring at various sheets of paper neatly laid out on the table in front of her. I suppose I should have been doing the same but Tracy was standing by her side and when I had arrived, she had given me a smile that could have melted an iceberg so I was distracted.

'It's the same printer.'

That got my attention. 'What!'

'Pay attention, Marco.' Alvine sounded exasperated. 'The printer responsible for the leaflet is the same as the one that printed the note you found on Dolman's body.'

I stepped towards the table and peered down, recognising the leaflet I had picked up in Henson's office.

'Bloody hell.'

'What's wrong? You've got your evidence. Go and arrest the bad guys.'

'It's not that …'

'This is evidence.' Alvine raised her voice. Then she tilted her head and glared at me. 'Of course. This is *inadmissible* as evidence. Detective Inspector Marco picks up a leaflet and brings it here hoping he'll make a connection.' She scowled.

'It wasn't like that.'

'Then how *was* it?'

I fell into an embarrassed silence. Then I passed her the folder with Deborah Bowen's messages, which she opened and read. 'And where did you get these?'

'They were sent to Deborah Bowen.'

'And who is she?'

'She's Matthew Dolman's mistress. She received them over the last three weeks.'

Alvine peered at them as though there was a message in invisible ink that she might be able to decipher.

'So you want me to compare these to the original messages?'

'And the one on Dolman's lanyard. And see—'

'If it matches the printer.'

'Of course.'

Alvine unfolded her arms and rested her palms on the table. 'You know I'll have to make a report in due course,' she added.

Paperwork, it was always paperwork.

I marched back to the Incident Room, my pulse beating a little faster and the possibility that we had a breakthrough dominating my thoughts. Now we had something tangible and my excitement at the first direct evidence lifted my spirits.

Back in the Incident Room, I stood by the board and stared at Henson's name.

'Do we focus everything on Henson?' Lydia said.

I hesitated, my earlier enthusiasm dulled. 'We must be careful. Some things make little sense.' I turned to Lydia who was frowning. 'If Henson was responsible for the letters then why print them on his own printer?'

'Maybe he was just stupid.'

I mumbled. 'He would have guessed that we could work out he had printed the letters on his computer. He can't be that stupid.'

'I suppose ...' Lydia said. 'So who did print them?'

I ran a hand through my hair. 'I don't know. But let's keep an open mind. Someone might be wanting to pin the blame on Henson and use his printer to point the finger at him.'

'So it might be someone who knows Henson and wants to set him up?'

I nodded. 'Or it could just be Henson. In the meantime we've got the Stanway connection to investigate. Over the weekend I'll talk to Mrs Dolman again and find out about the flat in Nice.'

'I spoke to Mrs Stanway who told me she left for work just after seven. Her husband was fast asleep when she left.'

'So he could have jumped out of bed and travelled into the middle of Cardiff. Better requisition as much of the CCTV footage as you can. And talking about CCTV was there anything from the car park?'

'Nothing, boss. But I could recheck them.'

I shook my head. 'No. Let's get as much CCTV as we can get for all the streets in the immediate vicinity of the Royal Bell car park. And we need a mobile telephone number for Henson and Cleaver. We might track their movements.'

'They'll be using pay-as-you-go that'll make it impossible to pin down their locations.'

'What did Deborah say about the bank? She thought there were problems.'

'Not enough to prevent him buying a flat in Nice.'

I stepped back from the board and read the names of the Dolman family. 'I know it doesn't make sense. How could he afford it?'

Lydia returned to her desk and sat down. She drew a notepad from a drawer.

'I want to know as much as we can about the Dolman family. I need background checks on them all and I need you to double-check their movements on the morning Matthew Dolman was killed. Both men had parked their cars that morning. I need to know when they arrived at work. I'll call Boyd Pierce and get him to research the shareholding of the bank.'

Lydia finished making notes and looked up, expecting me to say something else. 'What about the other group of activists?'

I heaved a sigh. Chasing one set of shadows was bad enough but we already had two to go after. And they were all probably clever enough to use pay-as-you-go mobile telephones and applications that made it hard to trace their communications.

'I'll concentrate on Henson and the others.' My reply didn't sound convincing.

When I got back to my office it smelt stuffy so I opened the window a fraction and a sharp cold draught blew across my face so I pushed it closed. As I found Boyd Pierce's number I thought about Tracy and found my mobile among the papers on my desk. I tapped out a message. *Busy later? Mexican or Italian? J.* The reply came immediately. *Don't know any Mexicans. Suppose an Italian will have to do Tx.* I smiled to myself. She had a sense of humour that my father would appreciate and I wondered what my mother might make of her.

Then I called the economic crime department.

'Sergeant Pierce. Economic Crime.'

'Hello, Boyd. How's life in the fraud squad?'

I heard a gentle, impatient exhalation of breath from my former sergeant as I used the old-fashioned title for his new department. Although he had enjoyed working for me, a new baby and pressure from his wife for a regular nine-to-five day meant that Boyd had sought a transfer.

'Hello, sir. How is Lydia Flint fitting in?'

'Good, thanks. How's the family?'

'Great, although I'm not getting much sleep. And Mandy's hoping to get back to work next month. How can I help?'

'I need an analysis of the shareholding of the National Bank of Wales.'

His voice got serious. 'How urgent is this? Only I've got—'

'Today.'

Another groan. 'I'll see what I can do.'

Then he rang off and I turned my attention to the special branch reports on my desk. After an hour I had found no reference to mobile numbers for Henson or Cleaver. The telephone ringing on my desk was a welcome distraction.

I recognised the measured tone of Boyd's voice. 'The shareholding of the National Bank of Wales is divided between Matthew Dolman who owns fifty-five per cent, a charitable foundation owns twenty-five per cent and the rest is divided equally between Troy and Rex.'

'So does that mean that Matthew Dolman can do what he wants with the bank?'

'Depends on who controls the charitable foundation.'

'Can you find out—'

'You'll have to ask the trustees of the charity. And

without knowing exactly who runs the foundation it's impossible to know what the legal position might be.'

'Thanks, Boyd.'

It was late in the afternoon when I noticed Lydia leaving the Incident Room, suit bag in hand. It must have been half an hour later when she returned and stood in the door to my office. The blusher made her face look thinner, the high heels made her taller and her navy blue dress lay in smooth folds over her flat stomach.

'Night at the opera?' I said.

'*Carmen*.'

'You look very smart.'

'Thanks.'

Lydia bowed her head and as she smiled, I noticed a dimple on her right cheek.

By eight that evening I was standing with Tracy outside my mother's favourite restaurant in the brewery quarter. I stopped, tugged at Tracy's elbow and stepped towards the menu displayed in the window. One of the waiters gave me a brief smile of acknowledgement.

'You'll like this place,' I said.

She stood by my side; I could smell her perfume, it had rose petals combined with citrus.

'What's the food like?'

'My mother thinks it's the best Italian in Cardiff.'

An endorsement from an Italian woman did the trick. We stepped inside, the waiter shook my hand and welcomed me as a friend and then led us to a corner table. After fawning over Tracy he left, returning moments later with menus.

'Can I get you something to drink?'

'Water,' I said automatically. And I wondered if

Tracy had already heard about my past.

'I'll have a gin and tonic,' she said, giving me a glance that confirmed she did.

After a scan of the menu I chose Tuscan soup and lasagne. The waiter returned with our drinks and we ordered. The subdued lighting complemented her hair that occasionally she brushed away from her face.

'So you were brought up in Pontypridd?' I said.

'My parents lived in the same house for twenty years. The only house I remember.'

'You remember the Marco café in the middle of town?'

Tracy nodded.

'It was my grandfather, Nonno Marco, who ran the place originally.'

'So what does your family do now?'

I explained that my father – papà – was the industrious brother, the one who worked hard building his ice cream business. She sipped on her drink and looked interested as I talked about my family and my mother's home in Lucca. The Tuscan soup arrived with Tracy's pâté and I discovered why she had joined the Wales Police Service after a degree in criminology.

'I didn't want to be a police officer,' she explained. 'Like a lot of CSIs I just love the analysis side of the work. So how long have you been in the WPS?'

Her leg brushed my trousers. I didn't move and she kept her leg exactly where I hoped she would.

'It feels like a long time. After leaving school I drifted for a while, spent time in Italy with my family and then joined the old South Wales Police Force.'

I told her about my time in Merthyr Tydfil as a constable, the two years as a custody sergeant in Pontypridd before my promotion to CID. She didn't ask about my family, and it made me think that Alvine had already told her all about me, all about Jackie and Dean.

The restaurant was quiet for a Friday night. Our main course arrived and Tracy talked about working with Alvine.

'So have you got any suspects for Dolman's death?' She finished a mouthful of carbonara.

'There's a list of persons of interest.'

'And do you think the stiletto fits in?'

'Somebody must have been practising the movement needed to kill Dolman.'

'Really?' She leant a little further over the table, and opened her eyes; they were a warm turquoise colour. 'Is it one of those extremists from the YouTube video? So what was the motive?'

I shrugged. The waiter returned after clearing away the main courses and we ordered ice cream – another recommendation from my mother.

'Are you looking into the death threats against Matthew Dolman?' Tracy said, her eyes wide.

'At the time they were investigated fully. Nobody took them seriously, but now everything is being looked into.'

Tracy made no objection when I paid the bill.

'I've got a great coffee machine.' It had to be the cheesiest line ever. She gave me another smile. We walked over towards Mary Street in the hope of a taxi.

I dawdled and she was a few steps in front of me. 'I wouldn't recognise most CSIs without their boiler suits, in the flesh, so to speak,' I said, hailing a taxi.

'And how much flesh do you like to see, Inspector?'

Her smile sent me all sorts of signals and stretched my patience during the journey to my apartment. Her skirt rolled up over her knees exposing a few inches of immaculate thigh. I passed the time of day with a driver who gave me the results of Cardiff City's competitors – it wasn't good news.

I scrambled for the right change, giving the driver a generous tip.

On the stairs to the flat Tracy had taken her coat off, draping it over one arm. I fumbled the key into the lock and then I slammed the door behind us before I threw my jacket into a corner and pulled Tracy towards me. My tongue found hers and we huddled breathless in the hallway. I struggled with the buttons of her blouse as she undid my belt. Then I gasped as she squeezed me, really hard. We left a trail of shoes and clothes before I pushed open the bedroom door.

Chapter 14

It was Sunday morning and I arrived early at Queen Street. I had to finish the work that I had started yesterday before I could justify my evening in the Cardiff City stadium watching Cardiff play Fulham. By mid-morning I had a more complete picture of Jamie Henson and an understanding of Neil Cleaver. The name of Paul Youlden, the ringleader of the other activist group in South Wales, had been pinned to the board. The special branch report had been sketchy on the details of the others involved.

Something niggled about the way the messages could so easily be linked to Henson. I found the printed sheets and scanned them again. Then I turned back to the special branch file and reread the comments about the myriad relationships between the various individuals. I realised it would be difficult to build a complete picture of everyone involved. It didn't mean I would ignore Henson.

By mid-morning Lydia appeared at my office door with two cups of coffee and sat down uninvited.

'The Dolman family seem to get everywhere. There is a Dolman charitable foundation that helps disadvantaged children through school, offers scholarships to university. All very philanthropic and funded by the bank.'

'Is it the same trust that owns the bank shares?'

'No. That's a different one. In fact there are half a dozen and Mrs Dolman gets her name everywhere.'

I took my first mouthful of coffee. 'Did you check up on the Dolman brothers on the morning of their father's death?'

She nodded. 'They were both in the bank and at their desks at the time he was killed. I checked with various members of staff who all confirmed the same.'

Lydia was busy dunking a biscuit in her drink.

Sodden bits fell off into the hot liquid. She continued once she'd finished a mouthful. 'Both Troy and Rex went to fee-paying schools and then on to university before returning to work in the bank. Troy did a short commission in the Welsh Guards. And he's still in the Territorial Army now. I should have his service record early next week. He's single, lives alone near Abergavenny and has a box at Cardiff City football club.

'Anything on Rex?'

'Rex has an address not far from his parents in Penarth but apart from a caution for smoking cannabis when he was at university there was nothing to suggest he was anything other than a rich banker.'

'We'll need to talk to them about the charitable trusts. In fact let's go and talk to Mrs Dolman now.'

Lydia gave me a surprised look before gathering up both mugs and making for the Incident Room. I stood up and found my car keys. I strode out to the Incident Room where Lydia was gathering papers and a ballpoint before shrugging on a light jacket.

'Do you think we should call in advance?'

'This isn't a social call.'

We trooped down to the car park. It was a pleasant enough morning: not raining nor too cold. The odd smell I'd noticed first thing in my Mondeo was still there and I could see Lydia turn up her nose as she scanned the detritus in the foot well. I fired the engine into life and we headed towards Penarth. The traffic was light, the occasional taxi passing us from the Bay.

'How was the opera on Friday night?' I asked as we drove down Central Link.

'It was wonderful.' She relaxed for a moment into her seat as though the recollection was calming in itself.

A few minutes later I pulled the car to a halt at the

pavement near the Dolman's detached property. I stepped out and noticed that the gravelled drive glistened as though each pebble had been hand polished. Then I saw movement by the rear door. I shouted a greeting.

'Is Mrs Dolman at home?'

A woman dressed in a housecoat, her hair pulled into a knot behind her head, turned towards me. I repeated my question and she walked over.

'Mrs Dolman no here.' The accent was Eastern European. She stood well back from the gate and stared at me. I pressed my warrant card to the gate and she squinted over. 'I'm a police officer. I wanted to talk to Mrs Dolman.'

'She is out.'

'I need to see her urgently. It is police business.'

Even from a distance I could see her frown. 'She is in tennis club.' Then she turned and walked back to the house, her shoes crunching on the gravel.

I turned to Lydia. 'It looks like we've got another visit to the Vale of Glamorgan Racquets Club.'

Twenty minutes later we passed two gardeners working on the shrubbery as we drove up towards the entrance of the club. I had to slow to let a Mercedes Benz saloon pass us as it left the club and then I drew into the car park. I scanned for a free slot but Lydia interrupted my search.

'That's Mrs Dolman over there.' She gesticulated towards a couple standing by a black Range Rover. I slowed the car to a halt and stared over towards the pair deep in conversation. By her side was a tall man with a receding hairline. He was slim and healthy looking. From the body language, they were on good terms, formal without being too friendly and she shook his hand neatly when they finished, no peck on the cheek, and he drove away. I parked and we walked over to the club. Inside Mrs Dolman was standing in the foyer.

She glared over at us. The steward we'd met the first time stood next to her and gave us a neutral stare.

'Mrs Dolman, good morning. I was wondering if we could have a moment of your time.'

'How did ...?' She guessed the answer and said no more. Instead she stepped into the large reception room. It was empty and she pointed to one of the chesterfield sofas, sitting herself down opposite.

'How is your investigation proceeding?' she said, staring at me and then Lydia.

'We want to discuss some of the details regarding your late husband's affairs.'

'I hope I can be of help.'

I decided on a roundabout approach. 'How many charitable foundations do you run?'

'Several.'

'And what is your involvement in all of them?'

She sighed, folded the fingers of both hands together and started a detailed explanation. Lydia scribbled notes and occasionally I asked a question for clarification, sometimes pausing for Lydia to catch up.

'Nobody involved would have any reason to kill Matthew.' She made it sound like an announcement in a railway station.

'Of course. We have to check.'

I turned to Lydia who knew the prompt that we had agreed on during the car journey from Queen Street.

'The bank shares weren't all owned by Mr Dolman,' Lydia said, her voice smooth and calm. I kept my eye contact direct but Mrs Dolman didn't blink or avert her gaze. 'A charitable trust of some sort owns twenty-five per cent. Can you tell me about that trust?'

Now she blinked and looked away. 'That has

nothing to do with my husband's death.'

Brenda Dolman turned a fountain pen through her fingers.

'I am sure you appreciate that we have to investigate every line of inquiry. Consider everything that might be relevant to find his killer.'

She didn't flinch. No blinking or quivering lips. Nothing to suggest that her husband's death was anything except a footnote in her life.

Lydia pressed on. 'Who are the beneficiaries of the trust?'

'I shall need to discuss this with the trustees before I could ...'

Her fist curled around the pen more tightly now.

'We'll need to establish the position quickly.'

'Of course. I'll talk to Troy.'

A brief silence followed as we watched Mrs Dolman's discomfort. She was hiding something. I had one more question. 'Can you give us some details about the ownership of the flat in Nice?'

There was a look of genuine disbelief in her eyes.

'What on earth are you talking about?'

'The flat that your husband owned in Nice.'

'Complete nonsense. He didn't own any such property.'

'You knew that he was having a relationship with Miss Deborah Bowen?'

She stood up. 'Now if we're finished. I have a lot to do.'

She led us to the front door. We returned to the car and we drove back to Cardiff.

'She knows all about the shares owned by the trust,' Lydia said. 'She got all evasive when I asked her.'

I nodded. 'We haven't had the truth from her. Yet.'

I spent the rest of the afternoon in Queen Street making various calls. Deborah Bowen was top of the list. She rang back within an hour with the address of the property in France and another hour passed until I found the right street view. Another search of estate agents selling property in the Riviera killed more time before I realised it was time for me to leave. I headed back to my apartment and found my jacket and a Cardiff City supporter's scarf. I had already texted my friend Robbie, another Cardiff City supporter, and we had agreed a time to meet before the game. Playing Fulham did not have the same excitement as the local derby game had against Swansea. And with Fulham at the bottom of the table Cardiff should win easily enough.

After a change of clothes, I left the flat, walked down to the car park, and then off towards the ground. I passed families walking down to the Bay for a Sunday afternoon outing. I crossed the Taff and walked on through Grangetown realising that the Dolmans lived in a world removed from the mundane trials of everyday life like paying the mortgage or walking the dog. Supporters arriving for the game choked Ninian Park railway station so I had to slow my pace and I joined the mass heading for the ground. I peeled off before the entrance and waited for Robbie who joined me after a couple of minutes. He worked for an IT consultancy and the office politics he recounted sounded just like the atmosphere in Queen Street. We reached the inside of the stadium and headed for the bar. Robbie returned with a pint of lager and an orange juice. He told me about his recent appraisal where his boss had suggested that he needed to develop his 'managerial ambitions'.

'What's that supposed to mean?' I said.

'Fucked if I know.'

Robbie leant on the window overlooking the car park and supped heavily on his pint. Fathers with boys grasping their hands jostled with groups of teenagers and older men. It made me think about the time Dean and I had watched Queens Park Rangers. The only time. An event I hadn't repeated although Trish, my girlfriend at the time, had made it clear that she thought I was a useless parent for not trying any harder. I listened and contributed occasionally to the conversation with Robbie. He finished his drink and we trooped into the stadium. A scrappy first half was made worse by Cardiff failing to work the channels effectively and finding themselves at the wrong end of two free kicks, one of which Fulham managed to convert into a goal. It did not improve Robbie's mood who went in search of another drink as I munched on a chocolate bar. After ten minutes of the second half, it was clear that the team talk at half-time had been effective. The Cardiff City players were in full attacking mode with three players driving at the Fulham goalkeeper in quick succession. The visitors looked shell-shocked after conceding two quick goals and the smiles on the Cardiff players had the effect of energising the crowd.

A light drizzle fell as we left the stadium. Pale yellow lights shrouded the contented crowd snaking its way home from the game. It was a short walk round to the bar. I had walked no more than a few steps when my mobile rang.

'DI Marco.'

'This is Troy Dolman.' He was almost shouting. 'How dare you harass my mother!'

I slowed and Robbie turned towards me.

'I'm not certain I understand—'

'She's been telling me all about your insinuations about my father and Deborah Bowen. It really must stop.'

'This is a police inquiry—'

'And another thing. My father doesn't own any property in Nice. I haven't spoken to Rex as he's away on business until Wednesday but when he gets back he'll be furious.'

I gave Robbie a vague sort of grin that he had probably seen a dozen times.

'Work?' he said.

No sooner I had I put the mobile in my pocket than it rang again. I snatched at the handset and it almost fell onto the pavement.

'DI Marco. Area Control. You're needed at a murder scene.'

Chapter 15

Alan Turner wore a Gant shirt; I could just about make out the logo and I guessed that the denims were the same expensive American brand. The brogues looked pristine, as though he had bought them that afternoon. He sat crumpled on the floor of the lift at the exclusive development where he had a penthouse apartment.

Around Turner's neck was a lanyard, similar to the one I'd found on Matthew Dolman. The typed message on the paper in the plastic pouch attached to it had 'ANOTHER GREEDY BASTARD' printed in large font. I snapped on a pair of latex gloves, leant down and moved the pouch to one side. A large red stain covered most of the expensive shirt.

Lydia stood to one side. 'This looks exactly the same MO as Matthew Dolman.'

I turned towards her. 'Once the CSI team have arrived we'll visit his apartment.'

Lydia yawned. I could feel the tiredness in the small of my back. I should have been eating a curry with Robbie, dissecting the game, recharging my mind for the following morning. Instead, we had hours more work. A crowd had gathered outside the main entrance, faces peering in, hands raised, fingers pointing. Moments later, I saw Alvine barging her away through the crowd. I looked for Tracy but she wasn't there; two of Alvine's regular investigators followed her, carrying bags of equipment.

'There's another message attached to the lanyard around his neck,' I said, looking down at Turner. 'I'll need a forensic examination as soon as possible.'

'Do you realise the time?' Alvine said.

'There's nothing I can do about that,' I replied. 'I've got two deaths in less than a week and all I'm asking is that you get on with things.'

'All right, all right.'

Alvine turned to look at the two CSIs with her. 'Let's get a perimeter set up.' She nodded to the front door. 'And let's cover the glass before we get any press interest.'

I turned to the uniformed officer by my side. 'Who found the body?'

'One of the residents.' He fumbled with his notebook. 'Mrs Carrington from the second floor. She was returning from walking the dog. She's very upset.'

I left Alvine and her team and walked up to the penthouse apartment clutching a set of keys while Lydia took the door to the second floor.

There was a light on in the penthouse, and classical music played quietly. It sounded orchestral, definitely not operatic. The hallway was a grand affair with several impressive-looking prints hanging on the wall. I found the kitchen through a door on the left-hand side of the hallway. Subdued under-the-counter lighting accentuated the high-end equipment, including a pistachio-coloured coffee machine placed next to a toaster of the same colour. An opened bottle of Chianti stood on the worktop but there were no glasses and no sign that Alan Turner was expecting company.

Back in the hallway, I pushed open one of the two oak doors and found myself in a large comfortable sitting room. An elevated section of the floor had an oak dining table with six matching chairs. I walked around the room; there were large cream leather sofas and pottery and glass strategically placed on shelving and sideboards. I reached large full-height windows, cupped my hands to the glass and squinted out. None of the keys on Turner's key fob opened the doors to the balcony so I had to imagine the view from the penthouse decking over the city. I heard a tapping on the door behind me and I strode over to allow

Lydia inside.

'Mrs Carrington was pretty upset. She didn't see anything. Once she saw Turner's body she screamed, then the dog barked. It was a miracle she could call 999.'

'We'll get a proper statement from her in the morning.'

She scanned the room before wandering over to a door leading into another landing. I followed her through to the bedrooms. Each was sumptuously decorated, not a piece of furniture out of place and no dust within a mile.

'It's very sterile,' Lydia said.

'I wonder if he has a family.'

We pulled each door closed behind us and made our way back to the hallway. In the study a bank of three computer screens hummed on a large desk. One displayed the latest stock market information, another Turner's email inbox and a third was open to a news page. I picked my way through the pockets of the jacket draped over the back of an office chair. I found Turner's smartphone and worked my way through his contacts.

'We'll need to go through his personal papers. There must be something that will tell us if he had wife or children or …'

There were frequent calls to various mobile telephones, all with Christian names but no other details. Lydia rummaged through various drawers assembling a small pile of folders on a table.

'Any luck?' I said.

She shook her head. 'I can't find any reference to family so far.'

'He must have had staff. I remember calling his office.'

In an old-fashioned telephone index book we found the contact details for Hannah Peters at an address in

Roath. Before we left Lydia checked all the windows and we switched off the radio and the lights. Alvine was standing by the lift door staring down at Turner, a stern look on her face. The pathologist looked up as he knelt by Turner's body.

'Hello, John.'

'Hi, Paddy.'

He got up. 'No reason why you can't move him.' He fastened the zip of his Barbour. Then he looked over at me. 'Another good killing I'd say.'

'I beg your pardon?' The realisation of what Paddy meant becoming clear.

'It looks like the same weapon. A small stiletto-like blade. The post mortem will confirm.'

'Could it be the same—?'

'Impossible to be certain. But how many killers are there in Cardiff using a stiletto?'

He turned to leave and I walked to the door with him. Outside the temperature had fallen by two degrees. He raised the zip of his jacket to his chin. I buttoned my coat and Lydia shivered.

'When are you going to do the post mortem?'

He glanced at his watch. 'First thing in the morning.'

Paddy marched off and I spoke briefly to the uniformed officer who looked tired. The other residents had been complaining about getting access to their flats. Some had even threatened making a complaint. 'Tell them to contact Superintendent Cornock,' I said.

The officer nodded nervously.

I manoeuvred the car away from the Scientific Support Vehicles and the patrol car and then headed north before passing the prison and skirting around Adam Street and then up Fitzalan Place before taking a right onto Newport Road and then up towards Roath. The sat-nav gave us directions although I had a fair idea where Hannah Peters lived. I pulled the car onto a pavement in a nearby side street and we headed towards the address.

At the top of a short flight of stairs were two doors. One had the name Appleby written under the doorbell and the second Peters. I heard a sleepy, worried voice through the intercom. 'Who is it?'

'I'm sorry to disturb you at this time of night. My name is Detective Inspector John Marco. Are you the Hannah Peters that works with Alan Turner?'

'Yes.'

'I need to speak to you on a private matter.'

There was a dour electronic buzzing as the front door opened. Hannah Peters was waiting for us at the top of stairs. 'Do you have some form of identification?'

I pulled out my warrant card and Lydia did the same. 'This is Detective Sergeant Flint.'

'What do you want?'

I looked over her shoulder. 'Is there somewhere we can sit down?'

She led us into a small kitchen and we sat by a table. 'I'm afraid I have bad news. Alan Turner was murdered tonight.'

Her eyes opened wide, and then she pulled her right hand over her mouth as her eyes filled with tears. 'When did this happen? This is terrible.' Hannah sobbed; Lydia tore a few squares from the kitchen towel on the worktop and passed them over.

'Could you tell us about his next of kin?'

Hannah blew her nose noisily. 'He had a son. His wife died in a car accident a few years ago. He doesn't see his son very often. He lives in London. And he had a brother who lives somewhere in Australia but they were never in contact.'

'Do you have the contact details for his son?'

'They're probably in the office somewhere.' She sounded exasperated.

Lydia stood up and fetched Hannah a glass of water. She drank half without stopping and then wiped away some of her tears. 'Has this got anything to do with what happened to Matthew Dolman?' Her eyes opened wide and her speech slowed.

'It's far too early to tell.'

We left Hannah clutching a handkerchief. Outside, a police siren sounded in the distance, quickly followed by an ambulance. A light drizzle fell as we made our way back to the car. It was after midnight when I got back to my apartment in the Bay.

I discarded my clothes on the bed and then stood in a hot shower. Trying to keep hunger at bay I trimmed spots of mould from some cheese in the fridge and made a sandwich. I sat down and flicked through the channels hoping to find some old *Top Gear* but it was a Liam Neeson film that caught my attention – I had seen it before, having lost count of the people he killed. I realised after a while that sleep would elude me. I tried reading a Harlan Coben novel, one of those that Trish had encouraged me to read. I even played an Elvis CD but my thoughts kept flicking back to Matthew Dolman and Alan Turner. There had to be something connecting both men. And if Paddy was right about the murder weapon somebody had a very specific motive.

Chapter 16

Hannah's swollen eyes and the smell of stale alcohol on her breath suggested she had slept little after we left her the night before. At the discreet third-floor offices near the centre of town, she led us through a corridor past a small conference suite to Turner's room. It was large and comfortable with a smart black leather sofa in one corner.

'What was he like to work with?' I said.

Her lip quivered. 'He was a great boss.'

'What was he working on?'

Lydia had opened the doors of a cupboard and pulled out box files and folders.

'He was working on the sale of Silverwood Engineering.'

The name sounded familiar. 'Was that the business that bought out Stanway Engineering?'

She nodded.

'Did he ever receive any hate mail or abusive letters?'

'Not that I knew.'

Lydia turned her head towards me. 'These boxes are full of papers relating to some contract for the electrification of the railways in the Valleys.'

Hannah nodded again. 'He worked on that for a long time. I don't know why really. He got a fee but it was nothing like what he normally charged. And he spent an enormous amount of time on it.'

'Was the bank involved in that too?'

'Yes. They were involved in nearly everything he did.'

'We'll need all the papers on the Silverwood deal and everything on the electrification contract.' I turned my attention back to the desk drawers. 'Where will I find details of his family?'

'Try his computer. He kept everything on that.' Then she left me booting up Turner's computer.

'What do you make of that Silverwood business, boss?' Lydia said.

I was scanning Turner's Outlook contacts page. 'There's a connection between Dolman and Turner. Something that got them killed.' I found the contact details for David Turner in London. 'We'll need to talk to the Dolman family again.' I picked up the telephone. 'First I need to call Turner's son.'

I walked back to the Incident Room from another meeting with Cornock, pleased that he had allocated additional resources for the double murder, but every time he used the word *budget* he grimaced as though he were sitting on something very sharp.

Two large stacks of plastic boxes stood in one corner. Lydia was already busy on some papers laid out on her desk. I found the file relating to the electrification contract for the Valleys railway line. There were dozens of formal documents in ring binders and lever arch files all with indexed sections and colour-coded dividers. I spent an hour trawling through the papers, not really knowing what I was looking for but hoping there'd be a thread to connect both murders. I scanned the environmental reports and then in a separate file there was a document summarising the long-term economic benefits for the Valleys.

It had been an enormous contract worth several million pounds and a local company, Frost Enterprises, advised by Matthew Dolman and the National Bank of Wales, had been very high profile in its press releases about their plans to deliver the contract on time and on budget.

After arguments between the politicians in Cardiff and Westminster about who would pay, a compromise had been reached. I struggled to work out how saving a few minutes on the journey from Cardiff to London would generate thousands of jobs. An article headed 'local jobs hope' suggested that local companies would share in the £350 million project. Matthew Dolman's clients must have hoped for a serious slice of that money.

Frost Enterprises had been one of the preferred bidders for the project. Malcolm Frost appeared shaking hands with various subcontractors, local union bosses and the directors of the company responsible for managing the railway tracks. The *Western Mail* carried a flattering portrayal of Frost as a local man made good. I absently bookmarked several websites. Two other companies were mentioned and there was controversy when the decision was made to award the contract to a business based in London. I tried another Google search for comments about the company that won the tender and found a blog suggesting links to various offshore companies and comments about the English fascist state and the conspiracy to denude Welsh people of jobs and wealth. I continued reading about Malcolm Frost. It was the entry about his suicide that drew my attention and reminded me that Stanway had named Frost when I first spoke to him. After Frost Enterprises had lost the tender, it had been three months before financial difficulties had caused the company to go into receivership.

The morning passed in a blur of paperwork. Lydia made coffee, the telephone rang occasionally and Superintendent Cornock emailed a notification that two additional detectives would arrive that afternoon. I punched in the number of the civil servant responsible for the contract negotiations and, after various voices that all sounded bored and disinterested, I found a Dr Vincent Owen.

'Dr Owen. Detective Inspector Marco of the Wales Police Service. I'm investigating the deaths of Matthew Dolman and Alan Turner.'

'How can I help?'

'Both men had worked on the contract for the electrification of the Valleys line. But the business that seemed firm favourite didn't get the contract. Can you tell me anything about that?'

'You should know, Inspector, that I cannot tell you *anything*. It was all a commercial transaction that went through a competitive tendering process. The company that the National Bank of Wales supported did not win the contract. And I know nothing about a Mr Turner.'

'He was killed yesterday evening. It was on the news.'

'Really. I dealt with the original owner of the company – Mr Frost and his colleague James Harding. I cannot help.'

'I was wondering—'

But all I heard was the dialling tone.

It was harder than I had thought tracking down anyone to do with Frost Enterprises. The receivers thought that Harding had moved to work in Edinburgh. Several telephone conversations later, I spoke to a woman in Glasgow who recognised the name but her accent made it difficult to follow her.

'It's a very bad line,' I said, hoping it would get her to slow down. It didn't. 'Do you have a contact number for him?'

'He's back in Wales.'

I scribbled down a number and then punched it into the telephone on my desk. My annoyance built as the call rang out.

My stomach turned over, reminding me it was lunchtime so I strolled out to Lydia's desk.

'I'm starving. Let's go for lunch.'

Lydia picked up her bag and collected her coat and fifteen minutes later we were sitting in Mario's. A crowd of office workers were standing by the counter making a racket so we moved to a quieter table.

'How did you get on this morning, boss?'

'There's paperwork three feet thick. I don't think I could ever have been a banker or a lawyer. I've been trying to track down one of the men involved in the electrification contract.'

'Do you think it might be helpful?'

'It's one of the things that links Dolman and Turner.'

Lydia shook her head slowly. 'There's something else I found out about both men. They each contributed to a homeless charity in Pontypridd. They made generous donations.'

Our meal arrived and Lydia gave my bacon sandwich a severe look. There was a lot of lettuce involved in her lunch.

'So maybe they were both being philanthropic.'

She started on a large piece of cucumber. 'Maybe. I've made an appointment to see the hostel later.'

'I'm going back to Turner's place to speak to his neighbours.'

We finished lunch and I left Lydia in the car park making for her car and took the stairs back to the Incident Room. I found a set of keys to Turner's apartment and checked with the search team supervisor that he had finished in the flat, before making the short journey to Alan Turner's apartment block.

There was a strong smell of antiseptic and bleach in

the main foyer of the building. But otherwise there was no trace of the events of the night before. I called the lift and when the doors clattered open I stared at the floor, half-expecting there to be some evidence that Turner had been killed there.

After I opened the door to his apartment I stood in the hallway, trying to imagine his routine. Did he put his keys on the table under the mirror? Where did he have his coat? Perhaps he dumped a briefcase on the floor behind the entrance door. Then I tried to build a mental picture of why Turner was in the lift last night. I stepped over towards the kitchen.

I knew that the search team would have completed a detailed analysis of everything in the apartment but I opened the fridge door out of interest. It had a bag of rocket, another of watercress and various components for a salad. Standing upright in the door were two bottles of white wine and sparkling water.

Nothing much had changed. The expensive domestic equipment was still in place and I drew a finger along the cool granite worktop of the island in the middle of the floor. The only thing that was missing was the opened bottle of wine. I wondered whether Turner had been expecting guests. But there was nothing to suggest that he was preparing a meal.

And then I realised he might have ordered a takeaway.

I searched through every drawer in the kitchen. Then every cupboard but I couldn't find a menu for a takeaway restaurant. Then I strode out of the kitchen, threw open the study door and rummaged through the drawers of his desk.

It drew another blank. Forensics would have taken his mobile to Queen Street so I called Alvine.

'Good morning, Marco,' Alvine said.

'There's something I want done urgently,' I said before explaining in detail.

In the meantime I left the apartment and visited all of Turner's neighbours. After two hours with the various flat owners who all wanted to be reassured that there wasn't a serial killer loose in their apartment complex I reached the first floor and texted Alvine. *Any news?*

There was no immediate reply so I knocked on the door of one of the flats, having checked the names of the owners. I sensed movement behind the door and then an elderly man answered. I had my warrant card ready. 'Mr Kennedy. Detective Inspector Marco. I'm investigating—'

'Of course, come in.' He opened the door and I stepped in just as he scanned the hallway behind me.

The sitting room was comfortable and well furnished. I sat opposite Mr Kennedy and his wife. 'I was hoping that you might help me with the inquiry into Mr Turner's death.'

'Of course,' Kennedy said.

'I was wondering if you have ever seen Mr Turner taking delivery of a takeaway meal?'

'What, like fish and chips you mean?'

'Anything really. He must have been in the foyer for some reason and we suspect that he might have ordered a takeaway meal.'

'Let me think.'

His wife, silent until now, interrupted. 'I think I saw Mr Turner with one of those pizza boxes.'

My throat constricted. 'Do you remember the name of the delivery company?'

'Good lord no,' Kennedy said. 'But you see the empty boxes all over the street.'

I tried a couple more questions to see if they could

add any more details, then I made excuses and left. The front door closed behind me with a reassuring thud as my mobile rang. I recognised Alvine's number.

'Top of the class, Marco. Looks like Mr Turner was a regular with Pizza House.'

Chapter 17

In my haste I crunched the gears of my Mondeo before I accelerated away from Turner's apartment. The traffic was building up by now and my impatience got the better of me as I sounded the horn hoping that it would help to clear the traffic. It didn't and my irritation grew. I double-parked outside the Pizza House restaurant and, after leaving the car, jogged inside. I gave the girls standing behind the counter a cursory nod as I strode towards the office at the rear. I barged in and the same woman was sitting behind the desk, her elbow propped on the surface, a cigarette perched between two fingers.

'Back again love?'

'Is George Stanway here?'

'He's delivering. I'll get him to call you if you want.'

I stepped towards the desk. Then I leant forward. 'Do you know Alan Turner?'

'Can't say I do? Does he play rugby for Wales?'

I could feel her attitude shredding my patience.

'Do you keep a list of the addresses for your regular customers?'

She dragged heavily on the cigarette. 'Some of them. Most of the lads know the regular deliveries.'

I gave her the details of Alan Turner's address and she gave me a blank stare. 'Ask the girls.'

I stepped back outside and repeated the details to each of the girls in turn. After I had explained where the apartment block was located they confirmed that Alan Turner was a regular. He particularly liked ten-inch pizzas with extra pepperoni and mushrooms.

'Did he order a pizza last night?'

They exchanged glances.

'It's urgent.'

The first girl gave a noncommittal shrug; the second looked blank. I was waiting for the third to say something when George Stanway walked in through the door.

'What the hell are you doing here?'

I pushed him back out of the Pizza House and led him by the arm towards my car. 'I've got some questions.'

Within half an hour I had settled Stanway into one of the interview rooms at Queen Street. A duty lawyer had been called and I was expecting Lydia to arrive any minute. I sat in the custody suite sipping a plastic beaker of insipid coffee. The telephone rang incessantly, there was a regular bleeping in the background and the occasional sob and moan from one of the cells.

Alvine had confirmed while I waited that Alan Turner had not telephoned the Pizza House on the night he was killed. It would have been too convenient for Stanway to have delivered a pizza and then murdered Alan Turner. And too easily discoverable. Even Stanway would not have been that foolish.

Lydia arrived, finishing an apple that she discarded in one of the plastic bins. I brought her up to date. She nodded occasionally.

'Anything constructive from that hostel you visited?' I said.

'The Dolman family made a generous donation when the place was established. They've made regular contributions since and Mrs Dolman sits on their board of trustees. Otherwise it was a complete waste of time.'

I collected the tapes we needed and gathered my papers before trooping off to the interview room. The duty lawyer sat alongside Stanway. He was a young pimply man and I was almost tempted to ask him to prove his accreditation. I sat down by the table and fidgeted with removing the cellophane covering of the tapes. Lydia busied herself with tidying the papers into neat order.

'Is this an interview under caution?' the lawyer asked.

'There are certain matters which we want to put to Mr Stanway that will help us with the ongoing investigations into the deaths of Matthew Dolman and Alan Turner.'

The lawyer nodded briefly at Stanway.

'I want to start with your relationship with Matthew Dolman. You have started proceedings against the National Bank of Wales. It would be true to say that you have a vendetta against the bank and Matthew Dolman personally.'

Stanway folded his arms and glared at me. 'I certainly did. He was the man that ruined my life, my business and my family.'

'Can you explain exactly how you think that happened?'

Stanway settled both elbows on the table in front of him and launched into a detailed explanation. I hadn't expected candour. And by the end he had given us the perfect motive for killing Matthew Dolman.

'What do you do now Mr Stanway?'

'You know full well I work for a pizza delivery company.'

'What does your work entail?'

The lawyer was the first to reply. 'I think it involves delivering pizzas.'

I tried giving him an avuncular look, hoping it might shut him up.

'I deliver pizzas to the customers of the Pizza House.'

'Explain to me how the business works.'

Stanway gave me a puzzled look. 'The orders come over the telephone. Then I deliver them. It's not complicated.'

'You have regular customers?'

'Of course.'

I found a sheet of paper with Alan Turner's address and pushed it towards him. 'So you recognise this address?'

He stared at the text. 'I've delivered to houses on that street.'

'The address belongs to Alan Turner.'

Stanway nodded slowly.

'Do you know who I mean by Alan Turner?'

Although Stanway had stopped nodding, I could see the acknowledgement in his eyes, and the hate and the anger. He cleared his throat. 'Of course, I do.'

'Could you explain to us how you know Alan Turner?'

'He was involved with Matthew Dolman in cheating me out of my business.'

'Where were you last night?'

He settled back in his chair; I could see the confidence in his eyes now. 'I wasn't working.'

'Alan Turner was murdered last night.'

Stanway stared at me unblinkingly.

'I was in the Railway Club in Quakers Yard for most of the evening. There was a quiz night. I drank too much, got shit-faced drunk and I don't remember how I got home.'

It was early evening when we finally authorised Stanway's release. I had nothing to justify an arrest and I needed to have his alibi checked and all the CCTV coverage for the area immediately surrounding Alan Turner's apartment requisitioned. I sat with Lydia in the Incident Room gazing up at the various photographs pinned to the board.

'What did you make of Stanway, boss?'

I threaded my hands together behind my head and pressed back. It was no use. I wasn't going to get any inspiration.

'He happily admits that he's got the perfect motive for both deaths.'

Lydia nodded enthusiastically. 'And he doesn't have an alibi for the morning of Dolman's death.'

I knew that not having an alibi didn't mean he was guilty. But he had a gold-plated motive that he didn't hide but even so I was wary. 'So we need to check out his alibi for the night of Turner's death.' My mobile telephone interrupted my train of thought. It was reception. 'A Mr Turner's arrived to see you.'

'Find an empty conference room and I'll be down to see him.'

I turned to Lydia. 'David Turner has arrived.'

Lydia went back to her desk and I walked down to the ground-floor conference room that still smelt of gloss paint. David Turner stood up and reached out a hand when I walked in. He was tall and slim and I could see the family resemblance. He even had the same sort of spectacles.

'I'm very sorry for your loss.'

'Thank you. Tell me, Inspector, do you have any suspects for my father's death?' I had heard journalists in a press conference manage more emotion.

'It's too early just yet. Can you tell me anything that might help?'

'We weren't close.'

No surprise there.

'I hardly knew him, really. I was sent to boarding school and then my mother died when I was at university and my father never had much time for me. He was always working on some deal or another.'

'How often did you see him?'

He sat back in his chair and averted his gaze. 'A few of times a year. At Christmas, of course, and then if he was in London on business we'd meet up.'

'How often did he travel to London?'

'I can't really say. Perhaps his staff could help you. I would meet him in his hotel for a drink or dinner. I met him with Matthew Dolman and once I met him with a man called Frost. I remember the name, reminded me of that fictional detective.'

I nodded.

'I'm staying for a few days to sort out his affairs.' He slipped a heavily embossed card over the desk.

I saw David Turner to the door and went back to the Incident Room, worried if Dean would say the same thing about me if I died. Dean barely knew me and our lives never crossed in any meaningful way.

When I got back to the Incident Room Lydia raised her head and glanced over at me, her eyes wide. 'Something you should see.'

I stepped towards her desk.

She pointed at the folder on her desk. 'It's Troy's army service history. He left under a cloud.'

'Why?'

'There were complaints about his violent temper. The whole thing was hushed up.'

'Have you spoken to the commanding officer?'

'Not yet. He's calling me tomorrow.'

Chapter 18

'Fennel and nettle tea.' Lydia said as I wafted a hand in the air.

'Smells disgusting.'

'It helps keep me calm and there are lots of other benefits. You should try some.'

I gazed down at the chaos on my desk – so much for the paperless office. Then I checked my watch. The two detective constables assigned by Cornock were late. Then I heard the sound of movement in the Incident Room and saw two officers peering at the board and throwing inquisitive glances towards my office. I strode out of my room and Lydia followed behind me. A short woman with purple-framed glasses thrust out her hand.

'DC Jane Thorne. And this is DC Wyn Nuttall.'

Lydia was by my side now as we looked over at the young officer by Jane's side, a nervous look on his face.

'Good morning, sir.' Wyn had a North Walian accent, warm and rural just like Dave Hobbs. Ever since the police forces of Wales had merged into one force a stream of officers from the north came to work in Cardiff. Maybe it was too cold up there in the mountains. He had a brief rather limp handshake.

'So you're the cavalry,' I said.

Jane frowned, Wyn blinked nervously. I decided not to try humour again.

Wyn replied. 'Superintendent Cornock gave us orders to attend for a briefing. I am on Detective Inspector Hobbs' Cardiff city football taskforce. The superintendent wants me seconded to your investigation pro tem.'

I waved at the empty chairs and then I turned to look at the board.

'Matthew Dolman was killed in his car in the Royal

Bell car park.'

Both Jane and Wyn took notes.

'He was the managing director of the National Bank of Wales and very wealthy.'

I turned to the board and tapped the image of Jamie Henson. 'Initially we've been concentrating on Jamie Henson and Neil Cleaver of the Wales Against Poverty group. But there is a second group of anarchists that we'll need to focus on too. And yesterday Alan Turner was killed in the lift of his apartment block.'

'Are both deaths linked, sir?' Jane had a serious frown on her face.

'Same MO. And they were business associates. Last night we brought in for questioning a George Stanway. His company was forced into bankruptcy by the National Bank of Wales or so he alleges. Wyn, you check out his alibi and requisition all the CCTV coverage from near Turner's flat.' I nodded at Lydia. 'Lydia will give you the details you need.'

'And Dolman had a flat in Nice that his wife and family know nothing about. So Jane, you get started with finding out everything you can about that. And the expense account won't stretch as far as a trip out there either. Maybe a pack of Nice biscuits.'

Jane managed the barest of smiles, Lydia suppressed a chortle and Wyn looked utterly lost.

'We're focusing on what happened to Stanway Engineering too. And another contract Turner and Dolman had in common was the electrification of the Valleys railway.'

I spent a few minutes giving them both a summary of what we knew and where our priorities lay. Jane stared at me intently, occasionally opened her mouth as though she had something to ask but thought the better of it. The terrified look on Wyn's face only disappeared as I left.

The sat-nav kept bleeping instructions that annoyed me so I turned it off and called Harding himself for directions. After another five minutes, we found his home. He was a man who had enjoyed corporate entertainment judging by the size of his girth and the jowls under his chin. The small bungalow on the outskirts of Cardiff was an incongruous home for a man who had been involved in various multi-million-pound transactions. He heaved himself into a large leather armchair, and pressed a button by the right armrest, activating a section of the chair under his knees that raised up his calves.

'I've got bad circulation,' he said.

'We are investigating the murder of Matthew Dolman. He was the managing director of the National Bank of Wales.'

Harding nodded vigorously.

'And also the recent death of Alan Turner. He was one of Matthew Dolman's associates.'

Harding continued to exercise his neck muscles. 'I met them when I was working for Frost Enterprises.'

'I want some background into the relationship between the three men.'

'Frost had his entire business riding on the successful outcome of the tender to win the electrification contract. Dolman and Turner made him believe that he was guaranteed to win. They had all the right contacts. They knew people in the government, people who would scrutinise the tender process, people who could put the tender together. It was supposed to have been a guaranteed success. Frost paid Dolman and Turner huge amounts in fees which he raised by mortgaging the business and his house to the bank.'

'So what went wrong?'

'Turner was supposed to smooth things along. He was an operator. He knew the right people to take for lunch, the right hands to shake.'

Harding reached for a glass of water on a small table by the side of his chair.

'I was amazed when the contract was awarded to that company from London especially as they were connected to some offshore outfit.'

'How did Frost react?' Lydia asked.

'He was utterly shocked. And I mean lost for words. I haven't seen him so upset since he'd lost his wife.'

I sat back in the sofa. 'So what happened to the business?'

'It was only a matter of time. Frost didn't wait around. He parked his Bentley near the Cefn Coed viaduct in Merthyr Tydfil and then threw himself off. Some walkers said that he smiled at them before he jumped.'

We sat silently for a few seconds. Neither Lydia nor I knew what to say. I could barely imagine the pain of a man driven to suicide. How could a person face that?

'When did his wife die?'

Harding took a sip of water. 'I can't be certain about the date. A year before he died, maybe more. A journalist confronted her on her doorstep about revelations she was going to make about Frost and some rent boys in London. He'd been there with Dolman. One of those freebie weekends. This journalist had the TV crew with cameras ready. But Agnes Frost had a heart attack on the spot. The journalists were sick enough to carry on filming whilst she was lying on the floor. The paramedics couldn't revive her.'

'Did they have any children?'

'No. But Frost had been married before. I don't know the details but he had a daughter I believe.'

My mobile rang and I fished it out of my pocket. I recognised the pathologist's number. 'I'm busy right now. Let me call you back in five minutes.'

We thanked Harding for his time and left. As soon as we were outside, I rang Paddy.

He launched immediately into an explanation of the post mortem. 'Turner must have struggled. There are several defensive wounds to the hands and arms. And the trajectory of the blade is downwards. There is evidence from the US that suggests a woman tends to stab downwards whereas a man will thrust upwards.'

'Come off it, Paddy. It would have needed a lot of force to kill Turner.'

'Still doesn't rule out a woman. But it was the same sort of weapon – even the same one.'

'Can you be certain?'

'Nothing certain in this line of work. You know that, John. The killer knew where to strike but was caught off guard.'

'How likely do you think it is that it was the same killer?'

He paused. 'I would say that on the balance of probabilities it was the same type of blade used in a similar way with the same result.'

'For Christ's sake, Paddy. Was it the same killer? Am I definitely looking for the same killer?'

'I'd say so.'

I ate a stale chicken sandwich at my desk as I scanned the post mortem report on Turner. Then I deleted most of the emails in my inbox although I dwelt on the briefing note from Dave Hobbs. He used all the usual jargon: 'stakeholders', 'measurable outcomes' and 'resource management' that made me realise why I'd never be promoted. I was halfway through when the telephone rang. It was a welcome distraction.

'DI Marco.'

'Hannah Peters, Inspector. There's something wrong.'

I put the rest of my sandwich on the wrapping on my desk. 'What do you mean?'

'My papers are all out of order as if someone has been rifling through them.'

'Are you certain?'

'Of course. It must have happened over the weekend before Alan was killed.'

'You didn't notice anything yesterday?'

'I didn't stay after seeing you. I just couldn't bear it.'

'Stay where you are. I'll get a forensic team there straight away.'

I dialled Alvine. 'I need a full forensic search of Turner's office. There's been a break-in there last night.'

'I can't just ...' It sounded like her mouth was full.

'And Alvine, it's urgent.'

'I'm in the middle—'

'I'll tell Hannah Peters to expect you.'

Alvine's muffled protests continued as I slammed the receiver down.

On my way out of the Incident Room I delegated Lydia to visit Hannah. I needed to complete the picture of Alan Turner's current workload so I found my car keys and headed out for the offices of Silverwood. A preliminary search before I left had told me that Keith Wood, the owner of the business, lived in one of the expensive suburbs in the north of the city and that he and his wife were the main shareholders of the business. I wondered who was behind the anonymous-sounding company that owned twenty per cent of the shares, so I had emailed Boyd Pierce to ask him to investigate.

In an industrial unit to the north of the city Silverwood had a large office building with a yard behind it that had a collection of plant and equipment. I parked in a slot reserved for visitors and made my way to reception. A yucca plant needed watering badly and there were old copies of various driving magazines on the table by some visitor chairs. The receptionist gave me a suspicious look as though I was the first visitor that week.

I pushed my warrant card towards her. 'I need to see the owner.'

She managed a narrow smile and pointed at the visitor chairs. 'Please sit down.'

I heard her talking over the telephone explaining that Mr Wood really needed to come to reception. I flicked through one of the well-thumbed magazines and scanned the images of the latest Range Rover.

'What can I do for you?' There was a loud booming voice from the other side of reception as a man in his forties, a white shirt straining at his girth, came striding over towards me. 'Keith Wood. I'm the MD here.' He stretched out a hand.

'I'm investigating the deaths of Matthew Dolman and Alan Turner. Is there somewhere private where we can talk?'

He turned on his heels and led me into a small conference room off reception. 'Now what's this about?' He sat down and leant over the table. A dull band of light fell on his face highlighting his pasty complexion.

'Matthew Dolman and Alan Turner were involved when the Stanway business was sold to you.'

'Certainly were.'

'How much did you pay?'

'A pound and the debts.'

I frowned. 'Can you explain?'

'Of course. There some debts that my company assumed and then I paid a pound for the actual business. But I had to take on the liabilities.'

'And now I understand that you're selling up.'

'Certainly am.' He patted his sizeable belly. 'Can't go on like this for ever. Got to get out and start getting healthy.'

'How much are you selling the business for?'

Wood sat back and inclined his head slightly. 'That's confidential. I'm sure you understand.'

'Does the National Bank of Wales support your business? Do you have loans with them?'

I could see him thinking. 'The bank has supported us right from the beginning.'

He had a dark brooding edge to his eyes behind the bluff personality.

'And Alan Turner?'

'It's terribly sad. He got things done smoothly.'

'Would it be true to say that you're making a lot of money from the sale of the business?'

Wood smirked. 'Certainly am.' He added without any reservation, 'Can't wait to retire.'

Keith Wood answered all my questions about the business and I skirted around asking him about Stanway Engineering half-expecting him to be evasive but he had no hesitation in telling me how he had capitalised on their reputation and expertise to grow Silverwood.

I shook Keith Wood's rather sweaty hand after thanking him for his help and went back to my car. I smoked a cigarette and thought about Stanway and the small house he rented. Then my mobile rang and I recognised Cornock's number.

'Get back here. Another video's been released.'

Chapter 19

Superintendent Cornock stared at the screen clutching the remote. Susan Peel from the public relations department stood by his side chewing her lip. She gave me a dark glance as I mumbled a greeting.

The screen came to life and two hooded individuals stood for the camera. I stared at the screen hoping that I could visualise that one of these men was Henson. But, again, there was nothing to identify gender. They wore black head to toe, even thick black fleecy gloves.

The taller one recited a monologue to the camera.

'Another greedy bastard has been killed. A man who thought nothing of taking advantage of the weak and helpless in society by being involved with the banking establishment. He had made himself indispensable to the corrupt, monied elite that rule our country. But he wasn't indispensable to the people of Wales or the people of the United Kingdom who have suffered because of the greed of the bankers.'

Cornock pressed pause, and turned to me, lips clasped closely together, his eyes narrowed. 'This is absolute madness.' He drew the tips of two fingers across his furrowed brow as if trying to find a pressure point. 'We need to find these people. And we need to stop them.'

'When was this released?' I said.

'An hour ago,' Peel said without taking her eyes off the screen.

'Is it the same group as before?'

Peel nodded quickly. 'When this goes viral then we are all in deep shit.'

Cornock turned back to the screen, pressed play and watched intensely as the two figures started again.

'It is time for the corrupt banking elite to realise that

the ordinary people cannot bail them out for their corrupt practices. The bankers who have lined their pockets and continue to do so will not be tolerated any longer. Everyone associated with them is tainted in the same way. It is time for things to change.'

Cornock pressed pause again. He spoke slowly this time. 'It's *got* to be the same group.'

I could remember the smugness on Dolman's face as he destroyed every argument that Henson put forward in their television debate. Henson had looked incoherent and the interview had turned him into a laughing stock. But was it enough to kill Dolman? And why kill Alan Turner?

'There isn't much more,' Cornock said.

The screen came to life again with the sound of the electronically altered voices filling the silence of Cornock's office. We listened to a long catalogue of statistics and facts about the impact of the financial bailout that had rescued the banks in 2008 and how the level of bankers' bonuses hadn't been curbed as a result. It sounded like propaganda always did, plausible on one level, even compelling and probably persuasive for some people. Individuals like Henson were on a mission to change society for the better or certainly their view of it. I was waiting for some demand, a reason to justify the deaths of Matthew Dolman and Alan Turner. The final part of the video explained that a Robin Hood tax on the profits of the bankers and additional profits on their bonuses was the only way to secure a stable banking sector.

'This probably means that they are capable of killing again,' Cornock said as the tape finished. He sat down heavily in the chair behind his desk and looked over at Peel perched on the edge of one of the visitor chairs. 'How are you going to respond?'

'We've drafted a brief announcement. This time

around there won't be any press conference. We are not going to give this group any extra publicity.'

Cornock nodded. I stepped over towards the window and leant on the sill. The evening had drawn in; light pollution formed a pale white mask over the city centre. Drizzle fell against the window pane.

'I've spoken to the assistant chief constable,' Cornock said. 'Forensics is going to do everything to analyse this video. It's already with psychologists and a specialist forensic team. Hopefully they will give us some idea of who these people are. They reckon they might be able to filter out some of this electronic crap. If that's the case we might identify an accent.'

It all sounded very positive. But I preferred to rely on old-fashioned police work. Doing the hard graft of knocking on doors and talking to people who might know something.

'What do you think, John?' Cornock said.

I stepped away from the window. 'I'm not sure I believe all this corrupt banker nonsense.' I was thinking about the messages printed on Henson's computer. It just didn't fit. The link to Henson was too convenient and a gut feeling held me back from charging off to arrest him.

Cornock leant back in his chair. Peel sat more upright.

'Why kill Alan Turner? He's not a banker,' I said.

'But he was closely associated with Matthew Dolman,' Cornock said.

'These activists are on a campaign against the corrupt bankers. It just doesn't make sense that they go round killing someone like Alan Turner.'

Peel piped up. 'Then why make these videos and distribute them all over the internet? The whole world has seen them.'

I shrugged. I knew that the forensic analysis on the videotapes might give us some clues, something we could use. In the meantime, I could keep joining the dots, hoping to make sense of why Dolman and Turner had been killed and more importantly, what connected them. When Peel left, she gave Cornock a limp-looking handshake that she repeated with me.

Cornock waved a hand to one of the visitor chairs.

'We need answers soon, John. The ACC is getting a shed load of pressure. More pressure than you would ever imagine.'

I nodded slowly. I couldn't remember seeing Superintendent Cornock so agitated.

'I'm going to speak to Troy and Rex Dolman again—'

'Don't you think you should be concentrating on these activist groups?'

'There are questions I need clarified with the Dolman brothers first.'

Cornock raised his eyebrows, sat back in his chair and said slowly, 'I really hope you are right, John.'

By the time I got back to the Incident Room, the place was quiet. I switched on the light and the fluorescent tube flickered into life. Chairs had been tucked under desks, papers neatly stored away. I stepped over towards the board and looked at the images of Matthew Dolman and Alan Turner. I sat down in the chair Wyn used, put my feet on the desk, threaded my fingers together and propped my head back, hoping it might encourage clear thinking.

It would take days for the psychologists to analyse each sentence and every paragraph, as they looked for some hidden meaning in the individual words on the video recordings. And among the various names on the board was the answer.

I left the police station and walked over to my car.

I tried not to miss a meeting. It was the comfort of sitting in a group of strangers, who had become friends, of sorts. In the old days I could persuade myself that I could have one drink and stop right there. Just to be sociable. Before my promotion, heavy drinking was an essential part of my curriculum vitae as a detective sergeant. It had to be done, at least every Friday night. And then there were the weeknights when I'd be working late and somebody would suggest a nightcap. One drink became five and then eight and by the end of the evening, all I could remember would be somebody pushing me into a mini cab.

Streetlights came on as the traffic thinned and I indicated into the car park of the hotel. I pulled up alongside a Jaguar that had just extinguished its parking lights. I recognised the number plate and the driver who emerged from the car.

'Hello, Richard.'

Judge Richard Patricks would normally have balked at the use of his Christian name by a police officer. Our paths had crossed professionally many times. I had given evidence in court when he was the presiding judge, sitting before him in his chambers when he had considered bail applications and each time there had never been a glimmer of acknowledgement.

'Good evening, John.'

We locked our cars and meandered over to the hotel.

'I hear you're the senior investigating officer on Matthew Dolman's murder.'

'Did you know him?'

'I'd met him a few times at various dinners. I could never make him out. Never took to the man personally. He had done very well for himself after devolution. He turned the National Bank of Wales into quite an institution. One of his sons is engaged to Charlotte Parkinson. She's got a bright future ahead of her in the legal profession. I was in college with the lawyer that she trained with in London. He was surprised when she moved to Cardiff. But with all this devolution business there's a lot of government work and big contracts flying around.'

We reached the door and I yanked the handle open. Judge Patricks continued. 'I suppose you know about Dolman and Deborah Bowen. That was the worst-kept secret in Cardiff.'

I followed Judge Patricks through the hotel lobby and into a private room at the rear. A small group had gathered around a table, helping themselves to coffee and tea from various flasks. There were greetings, the occasional brisk handshake and encouraging smiles. We sat around, each of us nursing a cup or mug as a prop.

I was ready when my time came. 'My name is John, I'm an alcoholic.'

Chapter 20

Reports about the second video dominated the morning news. Journalists stood in the rain outside Queen Street squinting into the cameras, sheltering under umbrellas. They used words like 'police baffled' and 'murders still a mystery'. I sat watching the television first thing that morning realising that Cornock and the senior management team would be furious. I sipped on my double espresso and then finished some rubbery toast as I listened to interviews with various experts who claimed to be profilers. The television company had found former senior detectives who had words of wisdom that made it sound easy. Our own experts had promised to get us the information about where the original video had been uploaded onto the internet by the end of the day but it would probably be exactly the same as the first video – a laptop or PC somewhere in the UK.

After clearing away my breakfast I left the flat and drove into town hoping that the TV crews would have left by the time I arrived. I turned towards Queen Street police station and noticed several large vans with enormous satellite dishes parked along the roads nearby. I swung the car into the car park and then found my way up to the Incident Room.

I gazed at the photographs of Matthew Dolman and his wife that Lydia had assembled on the board. In one Brenda Dolman was actually smiling, at some black-tie charity event, both her sons by her side. There were intense smiles, all very convenient for the cameras. Scratching the surface of Matthew Dolman's domestic arrangements had soon uncovered family tensions. What else would come to the surface about this family? Despite the videos circulating on the internet something, a hunch maybe, perhaps instinct developed from too many years in the business of policing, told me I should focus on Matthew Dolman's life.

A noise from the staircase beyond the door alerted me to the presence of one of the team. Wyn was the first to arrive and looked surprised to see me. He was wearing a white shirt with a blue tie that had a few discreet red stripes. He could have been a civil servant or a bank clerk. Clutching one of those enormous plastic mugs of coffee he walked over to his desk and found a spot for his drink. Then he buttoned his jacket before he stood looking at me. Sometimes it was difficult to make him out, but I had never fathomed out people from North Wales.

'How are you fitting in?' It was the sort of question that I hoped might have helped me build our relationship. The brevity of his reply soon made that a distant possibility.

'Fine, thank you, sir.' And his tone suggested he wasn't going to discuss it any further.

Jane Thorne barged in sparing me the necessity of persevering. She was also holding a portable mug of coffee; it was even from the same outlet as Wyn's. 'Good morning, boss.'

I nodded. 'Jane.'

As she took off her light jacket, and tidied her desk for no apparent reason I sat on the edge of one of the desks. It had been barely two days since I had met them and my initial impression that they were an odd pair still remained.

'Bring me up to date,' I said.

Wyn cleared his throat, glancing over at Jane who gave him a brief nod as though she were in charge, giving him consent to go first.

'I've been checking George Stanway's alibi. I spoke to the landlord of the club where he alleges he was drinking on the night Alan Turner was killed. He couldn't remember very much. Apparently the place was rammed.'

'Is that up in Quakers Yard?'

Wyn nodded. 'They do a special on a Sunday night, selling cheap booze with a curry.'

'And what did he have to say?'

'He can't remember. But the place was so busy he was flat out changing barrels, making sure that there was enough food. He gave me the names of some of the bar staff and I tracked one of them down.'

Jane chortled. 'The suspense is killing me.'

Wyn gave her a hurt look. 'He remembers Stanway ordering a drink quite late.'

'So he can't confirm where Stanway was during the early part of the evening?'

'That's right boss. But last night I spoke to a couple of Stanway's mates, ones that he named when you interviewed him. And they confirmed that they had been in the club from about six o'clock onwards. Apparently there was a rugby game on the television. Then they drank themselves stupid.'

'They're all like that in Quakers Yard,' Jane announced, folding her arms.

'Did you check the television schedules?'

Wyn nodded.

'Damn.' I stood up, stepped over towards the board and looked at Stanway's photograph, pinned below Alan Turner's.

I turned to look at Jane. She was already assembling paperwork on her desk, realising that I expected her to tell me if she had made any progress.

'It's a nightmare, sir.' She paused, looked up at me, obviously preparing me for bad news. 'We've got protocols about requesting help from the French authorities. The woman I spoke to thought we'd have to go through the

Home Office.'

'You're joking?'

'Then she suggested we contact a department in the French police in Paris. So I gave them a ring because she thought that the *Gendarmerie Nationale* would be responsible for that sort of enquiry. Then when I contacted them they told me that it was the *Police Nationale* who dealt with urban city areas such as Nice.'

'How many police forces are in France?'

'Only two boss but they're both national and for some reason they can overlap.'

It reminded me of the problems that had arisen once policing and criminal justice had been devolved from London and the four police forces of Wales amalgamated. There had been predictions of chaos and criminals running riot but in the end nothing much had changed.

'And did they give you any idea of how long it will take to get information about this apartment?'

'Apparently it's quick according to French bureaucracy. These requests are quite common as part of anti-money-laundering regulations. I've got all the paperwork together for you to sign making the formal request for the relevant town hall to provide us with all the information we need.'

'We need it as soon as possible.'

Jane folded her arms, frowning and nodding simultaneously.

I continued. 'I want you both working on the CCTV coverage from Penarth to Cardiff on the morning Dolman was killed. I want to see anything unusual. He might have been followed. And do the same for CCTV coverage outside Alan Turner's place. And Wyn, there is a file relating to previous death threats that Dolman received. I want you to review that again.'

I left them both scribbling notes and headed to my office.

The paperwork on my desk was unchanged from the night before. A stale smell hung in the air so I opened the window. I had complained to the estates department but I'd been met with derision. One of them had even suggested that I hang up an air freshener like the things you see dangling from the rear view mirror of old cars. A gentle waft of fresh air blew across my desk.

It was late morning by the time I realised how much time I had spent Googling Malcolm Frost. His suicide had made the headlines for a day but he was quickly forgotten. I found all of the newspaper reports covering the announcement by the government that his company had not been awarded the electrification contract. Initially there had been comments that legal action was being contemplated and I could imagine the lawyers rubbing their hands in glee at the prospect of the fees involved. A YouTube clip had followed a journalist onto Cefn Coed viaduct to the exact spot where Malcolm Frost had thrown himself to his death. By the end I had an overwhelming feeling that I had wasted valuable time. The Frost link between Matthew Dolman and Turner seemed a dead end. Apart from Stanway Engineering it had been the only deal they had in common recently. Perhaps there was something else linking both men. Something that I was missing. I leant back, pitched my shoes onto my desk, an affectation I found often assisted clear thinking.

The telephone rang and I cursed before dragging my feet off the desk.

I reached over and scrambled for the handset. 'There's some foreign woman in reception asking for you.'

'Who?'

'How would I know?'

'Have you asked her name?'

I heard a groan. 'She says it's important, like.'

Although I felt annoyed with the interruption I knew that I was a world away from some eureka moment. 'Put her into a conference room.'

I stood up and rummaged for my papers and a ballpoint pen before making my way downstairs to reception. I pushed open the door to the conference room and recognised the face sitting at the table. The woman had broad cheekbones, narrow thin lips and eyes that stared at me intensely. Dark hair curtained her face but the apprehension I had seen the previous Sunday at Mrs Dolman's home had been replaced by puzzlement. Immediately she averted her eyes and fidgeted with her fingers.

I dragged a chair from underneath the table and sat down, my interest piqued. I held out a hand before sitting down. 'Inspector John Marco.'

She gave me a brief nod.

'Gabriele Vaitkus,' she spoke softly.

'You work for Mrs Dolman?'

Her nodding was more energetic now. I sat down and dropped my notepad onto the table.

'This is confidential, yes?'

I nodded in acknowledgement. 'What do you want to tell me?'

I didn't recognise her name from the preliminary reports. And I could sense her unease so I decided that taking this interview at Gabriele's pace would be best.

'Mr Dolman good man.'

I tried a brief smile. 'What do you do for the Dolman family?'

'I work in house. Clean and laundry.'

'Do you work every day?'

'Monday is my day off.'

That explained why there had been no mention of her from the preliminary reports after Dolman's death. I leant over the desk. 'Gabriele, why are you here? How can I help?'

'I hear things. Bad things in the house.'

Again I smiled hoping to put her at ease. 'What sort of things?'

She looked up at me and stared, locking eye contact with me. 'This is confidential, yes?'

'I'm investigating Mr Dolman's death,' I said softly. 'If you have any information that might help me catch the killer then it will be important.'

There was a moment's hesitation. 'There was much argument. Mr Troy and Mr Rex they argue much with Mr Dolman.' She sat up in her chair. 'They fight a lot and argue and I hear lots of bad things.'

'Did you hear what they were arguing about?'

She rolled her eyes and scanned the room. 'They argue about the bank and what was going to happen ... Mr Troy he was bad. He say really bad things and he want Mr Dolman ...'

'You'll have to tell me as much as you can.'

By the time Gabriele had finished I had a clear picture that the Dolman family had been warring about the future of the bank and that there had been frequent and repeated arguments when tempers had been frayed and there had been a shouting match between father and sons. She made a point of telling me that Troy Dolman had shouted the loudest and threatened his father.

'Why didn't you come to talk to us sooner?'

'Back in Lithuania police are shit.' She said it with a simple certainty. Then she shrugged. 'And Mrs Dolman, she tell me it is nothing.'

I sat back in my chair and smiled at Gabriele wondering what she thought of life in Wales. 'I'll need you to sign a statement in due course.'

She curled up her lips and nodded her understanding of the inevitable.

'I find another job.'

Lydia standing in the doorway of my office interrupted the various threads I was trying to connect. 'I've had Troy Dolman's former commanding officer on the telephone.'

I took my feet off the table and jerked my chair nearer my desk. Lydia stepped into the room. 'I wanted to speak to him about Troy's service record. But he refused point-blank to talk to me. He said he would have to speak to somebody of your rank or above.'

'What?'

She handed over a single sheet of paper with a telephone number. Without invitation she sat down, crossed one leg over the other knee and waited for me to make the call.

I grabbed the telephone handset and punched in the number.

After several officious-sounding voices, I reached the extension for Colonel Watkins-Pugh.

'Inspector John Marco, Wales Police Service. I understand you were the commanding officer when Troy Dolman was on a short service commission. We have his record and we would like something clarified.' I made it all sound very reasonable.

'I spoke to that sergeant of yours earlier today,' Watkins-Pugh said. If his name suggested some Welsh connection the accent suggested it was very tenuous indeed. He had a loud voice with crisp elongated vowels. It was like listening to a soundtrack from a 1950s documentary. 'She was in a terrible flap.' I glanced at Lydia, the epitome of calm. 'Wanted to know all about Troy Dolman's background, what were the nature of the complaints about him.'

'Well, I'm sure you can understand that we have to go through the motions of ticking all the boxes. There's more paperwork than you can imagine these days, Colonel.'

'No need to tell me about paperwork. Drowning in the stuff. Never used to be like this.'

'How well did you know Troy?'

'Well enough. Good, instinctive leader. Even if he could be, how can I put this …, robust.'

'Say no more, Colonel.'

I glanced over at Lydia again. This time she had a pained expression on her face. I was getting into the swing of this conversation, rather glad that Lydia couldn't hear the colonel's comments.

'You can treat this conversation in the utmost confidence but I was intrigued about some of the comments concerning Troy's familiarity with some of his men.'

I sensed Watkins-Pugh breathing rather slowly. He would never know that I was guessing about Troy's behaviour.

'Well, man-to-man. Christ, that's not what I meant to say. There was a certain corporal with whom Troy was over-friendly. I'm sure you understand what I mean. We live in an age of transparency and tolerance but even in the army we have to draw a line somewhere.'

'I understand, you have been very helpful Colonel Watkins-Pugh. Do you happen to have the name of the corporal involved. It'll help us to tie up loose ends. Make sure we can eliminate Troy from any ongoing inquiry and minimise any embarrassment.'

'Yes, of course. He was called Youlden, Paul Youlden.'

Chapter 21

We rearranged the photographs on the board in the Incident Room with Youlden's image earning promotion and it was now pinned alongside Henson's. I spent the evening reading again everything we knew about Youlden and his involvement with the extremist groups, while Lydia searched every database for information about him.

It was after midnight; my eyes were burning, so I left. In the morning, I would allocate tasks for Wyn and Jane but for now I needed to sleep.

By six-thirty the following morning I was sipping coffee, looking out over the Bay, cursing my mind for forcing me awake. After a shower, I dressed and then headed into the city. It was quiet, the occasional taxi, minibus and early morning commuter the only traffic. Lydia was already waiting for me when I arrived.

'Couldn't sleep?'

She nodded.

Our visit to the National Bank of Wales that morning had justified some additional attention to her make-up and her clothes. Her white blouse looked newly ironed and she had pulled her hair back into a ponytail that accentuated the carefully applied blusher, the lipstick brighter than I remembered.

She gave my second-best suit a quizzical examination. I had three and the one I was wearing was reserved for meetings with the CPS or lawyers and now bankers.

'Have you seen the news?' Lydia said.

'Cardiff is certainly making the headlines.'

'One of the journalists tried to stop me this morning when I arrived.'

'Just be careful.'

She tilted her head and scolded me with a raise of her eyebrows.

After a review of our plan for the discussion with the Dolmans and some detailed instructions for Jane and Wyn to build a complete picture of Youlden we left and headed for the bank. I was already smoking the second of my five-a-day when I reached the mobile vendor selling various e-cigarettes. I had read somewhere recently that the tobacco companies had been buying up the manufacturers of the electronic substitutes. No matter what sort of smoker you had become – traditional or electronic – your money ended up in the same place. I recognised the man behind the trolley: he was stamping his feet trying to keep warm. He was blowing into his hands as he gave me an interested look but before he started his sales pitch, I moved on. Outside a newsagent, there was an old-fashioned hoarding at street level with the words 'Anarchists Release Second Video' printed in bold letters.

We skirted around The Hayes, walked down to the end of St Mary Street and then dipped through a railway arch as a train rattled overhead before we reached the headquarters of the National Bank of Wales.

Inside two men approached me, both wearing dark suits, white shirts, and sombre ties, with an attitude straight from the boxing ring. I flashed my warrant card, Lydia did likewise and they gave us a brief nod. The girl in reception stared at my card and then spoke down the telephone. There was a tense frightened atmosphere not helped by the guards, standing, hands clasped in front of them, peering out through the revolving door.

I heard the lift door opening and glanced over, expecting to see the assistant again but Troy Dolman stepped out. I walked over towards him.

'Good morning, Inspector.'

'Mr Dolman.'

'We've seen the second video, of course. Isn't it possible to stop this stuff being put on the internet?'

We took the lift to the sixth floor and he led me to the same conference room that we had used on my first visit.

'You know my brother and Charlotte of course,' Troy said. 'And this is Tony Harper, our lawyer.'

I guessed Harper was mid-fifties. He was slim, short back-and-sides and small intense eyes. We shook hands. 'I was Matthew Dolman's lawyer and we did a lot of work for the bank. And I knew Alan Turner of course. Everything that has happened is just terrible. Are you any further forward in identifying who might be responsible?'

I gave Harper a brief, non-committal smile. 'I need to get some background cleared up. I'd like to know what will happen to the bank after Mr Dolman's death.'

From the glances that were fired across the table like static electricity between Rex and Troy and Tony Harper I knew that I wasn't going to get the truth. Charlotte focused on some paperwork on the table.

'It really is quite complicated,' Troy began.

Rex mumbled his agreement. Having someone take me for a fool wasn't recommended.

'Your father didn't own all the shares in the bank. A trust fund owns twenty-five per cent. I need details of how that fund operates.'

Harper replied. 'The fund is run as a private family trust. The dividends paid by the bank are all used for the beneficiaries of that fund.'

'And they are?'

'That is confidential I'm afraid.'

I wanted to raise my voice, shout even, but I curbed my anger. 'This is a murder inquiry. I need any relevant information. And I'll decide what's confidential.'

Harper glanced at Troy and then Charlotte. 'The trustees of the fund are Mrs Dolman and both Troy and Rex. The beneficiaries are the extended family.'

Charlotte looked over at me and smiled.

I had an uncomfortable feeling that it was only the barest of information and that there was far more that I needed to know. It was like fishing in a pond of deadly fish that occasionally came to the surface. 'Perhaps you can send me a briefing memorandum. You know, spell out the situation in simple layman's terms. I need to know the shareholding owned by your father and if it was used as security for any debts. And if so who the mortgagee might be. And more importantly who now has the controlling interest in the company?'

I was rather pleased with the look on the faces of the Dolman brothers. And even more pleased that I'd spent an hour that morning reading a simple guide of how companies operate and a lot of helpful websites about management structures.

'I'm sure that's something I can put together for you, Inspector,' Charlotte added.

I turned to look at Tony Harper. 'Did you do all of Mr Dolman's private work?'

'Yes.'

'Had he made a will?'

'Of course.'

'I'd like to see it.'

He glanced over at Troy and Rex who glared back at him.

'Is there a problem with me seeing the will?'

'No, of course not.' Harper was back into lawyer-mode. 'He was contemplating having it changed.'

'Can you tell me the changes he was considering?'

He blinked briskly, hesitated and then cleared his throat. 'He was going to leave more of his estate in trust for his various charities. And he was considering more generous provisions for Charles Bowen.'

I could sense everyone staring at me deliberately as though they had no idea where else to look. I let the tension drag out. 'Why did he want to make changes?'

I noticed Tony Harper swallowing hard before glancing at Charlotte. 'It was no secret that he and Mrs Dolman were having difficulties.'

'You mean he wanted to disinherit his wife?'

'No, of course not.'

'But she wouldn't have got as much under the new will?'

Harper adjusted his tie a centimetre or two before replying. 'I think that is a fair summary.'

'I'll need to see the file.'

'Of course,' Harper said.

'And have you made any progress with Mr Stanway?' Charlotte purred from the opposite side of the table.

'We have spoken with Mr Stanway, of course. And at the moment he is only one line of inquiry we are pursuing. I am more concerned with investigating the anti-capitalist groups active in South Wales. I think they are more likely to be the realistic suspects.'

Charlotte gave me another perfect-teeth smile. And yet another unreadable face. These people were good at hiding their emotions and concealing what was going on.

'Before I start with the staff, I'm interested in the homeless shelter that you funded in Pontypridd.'

Rex snorted. 'That was a bad decision. I don't know why my father wanted to support them. We've had nothing but adverse publicity.'

Troy stared over at me but said nothing.

'I understand that Alan Turner supported the shelter as well.'

Rex again. 'It wouldn't surprise me. He was probably roped into it.'

'There is one other question. I'll need the full details of the flat your father owned in the South of France.'

I couldn't look everyone in the eye simultaneously but I was certain that Rex and Charlotte were surprised. Tony Harper kept the emotionless face of an experienced poker player.

Rex pitched in. 'I don't know anything about a flat in the South of France. Where the hell did you get that sort of information?'

'That's confidential.'

They glared at me.

'I'll need to speak to the staff again. But first I need to clarify some things with Troy.'

Harper collected his papers and Charlotte walked out with him, Rex following. Troy leant on the table and clenched his jaw. 'This had better be quick. I've got an important meeting.' He motioned self-consciously at his watch.

Lydia opened the file of papers and scanned the first page. 'You were in the Welsh Guards for three years.'

'What the hell has that got to do with anything?'

She put one hand on top of another on the file and paused. 'I understand that you had difficulties with some of the enlisted men.'

Lydia was more diplomatic than I would have been.

Troy sat back, and folded his arms. 'Whatever you've been told it's a load of rubbish.'

The anger in his voice was inappropriate somehow.

'One of the men in your regiment was a Paul

Youlden. He's linked to one of the anti-capitalist groups.'

He guffawed in disbelief. 'The army has thousands of service men.'

'But he was in the same regiment. Did you know him?'

'You are wasting your time on this. You should know better. I've a good mind to telephone the chief constable and complain.' He stood up and towered over the table. 'You cannot come in here and accuse me of killing my father. It's utterly preposterous.'

He paced over to the door and left.

We watched him striding through the open-plan offices.

'Did you see them when you mentioned the flat in Nice?' Lydia said.

'Rex didn't know anything about it.'

'Charlotte looked astonished. Just for a moment though.'

'Let's talk to the staff.'

Lydia organised to call various members of staff. We spoke to over a dozen personal assistants, relationship managers and account managers and each confirmed what we knew already – Matthew Dolman had been a considerate, if tough, employer. When we asked about the relationship between Matthew and his sons, we met with less cooperation. One of the senior account managers told us how Matthew Dolman had boasted about his encounter with Henson on the television. He had even treated some of the staff to a celebration lunch.

It was late in the morning when Ann Roberts joined us round the table in the conference room. She brushed a hair out of her face and moved her lips self-consciously as she sat opposite us. I got straight to the point.

'Did you know about the flat that Matthew Dolman

owned in Nice?'

Fear and surprise combined in her face. She cast a surreptitious glance through the glass partitions. 'No. I don't know what you mean. There must be some mistake. Where did you hear about that?'

I paused, uncertain about her response.

'It seems that he kept the property a secret.'

She cast her gaze around the room. She was hiding something.

'Tell me about your relationship with Mr Dolman?' I sat back and smiled.

For ten minutes she skirted around telling us what was really on her mind. Lydia gave the barest of shrugs when I glanced at her as Ann stared at her hands curled up on her lap. I nodded back and was pleased when she asked the sort of question that might get Ann talking to us.

'It must have been upsetting hearing Troy and Rex argue with their father so much.'

Ann look non-plussed for a moment but the opportunity was gone for her to deny the truth. And had I asked the direct question she would have clammed up.

'I never meant to say anything.' She paused and looked intently at Lydia. 'Matthew was arguing a lot with Troy and Rex about the future of the business. They had endless meetings. I prepared reams of minutes.'

'Do you know what's going to happen to the bank now that he's dead?'

She chewed her lower lip. 'It's not for me to say. The business might be sold. Or taken over. It probably won't continue as it is.'

'Where is this paperwork?'

'It might take me some time to find it.'

She stood up and looked over her shoulder again but neither Troy nor Rex was in sight. I watched as she returned to her desk. I didn't know if I was any further forward. The flat in Nice remained a mystery and I recalled the surprise on Charlotte's face as well as Rex's. I wondered if anyone in the National Bank of Wales was telling me the truth.

Normally I kept a clean desk. But that afternoon I had the special branch files open in front of me again. I had relegated the papers on the electrification contract to a cupboard in one corner of my room. After Jamie Henson I would start on Paul Youlden and everyone associated with him. Wyn and Jane were working on the files from the National Bank of Wales and occasionally I heard them discussing terminology with the officers from economic crime.

I had just finished reading the Henson file when Lydia stood at my door. Through the window behind me, I could hear a deliveryman shouting instructions and then some swearing and a loud crash.

All the paperwork in front of me was having a soporific effect. 'I need a coffee and a doughnut.'

Lydia followed me out of Queen Street to Mario's around the corner. It was the end of the day and the place was quiet. I slipped into a bench and a tired-looking waitress came up to us.

'What can I get you?' She drawled.

'Double espresso and a doughnut.'

'Americano please,' Lydia said.

'I liked the way you got Ann Roberts to spill the beans on the Dolman family.'

'She was waiting for a reason to tell us. Once she thought we knew it was dead easy. So do you think it means that Troy is involved?'

'He knows Youlden. So he could have put him up to kill his father.'

'But why kill Turner?'

Sometimes Lydia could stop me mid-thought. 'I ... there must be something else.'

'He's got a temper. And we know they argued.'

The coffee arrived with an icing-sugar clad doughnut and a knife that I ignored. I enjoyed the sensation of the sugar hit.

'And Youlden could have used Henson's printer to plant evidence against him.' Lydia added, obviously pleased with her developing theory.

'But we also find out that Mrs Dolman had a gold-plated motive to kill her hubbie – he was planning on disinheriting her.' I turned my attention to the coffee.

Lydia paused and I could see her contemplating. 'But how could she have killed him? She was at home.'

'Do we have that verified?'

Lydia pondered and rolled her eyes. I continued. 'She might be in league with Youlden. Check out if he ever stayed at the hostel.'

Lydia nodded now. 'But Henson might have never thought we'd link the messages to his printer.'

'The printer is pretty conclusive evidence.'

Lydia didn't look convinced. And neither was I but we had nothing else to go on so Henson stayed high on the list of suspects.

Murderers never make it easy. I ran a napkin over my mouth. I gave the rest of the doughnut a hungry look.

'And what do you make of the electrification contract?' Lydia added.

'That's not taking us anywhere. Frost is dead and so is his company.' Even so, the details had been playing on my mind.

Lydia folded her hands around the cup and swilled the dregs of the coffee around the bottom. 'I agree. There are probably lots of contracts that Dolman lost. And who would have any motive – certainly not that Harding bloke.'

I said nothing. I dabbed a napkin to my lips and then scrunched it into a ball on the plate. My espresso was warm, just. I finished the coffee and after paying we returned to Queen Street. Jane looked up at us when we walked into the Incident Room.

'How far back do you want us to go, sir?'

'What do you mean?'

'We've been through all the papers from the NBW and there are dozens of contracts where Dolman was working with Turner and with that lawyers' firm where Harper works. And they know each other well. The emails between them are very matey.'

I sat on one of the chairs in the Incident Room listening to Jane and then Wyn explaining the work they had finished that afternoon. Wyn pinned on the board a large spider chart of how everyone was involved.

'Good work, Wyn,' I said.

He blushed before continuing. After an hour and several unsuccessful attempts to conceal yawns, I knew it was time to leave for the day. There had been various texts during the afternoon from Tracy confirming a dinner arrangement for tomorrow evening. Then I answered a couple more from my mother about the impending holiday with Dean.

As I shrugged on my jacket, my mobile rang.

'David Turner, Inspector. I've found something unexpected in my father's papers.'

Chapter 22

Lydia put her head around my office door the following morning to enquire what time David Turner was expected.

'He was in Swindon an hour ago,' I said.

I couldn't concentrate on work. I paced around the Incident Room gazing at the board and glancing at my watch. When the message came that he had arrived at Cardiff Central Station I shouted at Lydia and we headed off to Turner's offices.

The television crews had left Cardiff by now – we were yesterday's news. We strode down Churchill Way and soon found ourselves outside the office building. I pressed the intercom and it buzzed open almost immediately. David Turner was waiting for us and let us into reception. Packing boxes half-empty of stationery and office accessories crowded the tabletops and small labels hung from the furniture. There was no trace of the forensic work the CSI team had completed and no sign of Hannah.

I shivered. Lydia drew her coat lapels up to her face.

'I'm going to clear as much of dad's possessions this weekend as I can. I can then hand the keys back to the landlord.'

'What did you want to show us?' I said.

Turner led us into his father's office and sat down. He drew out a file from a tan leather briefcase and placed it on the desk in front of us.

'My father had an apartment in Sydney.'

Another overseas property.

'And you knew nothing about it?'

'Not a thing. I asked my uncle who lives in Tasmania and he was in the dark as well. I knew that my father had gone out there last year for a holiday. He met up with his brother – they never got on. But I had no inclination at all that he had bought a flat out there.'

'Have you got the details?'

He pushed the file towards me.

'How much did he pay for the flat?' Lydia asked.

'That's the thing. It overlooks Sydney harbour. I haven't been able to trace how much he paid for it but I did a Google search and similar ones go for the equivalent of half a million pounds.'

'*How much?*' I said.

Lydia tempered my surprise. 'We'll need to see all of your father's bank accounts and personal files.'

'Of course.'

David Turner spent an hour filling three boxes that sat on the desk in reception. His father's life had come to this: a pile of bank statements and investments certificates but no family to mourn him and no friends to grieve. Turner had no meaningful relationship with his son and I wondered what David must have felt. In truth, I should have known.

'Will I ever get the originals back? It's just that I might need them for the probate formalities.'

I looked up at David Turner. I hadn't paid attention to what he had said. I was thinking about my own family and wondering if Dean would grieve for me.

'Will the paperwork be returned to me?'

'Of course. Once our investigation is complete.'

We organised for civilians from Queen Street to remove the boxes and left Turner to the emptying office. I stood outside with Lydia who glared at me as I lit up.

I managed the stairs back to the Incident Room two at a time and by the top I could feel my smoking habit telling me that I had to stop as I gasped for breath. I strode over to the board and turned to face Jane and Wyn. Lydia was already at her desk.

'We've just been to see Alan Turner and his father had an apartment in Sydney nobody knew anything about.'

Jane was the first to give me a double-take. She straightened in her chair.

'Both dead men have overseas properties their families know nothing about. I need to know everything about them. And I need it now. No, yesterday. Jane, have you made progress on the French apartment?'

'I heard from the French authorities this morning. The flat is registered in the name of some company that's based in the Cayman Islands.'

'Can we get the full details?'

'That will be harder than you might think ...'

'For Christ's sake. I've got a double murder inquiry. Tell them to pull their finger out! When are we going to get the details?'

'Next week.'

I was getting breathless – too many cigarettes, but the tension dragging on my chest didn't help. I scribbled the name of the flat in Sydney on the board. Then I turned to Wyn and Jane. 'I want to know everything about this property today.'

Wyn was already trawling the internet. 'Sydney is nine hours ahead of us. That makes it almost midnight.'

'I don't care. The police in Sydney don't all go to bed at night.'

Lydia's voice had a soothing effect on my irritation. 'But the staff at their land registry probably do.'

She was right. I calmed my frustration and tried a measured tone. 'Then find someone in the Sydney police who can reach the land registry and extract the information we need.'

Jane and Wyn nodded.

I looked over at Lydia. 'Let's go through Alan Turner's financial records.'

He had more than I could imagine. And yet he died alone in the lift of his apartment block just after he had opened a bottle of Chianti. I knew from my past that drinking alone was a bad sign. One drink led to another and then another and then oblivion. Turner didn't need to worry about anything any longer and from the statements summarising his savings and his pension pot he had nothing to worry about when he was alive. Financially, at least. It amazed me how much paperwork could be generated by financial advisers and accountants. Turner probably thrived on it all. He was a hoarder which made it hard work trawling through all the stuff he had kept including the annual reports from the Vale of Glamorgan Racquets Club.

I realised what was missing from Turner's life: he had nothing in his papers about his family. Nothing to suggest he had any children, or grandchildren. No mementoes or photographs. All the comments my mother had made over the years about my parenting skills fell into place and suddenly I felt sad about Turner's life and my own. I turned to look at the telephone pondering whether I should call Dean there and then.

I got back to making detailed notes, resolving I would call him over the weekend.

The muffled conversations drifting in from the Incident Room had a tense edge and then I noticed the time, realising that not a great deal could be completed until the morning. I walked out into the Incident Room and the activity stopped.

I glanced over at Wyn. 'Did you make any progress with the CCTV coverage?'

'Nothing yet, boss.'

I turned to Jane. 'Any news from Australia?'

'I should have news in the morning. I'll be in first thing to chase them again.'

I nodded. 'It's going to be a long weekend. Get off home.'

Tracy wore a green dress with a zip down the entire length of the front. It finished just above her knees and her high heels completed the perfect sight for a Friday night. I stared at her legs, stared at all of her in fact. Her hair had been carefully brushed and lay in thick curly waves over her shoulder. I lingered over a kiss.

'You look sensational.'

She gave me another peck on the cheek. She threaded a hand through my arm as we strolled up Queen Street to the middle of town. Tonight I had booked one of the other places that had received my mother's seal of approval. The waiter remembered me as he led us to the table I'd asked for.

'How often do you come here?' Tracy whispered.

'It's my mother. She's a regular and being from Lucca she can tell them exactly how she wants things.'

Once we had decided I waved at the waiter who came back and jotted down the order. He returned moments later with a candle in a small glass jar with fancy decorations and a bottle of San Pellegrino.

'Isn't it terrible about the second video,' Tracy said, leaning forward.

The light caught the turquoise in her eyes: they almost glowed.

'Pretty sick.'

'Are you anywhere nearer catching the killers?'

'Not really. There are so many loose ends ...' The

waiter returned with some bread and olives.

'So why does your mother like this place?'

'Best Tuscan olive oil.'

'Your mother sounds quite a character.'

'She's an Italian at home in Wales. She misses the warm weather and the ice cream. Although she married my father – just for his ice cream.'

She laughed at all my jokes as we ate our ravioli starter. She drank wine and I got through half of the water. 'You don't drink wine?' She hadn't asked me that question on our first date and I'd assumed, maybe wrongly, that Alvine had given her an executive summary of my history. She must have sensed that now was the right time.

'It doesn't agree with me.'

It satisfied her, for now. 'Is it true that you're going after the anti-capitalist groups?'

Two plates of saltimbocca arrived and she carved off a small piece of veal, waiting for me to reply.

'They're the obvious suspects.'

'How many are there?'

'There are two groups. One based in the Valleys and another in Newport. Until now they were just agitators but obviously something has changed.'

'So we've got terrorists in Wales.' She made it sound like something we should be proud of.

The rosemary potatoes that assaulted my taste buds complemented the meat perfectly.

'Have you got other suspects? How does Turner fit into all of this?' She peered over the table, her eyes sparkling with curiosity.

I finished a mouthful of food. 'Let's not talk about work.' She pouted her feigned disappointment. 'Tell me about your family.'

Her father had worked in the same double-glazing

firm for thirty years. Her mother kept dropping hints that they wanted grandchildren before getting too old.

'Have you got any siblings?'

'A brother but he's ... single. Have you got any brothers or sisters?'

'No. Only child.'

The waiter cleared away the plates and returned with the pudding menu. We ordered lavender-flavoured panna cotta. The restaurant was full and the noise level had steadily increased to a pleasant hum. The candle light caught Tracy's cheeks. She smiled and I remembered the first time I'd seen her when she had been wearing a white boiler suit – it was the first time I had ever seen someone looking sexy in a CSI outfit.

'Did you read the PM report on Turner?' Tracy said.

'It was the same sort of knife that killed Dolman.'

She lowered her voice. 'A stiletto?'

I nodded.

'Do you think the same person killed Turner?' She finished the last of her wine. 'Maybe—'

The waiter arrived and placed the desserts on the table.

'Would you like coffees afterwards?'

Tracy giggled and put a hand to her mouth.

'Just the bill, thanks.'

I could still taste the lavender on my lips as I held Tracy's hand and we walked towards the castle. I flagged down a taxi and she held my hand as we drove down to the Bay. I wanted to lean over and kiss her, really hard, and then run my fingers through her hair and feel her tongue on mine. Traffic delayed us and the taxi had to slow at some lights. I could feel her body moving next to me, every sinew breathing and swaying in the half-light of the streetlights that darted into the taxi.

It was another ten minutes before I stood in the hallway of my apartment. I dropped my jacket on the floor before pushing the front door closed behind me. I pulled her close, her mouth was moist, the alcohol assaulted my lips. It wasn't like the first time where we almost fell headlong into the bedroom. Now I stood and slowly pulled down the zip as she fumbled for the fly of my trousers. My excitement pulsed a little harder as I noticed her lacy black underwear.

Chapter 23

A text woke me early. Tracy stirred by my side. I reached over and fumbled for the handset. I read the message from Terry, one of my regular informants, suggesting we meet for breakfast. I glanced at my watch. It was still early. I leant over and looked at Tracy. I drew back her hair and kissed her on the cheek. Her perfume still lingered in the bedclothes. She snuggled back under the duvet and I slipped out of bed.

It was a short walk from my flat to Gorge with George, a greasy spoon in the Bay, where the bacon was thick and the baps floury. Terry was sitting at a far table, a large mug in front of him. I slid into the seat opposite.

'This had better be worthwhile,' I said. 'I'm going to work this morning.'

'It's Saturday.'

'I'm busy.'

Terry gave me a puzzled look. 'I watched the telly the other night. About that banker – Dolman and those terrorists. Are you involved in that case?'

'What do you want, Terry?'

'There's an ongoing inquiry into the Cardiff City Soul Crew. You know those fucking nutters who go and beat the shit out of other team supporters.'

'I know who the Soul Crew are.'

I glanced over at the counter and mouthed a request for a mug of tea.

'It's just that I hear things that's all. And something's going on.' He leant forward over the table and whispered. 'I might have some information.'

'I'm not dealing with that inquiry. It's Detective Inspector Hobbs in charge. You'll have to speak to him.'

'That fucking knobhead. You must be joking.

Nobody can understand him talking.'

Two bacon rolls arrived with the teas and Terry chewed a large mouthful.

'He's the senior police officer in charge of that inquiry. So you talk to him or nobody.' I got a finality into my tone that even Terry should understand. He glared over at me.

'Okay. Keep your shirt on. I deal with you, Marco. Nobody else.'

'I've made it quite clear −'

'So if I have any valuable information then the WPS doesn't want to hear it?' He squinted his eyes, defying me to reply.

I finished my bacon roll in silence. 'What have you got?' I said.

'I need something in return.'

'Let's hear what you've got to tell me first.'

Terry gave a quick glance over his shoulder before straightening his posture. 'Doreen, my missus, is facing a blackmail charge. It's all fucking shit. I need you to make it go away.'

I sat back and crossed my arms. 'You must be mad.'

Terry shook his head.

'I can't make a charge like blackmail disappear. You know that.'

'It's that or nothing, Marco.'

We sat in silence. It felt like minutes but it was probably much less. I took another slurp of the tea before Terry got up and sidled out of the bench. He looked around the café and then over to George, safely out of earshot.

'I'll text you when I've got more. And then you're going to help the missus. Because that way it helps you.'

He left and I watched him raise the lapels of his jacket as he sauntered down the street. I reached for the mug of tea when a message reached my mobile. *Call me AD.*

It was another half an hour before I arrived at the Incident Room. Alvine was already waiting for me in my office.

'Where have you been?' She was wearing hiking trousers that had lots of different pockets and a thin navy fleece top.

'You're in early. Are you modelling a new CSI uniform?'

'Very funny Marco. I should have left half an hour ago.' She glanced at her watch.

'Going anywhere nice?'

She glared at me. 'We've finished the analysis of the forensics on Turner's office. The fingerprints of Troy Dolman are all over the place.'

'Really. He probably had meetings there.'

Alvine shook her head. 'They are all over the desks. And another thing. We've traced the computer.'

'What do you mean?'

There was irritation in Alvine's voice now. 'We know the location of the computer used to upload the second video.'

Tightness in my chest returned from the expectation that this could be a breakthrough. 'Where?'

I jotted down the name of the internet café in Pontypridd. It was near Henson's address. I raised a hand and waved at Lydia in the hope she would see me and then I shouted. 'In here, now.'

Seconds later Lydia stood in the door of my office, Wyn and Jane behind her. I stuck out my hand with the details of the property in Pontypridd. I gave them an instantaneous summary as I walked around my desk and reached for my jacket. 'Wyn and Jane. I want you to find as much as you can on the internet café. The owner etc. ... and then message me with anything you can find. Lydia, you're with me. And Wyn, find out who owns Turner's offices.'

I heard Alvine raising her voice and saying something about being glad she'd been able to help just as I yanked open the door to leave the Incident Room.

Luckily the heavy traffic was heading into the city so we reached the intersection with the M4 quickly and then I powered the car north up the A470. Soon I indicated left towards Pontypridd and broke the speed limit in my haste.

'I'm surprised that Henson would have used a café,' Lydia said.

'Maybe he just didn't want any trace to his laptop.'

'Still, using a public place is a bit risky.'

Lydia was right and it might just be too convenient that this evidence pointed to Henson once again. I spotted a sign for 'Computer Repairs and Internet Café' and drew the car to a halt by the kerb. Lydia had spoken to Jane once on the journey but she had nothing to report. I found my mobile and rang her again.

'I've just finished talking to one of the CID officers from Bridgend. Apparently Darren Williams, the man who runs the place, is known to them. They think he's a small-time fence for stolen laptops and other kit for computers. But they've never been able to prove anything. And he's got a profitable little sideline in selling films he's downloaded from the internet.'

I thanked her and finished the call.

A shower drenched the car and I peered out into the grey morning sky but the bleak weather had settled over the town. Thankfully the rain abated as we scampered over the road.

Half a dozen customers in the shop gazed at the computer screens and a couple drinking from enormous mugs gave us cursory glances.

A man with a long beard and an even longer ponytail sat behind a counter piled high with boxes of various computer accessories. Discreetly I flashed my warrant card. He grimaced. 'Is there somewhere we can talk privately?' I kept my voice soft but my eyes hard.

He jerked his head behind the counter.

We followed him through into a small room, boxes of PCs and monitors stacked to the ceiling. Darren wore a collarless shirt underneath a leather waistcoat. His corduroy trousers had lost all their shape.

'What's this about?'

'We need to trace someone who used one of your computers last week.'

'Why? I run a legit business here.'

I stepped towards Darren. 'I'm not interested if any of this stuff has been knocked off or in your little scam selling illegal films to the people of Ponty but unless you cooperate then I might be forced to take a different view.'

His poor complexion got worse.

'I've got nothing to hide.'

'Then you won't mind giving me the details I need.'

Standing so close to him, I could smell the cigarette smoke on his clothes and I noticed the acne scars over his cheeks.

'Do you keep a record of everyone who uses the computers?'

'It'll take me a while to get you that information.'

'We'll wait.' I smiled at Darren.

Back in the café, we sat down. Customers came and went, some giving us curious glances. It must have been almost an hour before Darren came over to us and sat down.

He pushed over a data stick. 'That's the record of

everyone who paid using a card.'

'Do you keep a record of the names of people who pay in cash?'

He shook his head. 'I've added the names of some of the regulars who come in and pay in cash.'

'Thanks.' We stood up and left the table.

'You can keep the data stick.'

We left the café and stepped into the windswept and wet Pontypridd morning.

'I found the details you wanted about Turner's office,' Wyn announced before I had barely got through the doors of the Incident Room. 'The landlord is the National Bank of Wales.'

It stopped me in my tracks. 'Bloody hell. So Troy Dolman could legitimately have a set of keys to the offices.'

The possibilities raced through my head. I stepped over to my office. Jane stood behind Wyn in the doorway.

'What motive would Troy have to kill Turner?' Jane said.

I was thinking the same. 'It must be something to do with the bank.'

Wyn again. 'But Hannah didn't mention that anything was missing.'

'Maybe Troy didn't find what he was looking for.'

I powered up my computer. 'Jane, you talk to Hannah again, and Wyn, check out the data on this stick.' I tossed it over the desk.

A commotion from the Incident Room interrupted my scanning of the emails in my inbox. I got up to see Lydia, hands on hips, glaring at one of the civilians from reception who had a sheepish look on her face.

'Why the hell did you open it?' Lydia said.

I reached her desk.

'It was … I don't know, I just didn't think … We get so much mail …'

I looked down at Lydia's desk and my heart missed a beat. *Bankers – when will they learn?* was printed on a piece of A4 paper. Now I realised why Lydia was angry. The envelope by its side had my name clearly printed on it.

'For Christ's sake, why the hell did you open this? It was clearly marked for me and now it's contaminated. Don't you understand the first thing about police work?'

The woman swallowed hard, opened her eyes wide and her lower lip quivered. She rushed out before the tears started. Lydia was already snapping on a pair of latex gloves and delicately put the paper into a plastic evidence pouch.

'You'd better get that to CSIs,' I said.

She nodded.

Wyn and Jane both stood quite still; each with a startled expression when my mobile rang.

I read Jackie's name.

'John. Dean's been rushed into hospital.'

Chapter 24

I stood by my desk and stared at the paperwork. I glanced over at the various boxes belonging to Alan Turner. Then I tried to remember Dean's face and I couldn't. I just fucking couldn't and I blinked hard. I turned away, knowing what I had to do. I grabbed my jacket, scrambled for my car keys and raced down the staircase to the car park.

I jumped in and within twenty minutes I reached the motorway and headed east. Once I was safely in the middle lane sticking to the limit I scrambled for my mobile and rang my mother.

'John! Where is he? When did he go in? Who's with him?'

I told my mother everything I knew while keeping a sharp eye out for traffic police.

'I'll call you once I know something.'

I knew that my mother would probably be calling the hospital every hour asking for updates but she'd still expect me to call her. Before reaching the Severn Bridge I called Lydia.

'Nothing is more important than family,' she said, deflecting me from talking about the investigation.

I switched off the mobile and threw it onto the passenger seat.

Family. Lydia was right of course but it made me realise what I had been missing. The regular contact with Dean, sharing family events, participating in his life.

I drove on and every time a to-do list formed in my mind it got pushed to one side. I tried Jackie again but it rang out. So I floored the accelerator and nudged the car nearer a hundred miles an hour. I passed streams of lorries and cars headed east towards Swindon. I dropped my speed when I passed a traffic car heading westwards. No pointing in courting trouble.

The sat-nav flickering on the dashboard told me I was approaching the junction for Basingstoke so I slowed down. I followed the instructions to the general hospital. I parked and ran over to the entrance. It was quiet; the main lights had been dimmed as they were preparing for the long hours of the night. My stomach tensed as I stepped over to the reception desk.

'My son has just been admitted.'

'Can I have his date of birth?'

I froze. My stomach tightened another notch.

'His name is Dean Marco ... But he's probably using the name Dean Alloway.'

The absence of a date of birth earned me a scowl. She clicked over the screen in front of her. 'He's been transferred to the Paediatric Intensive Care Unit in Southampton.'

'There must be some mistake.'

The woman shook her head. 'Your son was transferred by ambulance an hour ago.'

The words intensive care were like a piece of hot metal burning my skin. I wanted to swallow but my throat drew up into a heavy knot. I wanted to ask why and demand to know what was wrong with him.

'I can ask one of the medical staff here to talk to you if you like.'

I blanked out the sound of the telephone in reception. Southampton. I had to get there. All Jackie had said was that Dean was unconscious after an accident. I didn't have time to speak to a nurse.

'Mr Marco. Shall I call a doctor from A&E?'

I stared at her for a moment. 'No. No.'

'It's no trouble.' She reached for the handset.

I leant over the counter. 'How do I get to

Southampton?'

She scribbled the postcode on a card and I sprinted out to my car. I fumbled with the sat-nav until it listed the directions on the screen. I managed the journey in fifty minutes.

The receptionist pointed me in the direction of the PICU. I walked, then I broke into a mild jog before bounding down the empty corridors. A set of double doors led into an area before the main entrance and I found one of the staff nurses. She pointed me down the corridor towards two private rooms.

I pushed the door open and saw Jackie crumpled into a chair.

I couldn't move. I stared at the empty bed next to her.

'He's in theatre,' Jackie spluttered.

I managed to move, stepping towards the bed.

'He's in a coma.'

'What?'

'They had to put him into a coma.'

'What happened?'

She raised her head. She looked drawn and gaunt as though she hadn't eaten or slept well for days. A quick scan told me that Paul – Mr Alloway – wasn't there.

'He fell. He smashed his head against a rock. It looked terrible ...'

Her head sagged again; I reached for a chair and sat down by her side, holding her hand in mine.

'How long will he be in theatre?'

'They didn't say.'

I wanted to get up, march over to the nursing station along the corridor and demand a complete explanation. Instead I sat with Jackie. Gone was the confident woman that I had once loved, she looked haggard. Her hair was an unruly mass and her blouse creased. I heard the noise of a child coughing and then the sound of crying. A child was sick but it was my son who was in theatre. After a while I got up and found Jackie some water. A nurse gave me a sympathetic smile.

'Any idea how long they'll be?'

She glanced at the watch. 'It's variable. We'll let you know as soon as he's out.'

It was after ten-thirty when we heard the sound of activity outside. The door opened and a nurse and another orderly strode in, wheeling out the bed. Jackie and I stood up and moved to one side. It was another twenty minutes before more staff appeared pushing a bed with Dean on it.

Jackie gasped. I held my breath as we noticed the tube sticking out of his mouth and a wire protruding from under a bandage covering his head. The nurses connected him to a variety of tubes – one under his collarbone and another in his wrist. The ventilator made his chest rise and fall rhythmically.

I stared at my son's face. Almost zoomed in on him, wanting to capture his features. I had never been one to have a photograph of him propped on my desk. In fact, I couldn't even remember whether I had one in my flat.

A nurse turned towards us. 'The surgeon will be along very shortly.'

My mobile made a sound. It was a text from my mother, asking after Dean. I tapped out a brief reply telling her I'd ring her later.

'Where's Paul?'

Jackie averted her eyes over my shoulder and then back to Dean. 'We've split up.'

Now I really didn't know what to say. What do you say when your ex has split up with her new husband?

'I didn't know.'

She crumpled her mouth and her shoulders sagged.

'Things haven't been working out. You know what it's like.' She raised an eyebrow as she stared at me.

I wasn't certain that I did. My father would harangue me about my drinking, telling me I would lose my family. But what did he know? I wanted to reach out to Jackie but I stumbled over the right thing to say. My discomfiture was postponed when a dapper man with the demeanour of an army officer entered the room. His chin was a fraction too long. His handshake was dry and firm.

'Hello, I'm Jim Holland, consultant neurosurgeon. Mr and Mrs Alloway?'

'John Marco,' I said. 'Dean's father.'

'What do you understand about what's happened so far?'

I glanced at Jackie. She was staring at Dean.

'Your son has had a significant brain injury.' It was like someone smacking me in the chest. 'As a result of the fall he's sustained a serious head injury; the CT scan showed what we call an extradural haemorrhage, bleeding between the brain and the skull, and a cerebral contusion, which is a bruise to the brain.'

Jim must have seen the incredulity on my face. 'Basically we needed to remove the blood clot as soon as possible to relieve the pressure on his brain. This is why he was transferred urgently from Basingstoke straight to theatre.'

'What's going to happen ...?'

'We removed the blood clot, and have managed to elevate the piece of skull which was broken; it's now a matter of letting things settle.'

'When will he come round from the anaesthetic?'

Jim moved a step nearer me. 'We'll be keeping him asleep in the intensive care unit for a few days, and keeping a close eye on the pressure inside his skull. We've left a small wire inside which measures this for us. We won't be waking him up until this pressure is stable.'

My mouth felt like sandpaper. 'Will he be all right?' I stammered.

'Unfortunately it's very early days yet. Many children with this sort of serious injury do very well but we need to wait and see how he behaves over the next few days. As soon as the pressure in his brain stabilises we'll aim to wake him up.'

'When do think that might be?'

'It won't be for at least 48 hours, but it could be longer depending on how things go.'

The doctor left and we sat again next to Dean's bed nestled below a bank of monitors and pumps and tubes and equipment that occasionally bleeped. An hour later I persuaded Jackie to get something to eat and I sat in her chair holding Dean's hand in my own, the regrets and recriminations of my time living with Jackie dominating my thoughts. And then Lydia's words that nothing was more important than family came back to me again and I cupped Dean's fingers with both hands. The years when Dean had not been the most important thing in my life suddenly came to haunt me and I settled into a resolve that the past had to be exactly that.

Jackie came back and I found my way to the café. I sat pushing some stale fish and chips around the plate but finished the meal without much enthusiasm. Afterwards I walked outside, found a corner near the main entrance where there was a pile of cigarette butts on the tarmac, and called my mother.

'He's had a severe crack to the head. They've had to operate on his brain and he's in a coma.'

My mother caught her breath.

'He's really sick.'

She whispered. 'Is he going to be all right?'

I heard myself repeating the same details the doctor had given us earlier. I promised to call if anything changed and then I lit my cigarette and watched visitors arriving at the hospital and ambulances parking at A&E. I got back to Dean's room as Jackie was talking to a nurse.

She turned to me. 'I was asking your wife.'

'We're not married.' I said it too quickly but by then it was too late.

'Oh … Well, do you need any pyjamas, toothbrushes for tonight?'

'Yes, thank you,' Jackie said.

The nurse left and we sat down. She returned a few minutes later and gave me a weak smile as she handed me a pile of nightwear. After some discussion Jackie insisted that I sleep first but I lay awake listening to the muffled conversations and activity of the night staff. I glanced at the clock occasionally, and tossed and turned until I acknowledged that sleep would elude me. I got up and walked back to the ward. Jackie had her head resting on the bed so I gently shook her and told her to get some sleep.

At first she refused until I promised to wake her if anything changed. But nothing did. I sat on the chair yawning, then I stood up and walked around before staring out of the window. Twice I made myself a coffee with lukewarm water from the parents' room. I had never thought about Dean being ill before but he must have had a cold or the flu or something. I didn't know and the emptiness of it all made me feel I had lost out on far too much of my son's life. And this was something I knew I had to change.

By lunchtime the following day a dark tinge highlighted the bags under Jackie's eyes. When I ran my

179

tongue over my teeth they felt furry. A nurse had sat at the end of Dean's bed throughout making regular notes on a large chart. Other times she'd fill syringes and check the pumps. Every hour they checked his pupils and she'd consult with the doctors as we sat there helpless. Jackie called her mother. I called mine. She had already packed a case if she was needed and she had contacted Jackie's mother too. I even called Lydia who asked about 'my son' and then I knew that she didn't even know his name.

At the end of the afternoon Jim Holland arrived. He spent an age checking the readings and discussing matters with the nursing staff. I hadn't noticed the Irish accent last night but today it sounded more pronounced. He asked to speak to us in a room off the main ward.

'It's more private in here,' Jim said, waving a hand at two chairs. 'The team have been trying to control the pressure in his brain but it's still high, they're now trying some different medication.'

'What if they don't work? Will you have to operate again?' I said, not thinking what I was saying.

'I've discussed that possibility with a colleague but for now we've decided against more surgery. What we're doing is trying to cool his body temperature a little by using a special mattress; we might have to relax his muscles with medication, so we'll attach him to another monitor which monitors his brain activity. That involves a few more wires attached to his head.'

'But he is going to be all right?' I said.

'Let's talk again tomorrow. In the meantime I suggest you go home and get some sleep.'

I could see Jackie's shoulders sag; in fact I almost went to catch her from falling.

Jackie gave him a pleading look.

'We'll call you if there's any change at all.'

We left after the evening visiting and made more calls to our parents. The conversation went much the same way with each and we promised several times to call them if there was any change.

It was strange pulling into the drive at Jackie's home. She flicked on the light switch and I followed her into the kitchen with the takeaway we'd bought on the journey from the hospital. We ate and talked but it was the conversation we had had a dozen times or more in the last two days and it was all about Dean.

Jackie showed me around the house, including Dean's room. There were posters of footballers and pouting faces from some band I didn't recognise. She pointed to the guest bedroom and then she paused. 'I'm glad you're here, John. Thank you.' Then she stepped over and gave me hug.

Later, I listened as Jackie padded round her bedroom. It felt odd sleeping in her house, under her roof. Eventually the house was still and I guessed she was sleeping. But I couldn't and I lay there staring into space, thinking about the investigation.

I heard a footfall on the landing and the door opening.

I looked up and Jackie came into the room.

'I'm scared, John.'

She sat on the side of the bed before sliding under the duvet wrapping her arms around my chest. I held her back and in seconds she was fast asleep. The feeling that I had missed this came as a surprise as did finding myself dwelling on our life together.

In the morning she woke and immediately her face was a mixture of embarrassment and surprise. 'I'm sorry. I didn't mean ...'

'Don't worry. Things will be all right.' I hoped my optimism was well founded.

We reached the hospital early. Dean lay there, tube in his mouth, wire protruding from his head. The air filled with the hum from the bank of equipment surrounding his bed. I'd bought a newspaper but felt little inclination to read it so I sat there and sometimes we managed banal conversation that petered out. I stepped out occasionally and made coffee. I passed small groups of family gathered around the bedside of ill children. I knew that after seeing the doctor tonight I'd have to decide about whether to stay or return to Wales. It was late afternoon when Jim Holland arrived with a younger colleague – a woman, mid-thirties with long permed hair and a bright cheerful face.

'This is Janet Palmer. I'm on leave for few days so Janet will be taking over,' Jim said.

It unsettled me to think of someone new being involved. The frown on Jackie's face told me she felt the same.

'Unfortunately the pressure in Dean's head is still a little high, although it is improving. At the moment the best course of action is to keep him asleep and wait for the pressure to improve.'

'Is he going to be all right? I mean, is he going to have brain damage after this?' I blurted it out.

'It's impossible to say how Dean will wake up. I know this is hard and I'm sorry that I can't be more concrete.'

During the day various texts from Lydia reminded me that I was in charge of a double murder inquiry. Later that afternoon Jackie gave me a resigned look. 'You need to get back to Cardiff.'

I didn't reply immediately. It was going to be difficult leaving Dean. I even thought that I should ring Cornock and tell him to assign someone else to act as senior investigating officer.

'He's going to be all right. You need to get back,' Jackie said. 'Your place is at work now. He's out of danger.'

My place should have been as a better father for Dean over the years. And now my place should be here with Dean. It was early evening when Jackie persuaded me to leave, promising to call if there was any change.

I left Southampton that evening driving on auto-pilot. The traffic was light, the weather dry. I drove, hoping Dean would recover. There was a good chance. And that meant I had a good chance to put things right: try and make amends for the years I had been a useless father. When I reached the junction for the motorway I negotiated the roundabout three times, debating with myself whether I should go back to Southampton. Superintendent Cornock could allocate someone else to take over the investigation. Maybe even Dave Hobbs. But giving up on my career wasn't the answer although I resolved then that never again would I give up on Dean.

I headed for the motorway and hammered the car towards Cardiff.

Chapter 25

Superintendent Cornock shook me warmly by the hand and suggested I sit down. I was tired despite having slept soundly; in fact I was convinced that I hadn't moved all night.

'How are things?'

This time I knew exactly what he meant. 'Dean is still in intensive care. Next few days are critical.'

'We've been thinking of you here, John.'

Cornock turned his attention to the tropical fish swimming in his tank. After a brief moment of rumination he straightened in his chair and looked over at me. 'Are you certain that you want to get back into the investigation? I could always assign Dave Hobbs to take command, although he seems to be enjoying his role in the Cardiff City Soul Crew inquiry far more than I'd expected.'

I raised a hand in the air. The last thing I wanted was Dave Hobbs interfering.

'There's a lot of pressure to get the two murders solved, John. So you need to make progress and I'm concerned that with Dean poorly you will not be focused enough.'

'No problem, sir. Lydia and the team are really on top of things. I'm expecting some progress from forensics later today.'

Cornock raised an eyebrow. 'Good. Keep me posted.'

As I left I glanced back at the superintendent, a silver Cross ballpoint already in hand, his gaze on the paperwork on his desk.

I reached the Incident Room and three sets of worried eyes looked over at me.

'I've been in a meeting with the super,' I said.

The concern disappeared from their faces and Lydia spoke first. 'How's Dean, boss?'

I gave them all a summary of what had happened in the hospital. I didn't tell them about the risk of complications and that Dean was still very ill.

'Anything from Australia?' I said to Jane.

'The flat is registered in Alan Turner's name.'

I hesitated. Jane continued. 'All the paperwork seems in order.'

I was thinking about all the bank accounts in Alan Turner's name and the surprise on David Turner's face when he told us about the apartment. 'We'll need to know where the money came from.'

'Sir?'

'Trace the source of the money. Someone should be able to tell you where the money came from.'

From the energy in Wyn's demeanour I could tell he had something on his mind. 'We've built a spreadsheet of the individuals that used the computers in that café last week, sir. You won't believe it but Paul Youlden is on the list.'

I stopped and turned to look at him.

He thrust the list at me.

I scanned down the names, straining to block out any sound, hoping this would be a small breakthrough. They could be collaborating with Henson, pretending to be different groups but in reality, they had the same aim.

'Good work. Is there an address?'

'A property in Newport.'

I turned to Lydia. 'Get your coat.'

She followed me downstairs to the car park. I punched the postcode into the sat-nav and fired the Mondeo into life.

'Is it going to be another waste of time?' Lydia said.

'If it is you can always blame special branch.'

It was another twenty minutes before we had negotiated the Brynglas tunnels and I took a junction down into the middle of the city. Newport was drab even on a spring morning with far too much post-industrial catching up to do. The sat-nav dictated and I followed the instructions until I drove down into a group of industrial units by the river.

I parked outside a large entrance door, plywood pinned to the original frame. I pulled the door open and it swung freely on its hinges. A radio played somewhere in the building. We walked down a bare corridor, rooms off either side, empty apart from some discarded old furniture and stacks of old timber. The final room was an improvised office; various old printers and a laptop were set out on a piece of plywood as a makeshift desk.

'What is this place?' Lydia said.

'It was an old knitting factory. It closed down years ago.'

At the end of the hall, I could hear the radio playing one of those annoying Coldplay songs that stays in your mind for hours. I kicked open the door and went through, Lydia following behind me. The radio was playing in a small room that must have been an office for a supervisor. I scanned the group of people sitting around a table in front of me. I counted three men and two women as well as a dog that scrambled to its feet when we entered.

A man who looked to be in charge got up and walked towards me. He was wiry, with a wispy beard and straggly hair. 'Who the fuck are you?' He had a strong Rhondda accent – it made me feel quite at home. I flashed my warrant card. Lydia did the same.

'Are you Paul Youlden?'

'What if I am?' I took that as confirmation.

One of the other men sitting by the table stood up. He was wearing a T-shirt with Che Guevara's face printed on it.

'So what's going on here? Plotting the revolution?' I said.

'This is a free country,' Youlden said.

The third man had neatly cut hair, a healthy-looking face and a small cross in his left ear lobe. 'What's your name?'

'Greg Jones and this is police harassment.'

One of the girls sitting by his side had a tattoo stencilled on her right neck and short pink hair. She was chewing gum energetically and gave me a hard, uncompromising stare. The other woman got up and turned her attention to the Labrador at her feet.

'I'm investigating the death of Matthew Dolman.' I turned my attention back to the other man. 'What's your name?'

'Locke.'

'Is this where you record your videos?' I said.

I turned back to Youlden who crossed his arms and stared at me defiantly. 'This factory was typical of the capitalist corruption that we have to put up with. A company comes to the back-end of Wales with the benefit of massive grants from the Welsh government. Stays around for a few years until the money runs out and then undertakes a *re-evaluation* of their business model which is a shortcut for saying they want to close the business and move back to England.'

'I didn't think they could do things like that these days,' Lydia piped up.

Now it was Locke's turn. 'It's happened for centuries. And the people of Wales just get poorer.'

I'd had enough of listening to this sort of rant. 'And

we're investigating the murder of Alan Turner.'

'Who?' Locke smiled.

I stepped towards him. I poked a finger into his chest. 'You know exactly who I mean. It's been all over the newspapers, television, internet.' I pitched my head towards the monitor. Then I turned to Youlden. 'I want to know where you were on the morning Dolman and the evening Turner were killed.'

Both men gave a lazy shrug. It succeeded in riling me. 'You can either answer my questions here and now or we can go back to Queen Street and you can cool off in a police cell overnight.'

'You've got no grounds to arrest us.'

'You were in the internet café in Pontypridd last Tuesday.' I stared at Youlden.

A brief spasm of worry crossed his face. 'This isn't a police state yet. I don't have to answer any of your questions.'

I fingered the handcuffs in my jacket pocket. 'Paul Youlden. I'm arresting you on suspicion of conspiracy to murder Alan Turner.'

Chapter 26

A search team took Youlden's premises apart, one piece of furniture at a time as he languished in a cell at Queen Street. Then they started on the floorboards before moving onto the walls.

I stayed and watched as the place was pulled apart methodically.

Inch by inch.

The search team supervisor was a short man with a thick neck and tattoos on his forearms. 'You shouldn't be here.' Adding as an afterthought. 'Sir.'

I glared down at him. 'If you've got a problem take it up with Superintendent Cornock or better still ACC Neary.'

It suited me just fine that he ignored me for the rest of the day. Early evening meant that Queen Street looked grey and drab in the half-light before dusk. An end-of-the-day feel pervaded the station and in the Incident Room Lydia had papers strewn on her desk. She gave me a tired smile when she saw me.

'I've been through the file from Harper's law firm regarding Matthew Dolman's will,' she said. 'It looks like Mrs Dolman would lose out big time if Matthew Dolman changed his will.'

I stepped over to the board, moving her photograph to give it more prominence. Lydia continued. 'And we double-checked the hostel record sir. Youlden was a resident.'

'So she could have met him there,' I said.

She nodded.

'So Troy and Mrs Dolman have a connection to Youlden who had a link to Henson. Small world.'

I turned to look at Lydia; behind her computers and boxes removed from Youlden's place covered the desks in the Incident Room. 'Anything on the computers?'

'There's nothing to suggest he has recorded either of the two videos linked to the deaths.' She nodded to the PCs on her desk. 'There is a video on this computer but it's the one that's shown on that website they host. You know, the same vitriolic bigotry against "capitalism".'

I sat down at Wyn's desk. 'We'll need *something* if we're going to interview him.'

'His lawyer's been on the phone six times at least asking what's happening.'

'Let's hope they find something at his house.'

I got up and went back to my office. I scrolled down the messages in my inbox. Cornock wanted an update and his email alluded to 'press interest' but the message from the public relations department was far more blunt – 'Urgent update needed'. Tracy had called me twice and must have given up as she'd texted me suggesting lunch tomorrow in the National Gallery.

The door of the Incident Room banged open and Wyn and Jane streamed in clutching a laptop. Jane was the first to speak. 'This laptop was found in Youlden's home address – stuffed into the bottom of a wardrobe. There are videos you need to see, boss.'

Wyn sat next to Jane by her desk. Lydia stood behind him and I noticed her perfume that evening. It had a fresh lavender sort of smell. After standing around a search team in an old factory unit all afternoon, the sweet perfume was relaxing. I recalled Alvine's mention of perfume after Dolman's death; since then I'd been searching for a link. I couldn't detect any perfume from Jane. She didn't seem the sort that might wear any.

The monitor lit up and an image of a car windscreen filled the screen.

I peered down and recognised the electronic gates

of the Dolman residence. There was shuffling as the occupants moved in their seats. One had a cough and their breath was audible.

'That's the Dolman place,' Lydia said.

'There's more,' Jane said.

The camera zoomed into the gates as a voice said, 'There he is'.

'Play that again,' I snapped.

Wyn obliged.

A man's voice, definitely. And another's. And conversation now: each encouraging the other. The video ran on and I watched with growing alarm as the cameras panned towards the Aston Martin before following it down the road into the middle of Penarth.

Then the camera moved as the car pulled out and followed Dolman.

We watched until the footage stopped as Dolman indicated for the Royal Bell car park.

'There are four more videos, boss,' Wyn said. 'Two more following Dolman driving into work and two as they follow him to the bank. They must have been using a small camera.'

Progress. I noted the time and calculated quickly that I had another eighteen hours to keep Youlden before having to consider his release.

'I need all the CCTV in Penarth and the middle of town looked at again for the few hours before Dolman's death. This time we know that we're looking for Youlden and at least one other. Get his car registration number and the number of everyone else involved so far – Henson, Cleaver and the others with Youlden this morning.'

I walked over to the board and tapped the space next to Henson.

'I want Youlden's photograph up here.'

'There must be a connection between them. Youlden could be helping Henson.' Lydia said.

I turned to face the team. 'Wyn, take the photographs of Henson and Youlden and go and talk to Darren Williams at the internet café. In fact take all the photographs we've got of anyone involved with these groups. Find out if he recognises anyone.'

I left the Incident Room and walked through to Cornock's room. Susan Peel had a drawn, hunted look in her eyes that darted around Cornock's room as I gave them an update.

'We've arrested Youlden and we should be able to interview him in the—'

'The press have got hold of this somehow,' Peel said.

Cornock looked at her and frowned. The light from his desk lamp cast deep shadows in the worry lines on his forehead. 'I'm sure that Inspector Marco has more to add.'

Peel glanced at her watch. 'I've got to have something for the evening news.'

'Tell them we're conducting a double murder investigation.'

'That simply won't do.'

'What the hell do you mean?' Cornock's raised voice startled her. She shifted in her chair. 'We're not here to entertain the press. Tell them we'll do a press release when we're good and ready.'

Peel gathered her papers and left in a huff.

'There's something linking Troy Dolman to his father's death. We've got eyewitness accounts that they had blazing arguments about the future of the bank. And he was in the same regiment as Youlden and there's an allegation he was in a relationship with Youlden.'

Cornock managed a long sigh.

'And Mrs Dolman has links to the homeless hostel that Turner and Dolman funded and she would lose out big time if Matthew Dolman changed his will.'

Cornock sat back in his chair, and drew a hand over his hair. 'This is a mess John. I hope you've got enough to make progress.'

I got back to the Incident Room knowing we had to scan the CCTV recordings again. Before starting, I closed the door of my office and called Jackie. Usually I spoke to her a few times a year but now things had changed. She was still at the hospital and I strained to identify the tone to her voice. I hoped I could detect optimism but from what she said about Dean, it was soon clear there had been little change.

I agreed to call my mother, which I did as soon as I'd finished with Jackie.

'You must tell me everything.'

I repeated everything twice for her and found myself pleased to be sharing with her the health updates on my son.

I stepped out into the Incident Room as the television news broadcast an item that announced *'Police refuse to confirm or deny reports that an arrest had been made in relation to the long-running double-murder inquiry.'*

Wyn arrived back just as the piece finished. He dropped his notepad onto the desk and blew out a lungful of breath. 'Darren Williams didn't recognise any of them. But the girl who usually works in the café is in Tenerife.'

Exhaustion got the better of me. 'What the fucking hell is she doing in Tenerife?'

'She's on holiday, boss.' Wyn said. 'She won't be back until next Monday.'

It was late in the evening when we finished viewing

the CCTV coverage for the route from the Dolman home to the middle of Cardiff. The number plates of the cars on the screen merged into each other by the end. It left me with the uncomfortable feeling that I had missed something obvious.

I left Queen Street and drove home, yawning most of the way.

Chapter 27

It was just after seven the following morning.

There was a double-double strength espresso in a small plastic cup from Mario's on my desk alongside the bare bones of an interview plan. Lydia looked surprisingly normal. Her make-up was fresh and her blouse and trousers newly ironed. I gave my battered chinos a cursory glance and then I grabbed my notes and headed downstairs to the custody suite. By now Youlden would have had eight hours' uninterrupted sleep and no doubt his lawyer would have enjoyed a decent night's sleep too.

Before I left for the custody suite I spoke to Wyn and Jane. 'I want you both to go over the CCTV again covering Dolman's journey into work.'

I could see their enthusiasm waning.

'We've missed something. And we need to find it quickly.'

I left them and as I walked down to the Incident Room I wondered how Dean had been overnight and my irritation at having to work after only a few hours' fitful sleep evaporated. I fumbled with my mobile and sent Jackie a text. I was signing for the tapes and talking to the custody sergeant when the reply came that he'd had a good night and that the medics were pleased.

I was still staring at the screen of my mobile and thinking that Dean couldn't not pull through. Lydia's voice interrupted.

'I'll bring Youlden from his cell.'

I put my phone back into my jacket and walked over to the interview room. The cork-lined room was cold and stuffy. A table with the tape recorder sat against one wall. I stepped over and switched it on. I put the case holding Youlden's laptop on the floor underneath the table.

I heard the sound of footsteps and Youlden entered with his lawyer. She was a tall woman with short hair and a pale complexion.

'Catherine Norman.' She had a firm handshake.

Youlden sat down on a plastic chair and folded his arms stiffly. I got on with the formalities and once the cassettes were safely into the machine I sat back and looked him in the eye. His eyes were more deep-set than I had remembered and he had thin, almost non-existent eyebrows.

'Do you know why you're here?'

He parted his lips then looked at Norman who nodded.

'I've been falsely arrested on specious grounds and once I'm out I'm going to sue. And take the story to every news outlet in the UK.'

Susan Peel would love this.

I started slowly. 'I'm interviewing you in relation to the murder of Matthew Dolman who was the managing director of the National Bank of Wales. Do you know who I mean?'

He sat and looked at me.

'Do you have any comment to make?'

Nothing.

I shuffled some of the papers on my desk. 'What do you do exactly?'

'None of your business.'

Making progress, at least he was answering my questions.

'Are you responsible for the website called Tax The Bankers?'

'Yes, what of it?'

'And you maintain the website and do all the posting to it. Blog entries, that sort of thing.'

Another glance at his lawyer.

'At the end of last week a video appeared on the internet just after the death of Alan Turner. That video was uploaded from an internet café in Pontypridd.'

There was a glimmer of recognition on Youlden's face.

'You used the same café a day earlier.'

'Is that a question?' Norman asked.

I ignored her, gazing at Youlden.

Norman stopped writing notes. 'Is that the only evidence you have to justify the arrest of my client?'

'I think your client would be well advised to answer my questions.' I turned back to Youlden. 'How often do you use the internet café?'

'Ask them.'

'I'm asking you.'

'No comment.'

'You see, it seems to me that it's too much of a coincidence. You have a website so you're accustomed to using the internet. There are videos on your site vilifying the bankers. And then the video that's been seen all over the world is posted from the internet café in Pontypridd.'

I looked over and saw the rage in his eyes.

'Did you post that video, Paul?'

He tensed and glared at his lawyer.

I reached for the laptop and handed it to Lydia who opened the screen.

'Do you recognise this laptop?'

'Ah ...'

'It was recovered from your home address.'

He sulked back into silence. The machine hummed into life.

'Please look at the video we found on your laptop.'

The colour drained from Youlden's face. 'That's not

what you think. And it ...'

Norman moved awkwardly in her chair.

'For the purposes of the tape the video is a film of Matthew Dolman being followed from his home one morning. There is a brief conversation and we're waiting for expert analysis of the voice to see if it's a match to the videos that have been released. And there are four more videos from the same laptop, two of which film Matthew Dolman walking to the bank.'

I showed each in turn, glancing at Youlden occasionally who had turned a sickly shade of grey by the end. 'Now is your opportunity to tell us your side of things.'

He didn't and by mid-morning I was having grave doubts. I finished the interview abruptly, ignoring the surprise on the face of Norman. She wanted to know when a decision would be made about bail and after noticing the time I told her we needed to review all the evidence before the custody time limits expired.

Pacing back to the Incident Room I hoped that by now Wyn and Jane would have found something to link Youlden's fifteen-year-old Vauxhall to Penarth or Cardiff at a time near to the deaths of either Dolman or Turner. But I was disappointed and as we had no prospect of having any immediate results on the voice analysis I knew what Cornock would say.

A fractious superintendent decided that Youlden would have to be released on bail. Susan Peel had sent me an acerbic email suggesting that PR should be left to the professionals. So I headed out of Queen Street deciding that I'd wander over early for my lunch with Tracy.

I walked through the Gorsedd Gardens. An enormous tractor lawn mower went round in circles. I had started to believe that my investigation was heading in ever decreasing circles with no hope of finding the culprit. I checked my watch knowing that I had more than enough time before meeting Tracy so I headed to the room that displayed one of my favourite paintings – *Running away with the Hairdresser* by Kevin Sinnott. I entered the first gallery and stopped dead in my tracks.

Tracy stood at the other end, deep in conversation. She had her arms folded severely and even from side-on I could tell she was angry. And then I recognised Greg Jones from Youlden's group standing by her side. I blanked out the noise from the room and just stared at her. My breathing became shallow and the spotlights on the gantry above me shone more intensely, a strong white colour that sparkled. I couldn't risk her seeing me so I turned my back, hoping she wouldn't notice but all the time thinking that I had to be certain. I wanted to convince myself that I was wrong.

A crowd of visiting French children gathered by my side. They were noisy and talkative but I didn't hear their chatter. I made to leave but then I turned and followed the group into the room, keeping myself tucked in behind one of the adults.

I stared over at them. Tracy had her hands in the air. Greg Jones leant over her. I wanted to rush over and demand an explanation. Greg raised a hand and then moved his head and I jerked myself to one side fearing he'd see me. The person by my side moved so I turned my back before stepping towards another group of visitors, hoping I could use them as a shield. Tracy was peering into his eyes. My lips dried, my stomach wanted to do cartwheels and it even occurred to me that I should arrest them both.

I left the gallery, jogged down the front steps of the main building, and then strode back towards Queen Street convinced that the first thing I had to do was find out everything I could about Greg Jones.

I stopped in the middle of the park and tapped a message to Tracy – *Sorry have to cancel. Too busy Jx.* I took a deep breath, recalling the last two conversations I'd had with her.

She had been interrogating me, of course; it was plain to see now and I cursed myself for sharing details of the investigation with her. How much pillow talk had she shared with Greg? How far had she imperilled the inquiry? Then I realised it meant I was in deep trouble.

A message reached my mobile but I didn't react immediately. I knew it would be from her. *Everything all right? XXT.* It was the kisses at the end of the text that really angered me. She had betrayed me and the whole case might now be compromised.

I was contemplating how to reply when my mobile rang.

It was Lydia. 'Something you need to see, boss. Can you get back here?'

Chapter 28

The three members of my team were huddled over the monitor on Wyn's desk. My annoyance hadn't abated in the time it had taken me to reach Queen Street and the tension was making me short of breath.

Lydia heard me enter the Incident Room and turned to face me. 'I thought you should see this.'

Jane moved to one side and Wyn clicked on the mouse on his desk.

'You were right about the tape, boss,' Wyn said. 'I found this coverage when I ran it on for a few minutes after Dolman left for work on the morning of his death.'

I watched as an Audi SUV appeared on the screen and made its way into town. Wyn clicked again and the same vehicle appeared at various stages of the journey. 'That's Mrs Dolman.' I said.

Wyn nodded. 'And she told us in her statement that she hadn't left the house that morning.'

'So she lied to us.'

I hate it when people lie to me.

'There's more, sir.' Wyn added. 'Once I knew what time she'd left I had a look at the other days of the week. And every Monday and Thursday she leaves the house at about the same time before travelling into Cardiff.'

'Where does she go?'

'She takes one of the exits off the dual carriageway before reaching town and the CCTV doesn't pick her up again.'

'For Christ's sake we need to know where she goes.'

Nobody replied. The monitor was still showing her driving the SUV. And for once I knew that my instinct, telling me we had missed something, was right.

'It's Thursday tomorrow. Time for us to find out

what Mrs Dolman is up to.'

I stepped over to the board and I rearranged the photographs, hoping for clarity. I put Henson and Youlden next to each other.

'Motive,' I said, not waiting for a reply. 'Troy wants his father dead so that he can take over the bank. And Mrs Dolman faces losing out if her husband changes his will. So one of them uses Youlden – a person they both have connections with – to do the killing. And they try and implicate Henson.'

'Or Henson is stupid enough to use his own printer,' Wyn chirped up. 'He is a nutcase.'

'But why would she kill Turner?' Lydia said.

I avoided answering Lydia. 'Whatever is happening we need to know more about Mrs Dolman. And we still have the properties in Nice and Sydney to resolve.'

A message bleeped on my mobile and I fished it out of a pocket. Alvine wanted me to call her. 'We need to organise a plan to follow Mrs Dolman in the morning.' I headed back to my office.

Quickly I dialled Alvine's number.

'Bad news.'

I stood by my chair. 'Tell me.'

'The letter you sent me over the weekend. It's not from the same printer as the originals. Same font and size but the printer on the latest one doesn't print as flat as the others. You can't see it with the naked eye.'

Immediately I thought that Henson was using a different printer. Or that Cleaver had a printer at home. But it was odd that the message had appeared when it did. If the killer was responsible then why had he sent it when he did? It didn't make sense. And if it was somebody else then ...?

'Any other DNA?'

'Nothing. The envelope and the paper were clean.'

'And was there a match to the printer we recovered from Youlden's place?'

'Dead end too.'

I finished the call, picked up my mobile, and read various messages from Tracy. Texting had an anonymity that could hide emotion but it seemed a poor substitute for real-world conversation. I turned the phone in my hand, composing a suitable message.

Protocols.

I didn't know of any protocol about how I should deal with Tracy Jones. Although I knew I should record the position to Superintendent Cornock, formally in writing, in a detailed memorandum. But that would take me hours, time I didn't have to spare.

I spent the rest of the afternoon allocating tasks. We had to trace the courier that had delivered the message the previous Saturday, interview all the staff on reception and watch hours more CCTV footage from outside Queen Street.

My mobile flickered with more messages and I read one from my mother asking me to call her and then another from Tracy. My annoyance grew when I read - *Missed you at lunch. Tonight? XT.* I tapped out a message to Tracy that I was too busy to meet up.

Before calling my mother I knew I had to speak to Jackie but as I reached for the handset it sprang into life.

'There's something terrible ...' Jackie sobbed hysterically down the telephone.

'What's wrong?'

I stood up, waiting for her to reply. I heard chatter in the background and raised voices. Anxious voices. I felt like screaming into the handset.

'It's Dean. He's ...' Then scuffling. I heard Jackie's

voice and then the sound of a nurse asking her did she want her to speak.

'Hello?'

'Who's that?' I said.

'It's Lyndsey, one of the nurses on PICU.'

'What the hell is happening?' An enormous lump had appeared in my throat.

'There's been a problem with Dean's breathing tube so we're just changing it, we've asked Jackie to pop outside whilst the doctor does that.'

'Is it dangerous?' My voice squeaked.

'It's a common procedure, I'll ask the doctor to call you shortly after he's finished.'

Then the line went dead and I spent the longest thirty minutes of my life wondering what was happening. When my mobile rang I snatched it off the desk. It was voice I didn't recognise.

'Hello, my name is Mike Ross, the on-call registrar for PICU.'

'What's happened?'

'We had to re-intubate your son. His breathing tube became blocked so we had to change it, it's not uncommon but something we have to react to immediately. Your wife was understandably a little upset so one of our nurses took her outside whilst I did it. The tube's sorted and Dean's stable.'

I fell back into my chair.

I squirmed, realising just how Jackie would have felt.

'When are you going to wake him up?'

I could hear him flicking through the notes.

'We need to see what my consultant Dr Palmer and the neurosurgical consultant think once they've seen Dean during the ward round in the morning.'

He handed the telephone to Jackie. She listened as I

explained what the doctor had told me. She said very little.

'Go home and get some sleep,' I said. 'I'll call first thing.'

Chapter 29

I had expected Penarth to be busier on a Thursday morning. The occasional pedestrian ambled along the pavement with small dogs on long leashes. Expensive cars drove past at a sedate pace. It was warm enough for me to open the window, letting the cool spring air brush my face. Lydia sat in the passenger seat glancing at her watch. I recalled the detailed briefing by Wyn outlining the exact times that Mrs Dolman left the house for her regular tryst.

There was another ten minutes before we expected her. I thought about a cigarette but regulations made it clear we couldn't smoke inside a car.

Then I saw the Audi in my side mirror.

Quickly I adjusted my position, checked the rear view mirror, fine-tuned the side mirrors and started the engine. I caught my first glimpse of Mrs Dolman when she'd pulled up by a pedestrian crossing a little way behind me. Then she passed me and I lowered my head just to avoid any possibility of her spotting me.

I indicated before pulling out and following her. There were two cars between my Mondeo and the Audi but I could still see the personalised number plate – 752 BD. Wyn and Jane would be somewhere behind us. I had to stop at the roundabout and I drummed my fingers on the wheel as I watched the Audi speeding away towards Cardiff.

A stream of traffic flowed through the roundabout and when the Audi disappeared from view I quelled my raising panic. Finally a space opened and I jerked the car forward. I raced through the roundabout, indicating for the exit before accelerating towards the city. The tension subsided when I caught sight of the Audi in the distance.

By the time I reached the elevated section of the link road into Cardiff that ran above some old industrial units along the muddy banks of the river Ely I spotted the Audi in the distance keeping a modest speed. She wasn't in a hurry obviously. I pressed the accelerator and overtook the car in front but then dropped back into the inside lane. I kept glancing in the mirrors, watching the traffic building up behind me, knowing I shouldn't get too close.

The more I thought about the circumstances the more I was relishing the opportunity to interview Mrs Dolman.

We approached the turning to the Cardiff City stadium and the shops nearby and I could see the pulsing indicator light from the Audi so I did likewise and we headed down towards the red lights at a junction. Being only two cars behind her I dropped back; just one glance in her rear view mirror and she might spot me.

I strengthened my grip on the wheel and then the lights changed. The Audi moved away but I stalled the car. Wyn overtook me and followed her. A worry gripped me that we might lose her but I restarted the engine and accelerated through the lights just as they changed back to red.

'Where on earth is she going?' Lydia thrust the mobile to her ear and she mouthed Wyn to me silently.

After a few seconds she started talking. 'Where is she?' There was a silence as she listened to Wyn and my impatience grew. 'She's going towards Llandaff.'

I paid little attention to the shops and delicatessens lining the route into Llandaff. The Audi was slowing now as she pulled into a small junction that had a no-through-road sign. Wyn dawdled and then followed her.

Seconds later the traffic cleared enough for me to negotiate the turn. Wyn was already parked on one side and he gave us a brief nod as we passed. We drew up a little way beyond Mrs Dolman's Audi. Lydia picked up her mobile.

She spoke quietly. 'Where is she?'

Then she turned her head and looked over at one of the detached houses. She finished the call. 'The first of those semis.'

'Let's go.' I yanked open the car door and waved at Wyn and Jane. I strode down the path to the main door and rang the bell. It had a civilised ring and I didn't have to wait long before the door was opened by a man in a dog collar. 'Some sort of party?' I said, barging in.

Mrs Dolman sat on a sofa with two other middle-aged women, coffee mugs and a plate of digestives on the table in front of them. Each had what looked like a bible opened on their laps and I started to feel very uncomfortable.

'I've just finished speaking to the archbishop of Wales.'

Cornock let out a long sigh as he finished. The clergyman I'd met was the archbishop's chaplain who was leading a confirmation class that Mrs Dolman attended.

'What *were* you thinking?' Cornock looked over at me.

'It was the best intelligence we had. She had lied to us about where she was the Monday morning that her husband had been killed and she had everything to gain from his death.'

I ran out of steam and let the last few words sort of hang in the air. It all sounded circumstantial when I listed them aloud.

'The archbishop wanted to apologise on behalf of Mrs Dolman. She was naturally distraught after her husband's death. She should have mentioned it, she realises that now.'

'And she was drunk.'

Cornock gave me a troubled patronising look as though I was a naughty child. He shook his head. 'The archbishop thought it was all rather unfortunate. I gather that his chaplain was rather less generous and wanted to make a complaint.'

Cornock must have seen the worry cross my face. 'Don't worry John. The archbishop has told me that it's not going to happen. He told me that Mrs Dolman has been taking confirmation classes for twelve months. Are you a religious man, John?'

'Ah …'

Cornock sat back in his chair and gazed over at his aquarium. My mother went to church three times a year but the congregation was small and she always complained about the women sniggering about her behind her back. I could still remember as a boy attending a Christmas carol concert in one of the large chapels that was a community centre now, running courses on multi-culturism, gender equality and pottery.

'My mother goes at Christmas and …'

Cornock was nodding. 'My wife was the same. Easter and harvest thanksgiving until … Well, after Sharon … she…'

It was the nearest that Superintendent Cornock had ever got to discussing personal details. Although he wasn't really discussing anything, he just sounded rather sad.

He shook himself out of the momentary melancholia. 'Count yourself lucky, John. Christian charity and all that.'

He had already started on another pile of papers on his desk when I left his room.

Outside I stood for a moment. I could imagine the comments from Troy and Rex Dolman. For now Mrs Dolman would definitely be off the official persons of interest list but I couldn't ignore that voice in my mind telling me that she might still be involved.

I climbed the stairs to the second floor of Queen Street and from outside the Incident Room I heard the tone of Dave Hobbs' voice. It took me a couple of seconds to realise that he was talking in Welsh to Wyn. They continued babbling on when I strode in.

Hobbs gave me a quick glance, and turned back to Wyn who frowned as he looked at me. I had expected Hobbs to have emailed in advance or texted and his presence in *my* Incident Room set my nerves on edge. But more than anything I wanted to know what they had been talking about. I had always dismissed as paranoia English people's complaints about being excluded in shops in parts of Wales where Welsh was spoken. Now I knew how they felt.

'I was telling DC Nuttall about my initial work on the letters Dolman received. And he was telling me all about the inquiry,' Hobbs announced.

Wyn blinked furiously.

That shredded more of my nerves. 'Thanks for taking the time to see me, Dave.'

'No trouble. I have some time this morning. I'm seeing the chief super later for an update so I thought that first thing would be a good time to meet.'

I walked over to my office, Hobbs following me. I sat down and Hobbs made himself comfortable in one of the visitor chairs. My conscience had got the better of me about Terry's offer of intelligence on the Cardiff City Soul Crew so I had emailed Hobbs.

'Did I tell you about my meetings with the Metropolitan Police?'

He knew that he hadn't. And then he launched into a barrage of name dropping the senior officers of the Met that he'd been meeting.

'There's even talk of a national task force ahead of the next World Cup. There might even be secondments available.'

Then Hobbs examined the nails of his left hand very carefully, allowing me to fully understand that he was vying for promotion, big time. All I could think of was that he was far too much of country boy to be mixing with the senior officers of the Met. They probably had a good snigger at him behind his back.

'You wanted to brief me on something.'

I sat back in my chair deciding how little I could tell him without risking a complaint. 'I spoke to one of my regular informants. He says he might be able to help. Terry has always been very reliable'

Hobbs nodded. 'And what does he want in return?'

I opened the palms of both hands.

Hobbs nodded. 'Don't waste your time, John. These toe-rags aren't worth the effort.'

Now I rolled my eyes. 'I had to tell you, Dave. Protocols and all that.'

Hobbs stood up and glanced at his watch. 'I hope you make progress with the Dolman case.'

Then he left and I pondered whether I should contact Terry again. Dave Hobbs always had the effect on me of getting me to do the direct opposite of what he suggested.

Chapter 30

Brenda Dolman's skin followed the contours of her cheeks more closely than I remembered. She gave me a dull, lifeless stare. A pack of Camel Blue sat on the table alongside her handbag and subconsciously I counted how many cigarettes I had smoked that day. Mid-morning sunshine filtered through the blinds covering the windows of the conference room in the National Bank of Wales. To her right sat Troy and on his right Charlotte who had a file of papers open in front of her. She gave me one of her perfect smiles, beguiling yet utterly devoid of warmth. Troy leant on the table, glaring at me as though he needed only the slightest provocation to jump over it and throttle me.

I avoided staring at Troy. What sort of name was that? The picture we had built of him didn't suggest the nobility of a warrior from Greek mythology – more of a wealthy spoilt thug.

Lydia sat by my side, her hands placed one on top of the other on the table.

'Thank you so much for attending,' Troy said.

I nodded, unimpressed with his attempt at charm.

'We don't for one minute want to hinder your inquiry into our father's death but we wanted you to be aware of the family's position in relation to Deborah Bowen.'

Brenda flinched, curled her lips and let out an impatient breath.

'As you're aware my father had a relationship with Ms Bowen.' He darted a glance at Brenda who stared straight ahead. 'And we know that you've taken an interest in the homeless shelter and the bank's connections with Alan Turner.'

'We have to pursue all lines of inquiry. It is a

murder—'

Troy raised his voice. 'I know that full well, Inspector.' Charlotte put a hand on his forearm. 'I'll let Charlotte give you the details.'

Charlotte looked up and gave me another professional smile. 'The family have decided to create a trust fund for Charlie Bowen. The terms will provide a generous—'

'*Very* generous,' Troy said.

'Settlement for the young boy so that his every need will be catered for, now and in the future. The trustees will be Deborah Bowen and both Troy and Rex. The sum provided will enable Ms Bowen to buy a bigger home that she can occupy while Charlie is still at school. It will enable her to maintain her career and the fund will pay for nannies and additional help while he's still so young. And then all of his school fees will be paid and university, of course.'

It sounded so cold and detached as though they were dealing with a commodity. Perhaps that's what a private education meant, disinterest from the nuts and bolts of real parenting. But it reminded me of the warmth in Deborah's voice as she described the holidays they'd spent in Nice. And I wondered why exactly we had been invited to this meeting.

'I've spoken with Assistant Chief Constable Neary,' Troy said, propping his chin on steepled forearms. 'She agreed with me that the original death threat letters my father received have to be the focus of your inquiries. It's a matter of concern to us that insufficient resources are being directed at the inquiry into these terrorists.'

I sat back in the comfortable chair and stared over at him. Now I knew why we were there. The trust fund was a carefully choreographed stunt that told us that the Dolman family were out of bounds.

'We certainly will,' I said.

Lydia turned to look at me.

'I don't think that we'd be breaking a confidence in saying that our inquiries into the various groups involved are making good progress.'

Charlotte peered over at me intently as Troy nodded his head.

'Pleased to hear it.'

'We have had some very interesting leads in the last few days.' I glanced at Lydia. I detected a frown in her eyes. 'These groups have been very active on the internet since Mr Dolman's death and it's only a matter of time before we find the culprits.'

'When do you anticipate an arrest?' Troy said.

I drew a hand in the air and rolled my eyes. 'Imminently.'

'Excellent.'

Troy stood up; Charlotte followed his example and then gathered her papers together. Brenda sat impassively before reaching for her cigarettes. Troy even managed some humour as we left the room. Brenda had no time for me – not even an attempt at small talk.

We headed back for Queen Street.

'You were very diplomatic, boss.'

I gave Lydia a broad smile. 'Exactly what he wanted to hear.'

Lydia snorted. 'Mrs Dolman looked wrecked.'

I was already reaching for the cigarettes in my pocket when Lydia added, 'Too many cigarettes are bad for you.'

'We'll have to report back to Cornock.'

'Name dropping the ACC was clever.'

I put a cigarette to my lips and stopped to spark my lighter into action. It annoyed me that Troy thought he could dictate the terms of the inquiry and it annoyed me even more that if I wasn't careful I could allow my judgement to be clouded by him; already clear thinking felt like a scarce commodity. I pulled deeply on the cigarette and let the smoke score my windpipe. 'Then we look at Troy Dolman in detail. Everything. We need a better picture of him.'

Back in Queen Street I checked the memorandum I had prepared for Cornock about Tracy. I pondered what exactly I could tell him in our appointment later that afternoon. I had ignored the messages from Tracy since I had seen her in the National Gallery but her message that morning suggested meeting for lunch. As I stared at the screen I realised I would have to tackle her. Confront her and then let her face the consequences.

I noted the time, and grabbed my jacket draped behind my chair. Walking gave me time to think about the timing of our relationship. She had made certain that she had a direct source into the heart of the inquiry. The prospect that she had fed details of the investigation back to Greg Jones and Henson filled me with rage. Rehearsing the questions I wanted to ask her only confused me even more. All I really wanted to do was to demand an explanation and let the usual disciplinary procedure take its course.

I reached the door of the public house and pushed it open. Tracy sat in a corner. My lips suddenly felt dry and cracked. Her mouth formed words of greeting but she said nothing. She gulped a mouthful of wine before replacing her glass on the table in front of her. She frowned so I guessed she must have seen the hard look in my eyes.

'What's going on?' she said.

I pulled a chair away from the table and sat down. There was a glossy sheen to her dark hair and it was just as I remembered it from that first morning, cascading over the pillow by my side.

'I could ask the same thing about you.'

She gave me a puzzled look. 'I don't know what I've done. I thought we were ...'

'So did I.'

'Then tell me what happened. What have I done?' There was a tear in one eye.

'You've got something to tell me.'

She reached for a handkerchief. 'Don't play games with me, John.'

I leant back in my chair. A group of rowdy girls came into the pub and ordered fancy cocktails, giggling hysterically.

'I saw you in the gallery on Wednesday. I was early.'

She gave me another puzzled look.

'I'll need to report everything to Superintendent Cornock. You know that don't you?'

'This is madness. I don't what you mean.'

'Come on Tracy. The man with you in the National Gallery is Greg Jones. He's associated with one of the persons of interest in our inquiry. I met him when he was with Paul Youlden in the old factory in Newport. And of course every time we've met we've talked about the case. You probably know as much about it as the DCs on my team.'

Tears rolled down her cheeks. The puzzled expression gave way to annoyance. She glanced over towards the bar but nobody was looking in our direction.

'And you think I've been sharing secrets. Betraying the trust of the WPS.'

'That's what it looks like, Tracy.'

She brushed away the tears and paused, drank more wine.

'He's my brother.'

Chapter 31

I didn't get a chance to see Cornock. At the time of our scheduled meeting I was heading for the Severn Bridge. Tracy's reassurance that her relationship with Greg was sporadic and that she hadn't seen him for weeks was scant comfort when I thought about all the details she knew of the case. And it only made me more annoyed that she was involved. After taking the call from Jackie I had made to leave and I had raised my voice unintentionally, demanding that Tracy promise me she wouldn't talk to Greg. I had read the dismay in her eyes when she realised that I didn't trust her.

Jackie had called to tell me that the hospital had stopped the sedatives and that the next twenty-four hours would be crucial. I dragged into my memory the words Jim Holland had said about his recovery. It all sounded so vague and uncertain. The heavy traffic delayed me reaching Southampton until late afternoon.

I rushed through into the PICU and then headed for Dean's private room.

Jackie was cradling his hand in hers. She looked up and gave me a welcoming smile. The banks of gadgetry and equipment behind Dean still flickered and bleeped. But the wire that had protruded from his head with such foreboding had been removed.

'They've stopped the sedation this afternoon,' Jackie said.

'How long …?'

'They don't know.'

I sat down on one of the hard plastic chairs.

My hearing adjusted itself to the sound of activity in the hospital. Nurses and doctors exchanged muffled conversations, trolleys and beds were wheeled in and out of the unit. I recognised a father from the previous weekend who looked exhausted at his daughter's bedside. He narrowed his eyes and gave me a weak smile.

Jim Holland arrived to see Dean before ten that evening. He breezed in, obviously revived by his leave. He looked at Dean, checked the charts and then gazed over at us.

'By the morning he should be stirring. The drugs can be unpredictable.'

Neither Jackie nor I knew what to say. We had to wait.

I persuaded Jackie to sleep first. Time dragged. I drank a lot of weak coffee, exchanged small talk with various nurses and touched my son's hand. But he didn't stir. Jackie yawned as she came back into the room, drawing a hand through her hair.

I slept fitfully, dreaming about Tracy. It made me wake up with a start, wondering what Cornock would say. I fell back onto the narrow bed but sleep eluded me so I wandered through to the parents' room.

The man I'd seen earlier was sitting in a soft chair scanning a back issue of a car magazine. On the television in one corner an old episode of *Top Gear* was playing.

'How's your lad?'

I sat down. 'He's off the sedation now and they hope he'll wake up in the morning.'

'Good.'

'And your daughter?'

A thin grey veil drew itself slowly over his eyes. 'She's very poorly.'

'I hope you get some good news soon.'

'So do I.'

We watched in silence as Jeremy Clarkson played with the controls of a car that the average person could never own.

My new friend pointed the remote at the television. 'This is a good bit. Clarkson goes off on a rant about the sat-nav and the screen. It's real boys and their toys stuff.'

We watched as the presenter poked the touchscreen and then fiddled with the dials, ending by telling his audience that you needed a PhD in astrophysics to understand how it worked.

I lost interest in the programme after that and wandered back to Dean's room. Jackie had her head propped on the bed and she was fast asleep. I sat down quietly and waited.

Morning bought more noise and the bustle of the PICU returned.

Dean lay there oblivious.

Jackie had woken with a stiff neck and sore back that had been eased by paracetamol. By mid-morning we'd both showered, but wearing the same clothes made me feel stale.

Jackie tried small talk. 'Are you very busy?'

'Frantic.'

She gave an enigmatic look as though she couldn't understand why I was there. 'Is it a murder case?'

I nodded.

'Is it someone who knew the victim?'

'We don't know who the killer is. It might be more than one.'

'Isn't it usually someone the victim knows?'

I nodded. My mind turned to the images of likely suspects pinned to the Incident Room board, who all knew the victims, and I wondered what we had missed and whether we were any nearer to finding the killer. It was mid-afternoon after Jim Holland had done his ward round when there was the first sign of movement. It hastened my pulse and Jackie drew shallow breaths. An hour passed as we waited for something else to happen and all the while the movement in his young body increased. As did my anticipation.

Finally he choked on the tube that was still firmly stuck in his throat.

The nurse rushed out and returned moments later with a doctor who removed it. Then he held a mask on Dean's face for a while until he was happy he was breathing normally, then he replaced this with another mask with a bag hanging from it. And my tension released like a coiled spring unwinding. Another agonisingly slow hour passed until he opened his eyes. Then the tears poured down Jackie's cheeks. He turned towards me weakly, smiled and then I too brushed away a tear.

Chapter 32

In the early hours I drove back to Cardiff elated that Dean was now out of danger. I woke the following morning in my apartment in the Bay after dreaming about Jeremy Clarkson gesticulating wildly at the dashboard of a car. I realised it had been the same episode I had seen the day before while squirming in the uncomfortable upright chair waiting for Dean to move.

The same feeling struck me again that there had to be something I was missing.

I sat on the edge of the bed. I was still tired and I needed to think clearly. What had Jackie said last night? Aren't murders committed by people known to the victim? I had ignored her comment – she'd watched too much television.

I decided I had to get back to the Royal Bell.

I missed most of the traffic because I was so early. After parking on a double yellow line, I walked over to the entrance. A man in his fifties stood up when I approached and the challenging look in his eyes soon waned when he saw my warrant card. I climbed the staircase to the top floor and stood for a moment as my chest tightened.

The early spring sunshine made Cardiff look warm. I turned around and scanned the top level. I counted five BMWs and a handful of 4x4s and a Jaguar coupé. After descending to the next level, I stood among the expensive cars, uncertain what I was hoping to achieve: some flash of inspiration? Another few minutes and I pushed open the door to Level 7A. I stood below the CCTV cameras. The attendant downstairs would probably think I had gone mad. Then I considered that perhaps there was more than one killer and that it had all been planned carefully. The cameras were taken out of action at exactly the right time, which meant that someone knew when Dolman could be expected. I heard the sound of a car taking the last steep turn before reaching level 7A and I stood to one side. A Mercedes saloon glided past.

The killer had walked over to Dolman as he'd parked his car and calmly stuck a stiletto into his aorta. I pondered how his killer had prepared. Checking the time that Dolman arrived each morning must have been an important part. The routine enquiries would have to be rechecked. Statements from the car park customers, nearby office workers and passers-by in the streets all reread.

I reached the bottom of the staircase and stepped out onto the pavement. Reaching for my cigarettes, I lit my second that morning. On the opposite side of the street were substantial mansions of three storeys that must have been the homes, decades before, of merchants or lawyers or bankers when Cardiff was smaller and the coal trade was booming.

On a typical Monday morning there must have been dozens of people walking past on their way to work. Watching the coverage from the CCTV cameras at either end of the street had produced no results, but the killer would have known to avoid walking down the street.

I turned around and noticed a narrow alley leading off down the side of the Royal Bell car park, easily accessible from the ground-floor level without walking onto the street. It didn't seem to lead anywhere but I walked down alongside the wall of the adjacent building. Ahead of me was a steel grille and beyond it a yard full of bins. I rattled it and it stayed firmly in place. There didn't seem to be any lock so I shook it again and then yanked it with both hands. It gave way and opened. I guessed that the uniformed officer who had checked must have given up when he reached the grille. Anticipation heightened my annoyance that the early stages of the inquiry had been less than thorough.

I stepped into the yard and, looking up, saw windowless walls. But if the killer had been here then there must have been an exit. I skirted around half a dozen bins; beyond them was a door that opened from the inside only. I marched on and then, after a few metres, was rewarded with the sight of another passageway leading away at right angles. At the end I spotted another grille-like gate. I didn't wait this time, I grabbed it and jerked it open.

I sprinted down to the end of the passage and emerged onto a street full of taxis and pedestrians. There were two CCTV cameras high up on the side of a building further down the street. I muffled a shout of elation before noting the names of the various shops, knowing that Wyn and Jane could call each one. There had to be someone that might have seen something.

Striding to the end of the road I turned back, trying to guess where the killer might have gone. I imagined a hurried walk tempered by the adrenalin that must have been bursting through his – or her – body.

Racing back to my car, I headed back for Queen Street police station. Wyn and Jane gave me surprised looks when I burst into the Incident Room.

'I need you to trace the CCTV coverage for the road at the back of the Royal Bell car park.'

'Which road is that, boss?'

I realised I hadn't read the name. 'I don't know. It's the one behind the bloody car park. I found an alleyway that leads around the back of the adjacent buildings and brings you out onto it … Just Google it or something. There are CCTV cameras at each end. And get working on calling all the shops. They might have their own systems.'

An hour later there was a shout from the Incident

Room and I rushed out to see Wyn and Lydia standing over Jane.

'We've had that CCTV coverage you wanted, boss,' Jane began. 'You should see one section in particular.'

I stood behind her, looking down at the monitor. I cut her explanation short. 'Just get on with it.'

'We started with the coverage from half an hour before Matthew Dolman arrived at the car park and we let it run on for ten minutes after he'd arrived.'

She clicked again on the screen and the images speeded up. 'As you can see, sir, there's no activity in that alleyway before Dolman arrives. But just look when we slow the tape down at nine thirty-five.'

A person emerged from the alleyway and strode into town, hands thrust deep into a jacket pocket, a dark beanie pulled down over his face, drainpipe jeans and Doc Martin-type boots.

'Stop it. Stop it,' I shouted.

I peered down at the image monitor. It had to be the killer. It was the closest we had so far.

I stalked over to the board and stared at the image of Matthew Dolman.

His post mortem had ruled out any possibility that he had been moved after his death. I tried to picture the scene. Closing my eyes took me back to that Monday morning, kneeling down by the open driver's side door, looking into the cabin. The sat-nav screen was elevated but I couldn't make out the images.

'What was on the screen in the car?' I said.

Behind me, Lydia cleared her throat. 'The sat-nav screen was upright.'

I opened my eyes and peered at her. She gave me a puzzled look.

I took a deep breath, despairing that my thought

process was so garbled. 'He must have switched off the engine when he parked. But the sat-nav was in an upright position. So he must have switched the ignition *on* again for the sat-nav screen to open.'

'Maybe he was listening to a radio programme or to the end of a CD,' Lydia said, dampening my excitement.

'But what if he was …' I thought about the presenters of *Top Gear*. Often they explained to their viewers how the dashboard of cars worked. It was a man thing – boys and their toys. 'He was showing someone.'

'What do you mean?'

'It had to be someone he knew.' I cursed for having missed the obvious. 'I need to see that street again.' I paced over to my room, and found my jacket before striding back to the Incident Room. The rest were still sitting by their desks. 'I meant all of you.' I yelled.

There was a scramble for coats and bags. Then we marched over to the alley where I stopped to get my breath back. I wanted to believe that we were nearer the killer than at any time during the investigation. He had walked on this pavement. I turned and looked over at the various shops and offices.

'We'll need to speak to everyone who works here.' I nodded towards the shops and offices.

I could sense the silent groans around me. 'Now that we suspect the killer left the car park this way we'll have to get everyone interviewed.'

'We'll need photographs of the person from the CCTV coverage, boss,' Lydia said.

I had barely started dictating instructions when my mobile rang. It was Tracy. Her voice trembled. 'My brother wants to see you.'

Chapter 33

Leftie's lounge was empty when I arrived. Alex Leftrowski was the only person behind the bar and his accent was still as thick and heavy as the day he left Russia for a better life in the West. It was debatable whether running a bar in Cardiff qualified. I had overstayed my welcome too many times in Leftie's, drunk too much, argued too much with the staff that refused to serve me but still Alex smiled at me as I walked in.

It was the sort of place that kept its secrets. Nothing that happened inside ever filtered out. Leftie made certain of that. His hands were his best advocates.

'John Marco,' he said. 'It is long time.'

I nodded. Being permanently sober turns you from social animal to social pariah very quickly.

'I'm busy. You know how it is.'

He nodded to the far end of the bar. 'Over there.' And then he pushed over a bottle of sparkling water and waved a hand at me when I offered to pay.

Tracy sat on the edge of a leather sofa, her brother by her side. She drew a hand through her hair and pulled it behind both ears. She tensed when I sat down and gave me a dark stare. I had checked the records for her brother's full name: Gregory Norman Jones. I had even memorised his date of birth. It had been a few days since a razor had met the skin on his face and just as long since he had showered from the look of his hair that stuck up in greasy lumps.

'It's not what you think.' Greg sipped from a green bottle of European lager.

'You have no idea what I'm thinking.'

'Don't be like that, John,' Tracy said.

I drank a mouthful of the sparkling water but I kept looking at her. There were bags under her eyes that hadn't been there before the weekend. 'I'm going to speak to Superintendent Cornock later.'

'That gives me an opportunity to explain.' Greg put the bottle down on the table. 'The bankers are to blame for so much that has gone wrong with our society. After the financial crisis, I thought it was time that things might change. But then the cuts started in public spending and the councils cut the funding for social services. I was working in the local council with frail elderly people as a carer. I loved what I was doing.'

He reached over for the bottle and began peeling the label. He looked up at me.

'It was terrible. Everyone frightened for their jobs. And then you realise that the bankers haven't changed. Massive bonuses and a complete disregard for the ordinary man in the street. And they accepted no responsibility for what they had done.'

'Why are you telling me all of this, Greg?'

He frowned now. 'I want you to understand.'

'Understand?' I got incredulity into my voice.

'Please, listen.' Tracy added quietly.

'I joined this group and they wanted to demonstrate peacefully. Make a point about the bankers. And how we could put things right if only the politicians saw sense and got balance into things. We made videos and there were public meetings ...'

'And your friend Henson had the debate with Dolman on the television.'

He nodded as his head drooped. 'That was stupid and I told him not to do it. He was never the same afterwards. Everything changed.' The label-peeling stopped. He looked up at me, a shadow crossed his eyes. 'That's when things got serious.'

'What do you mean?'

'There were a lot of arguments in the group about strategy.' He paused and I could sense the disappointment of the zealot ultimately disillusioned with his adopted cause. 'Some of them wanted more direct action.'

I leant forward. 'Who?'

'Jamie Henson. He believes in direct action. He said it was the only way that we could effect change and that the political system was bankrupt. He was convinced that kidnapping one of the bankers was the only way to secure change. Make an example of him and humiliate him in front of the cameras. Just like he was humiliated. It became an all-consuming hatred for him. So he split from our group and he went off with Cleaver.'

'Dolman received death threats. Could Henson have sent them?'

He shrugged. 'I suppose so.'

Tracy hadn't said a word since Greg started talking. I glanced at her. She curled her lips. The hardness had gone and there was a defiant edge to her expression.

'Who else was with Henson?' I said.

Greg reeled off the names of two others that I noted down in my pocket book.

'Is Henson capable of murder?' I said.

Greg stared at me through narrowed eyes. 'He's got a hell of a temper and he's mad enough to do anything. But kill someone ...? I don't know.'

I finished the water as Greg downed the last of his lager. Tracy sat massaging her fingers and avoiding my gaze. Jamie Henson had just turned from a person of interest into a formal suspect.

'I will need every piece of information you have about Henson including addresses, telephone numbers, friends, etc.'

He nodded and I spent the next hour jotting down

everything he told me. Afterwards I got up and made to leave but he turned to me again. 'You should know that there's a demonstration next Friday outside the bank's office. Henson's organised it and he's been boasting about the people he's got coming down from London.'

At the end of the afternoon I stood listening to Lydia summarising the preliminary work they had achieved from the shop-to-shop interviewing that afternoon. I soon realised that it would take days of work. Wyn and Jane wouldn't be able to start on the offices until the start of the week. And in the meantime we were no nearer to identifying the killer. Half an hour later I stood outside Cornock's office, rapped two knuckles on his door, and heard a shout from inside. He was standing over his desk reading the inside pages of one of the broadsheets.

'I need a word, sir.'

I sat in one of the low-backed visitor chairs and dragged a foot over the other knee. I noticed that my brown brogues were filthy so I uncrossed my leg and tried the other shoe, which was cleaner. 'It's about the Dolman and Turner murders—'

'Is it about Tracy Jones, the CSI?'

'Ah ... How did you ...?'

'Alvine sent me a report. It wasn't very complimentary about your handling of the position.' Cornock folded the paper neatly, placed it on top of a bookcase, and then sat down. He gave me a wary look. 'Tracy Jones has been informed that she should not be involved with any of your ongoing inquiries.'

'I was concerned that ...' I wasn't thinking clearly. Tracy had been to see Alvine before I had a chance to talk to Cornock. It made me look a complete idiot for not having reported the matter sooner. 'I was with Dean over the weekend.'

'Of course. How is he?'

'The doctors think he'll make a full recovery.'

'Pleased to hear that. So any developments on the Dolman case?'

Cornock nodded as I gave him an executive summary before I left. He raised an eyebrow when I mentioned the demonstration.

'Take care, John. No balls-ups.'

I got home late and rang Jackie to check on Dean, relieved to hear he was getting stronger every minute.

Chapter 34

The lawyer's offices where Lydia and I were meeting the Dolmans were next to the National Bank of Wales. It was early afternoon and still cold. Back at Queen Street Wyn and Jane were building a complete picture of all the names that Greg had given us with addresses and known aliases and contacts. They had instructions to make progress by the time we got back. I hesitated when we reached the open concrete area in front of the bank, wondering what exactly Henson had planned for Friday.

A woman at reception welcomed me as though I was a high-rolling client that needed star treatment. She picked up a telephone and I heard her say my name. Then a younger woman arrived, sat down and ran her identity card through a reader connected to her computer.

'Big Brother, eh?' I said, making conversation.

She gave me her welcoming smile. 'Everyone has to sign in. That way they know when we arrive. It means they can track the hours that the fee-earners work.' Then she rolled her eyes. Her colleague pushed a visitor name badge over the desk at Lydia and me.

From behind a large glass door the personal assistant I'd met at the bank emerged. A name badge dangled from a lanyard hanging around her neck. She wore a narrow pencil skirt, a crisp white blouse and neatly cut blond hair. Her high heels made her calves look lean and sculpted. Lydia gave her shoes a serious look.

'Mr Dolman was intrigued by your request for a visit,' the woman said, fishing for information.

'Why are we meeting here?' I asked.

'We're closing a big deal this morning.' Her tone implied I shouldn't ask any more.

We walked towards the lift and I kept my eyes

straight ahead but my nose was being assaulted by her perfume – citrus and fresh lemons. All of it reminded me of a holiday in Lucca and cycling along the city walls. And I decided then that I would take Dean there in the summer. Take time off. Do some well-overdue father–son bonding.

She led us out of the lift and then through an open-plan office into a room away from the prying eyes of the staff. Tony Harper stood waiting for me and reached out a hand. His white shirt had a cut-away collar complemented by a navy tie that had red and purple stripes. The Dolmans and Charlotte Parkinson were sitting around a highly polished oak conference table.

Charlotte smiled at me and another bank of expensive perfume invaded my personal space. This time it was sweet and sensuous and matched the wearer perfectly. It was like having a bath in strawberries and thick clotted cream.

'What's this about, Inspector?' Troy Dolman started.

Charlotte chipped in before he could continue what sounded like a tirade. 'We've a lot of work to get through today. And as always time is against us. I do hope you understand.' Her smile dimpled her cheeks and her eyes lit up. It had the desired result of making me feel warm and mellow inside. Just for moment, at least, until I looked over at Troy Dolman.

Lydia had already sat down and I followed suit. A bottle of Ty Nant water was open on the table with cut-glass tumblers. This was a different legal world from the cramped chaotic offices of the lawyers on Cathedral Road who handled the purchase of my flat.

'We have some intelligence that suggests there'll be a protest or demonstration of some sort outside the bank on Friday.'

Rex Dolman was the first to respond. 'How did you

find this out?'

'We have our sources.'

'Is that all?' Troy Dolman now.

'We suggest that it might be sensible for you to take some additional precautions. Perhaps warn your staff and arrange some additional security.'

'Are we targeted as well?' Harper said.

'Your buildings are next to each other so it will be hard to avoid any attention from this group. These people are good at getting publicity so they'll have tipped off the press.'

Troy Dolman threw a large fountain pen with a mottled barrel onto the pile of papers in front of him and snorted. 'Damn terrorists.'

I watched Terry's back as he left the café after an ill-tempered meeting where he had repeated his demands that I help his girlfriend and I had replied equally forcefully that it was impossible. I sat finishing my Americano when the call arrived from Hannah Peters.

'I'm sorry. I should have told you sooner ...'

Her voice trembled so I focused hard on what she was saying. I blanked out the noise from the café, my anticipation building. 'I've got some papers belonging to Alan that you need to see.'

I was on my feet, heading out of the café, my mobile still pinned to my ear.

'I know I should have mentioned this earlier.'

'For Christ sake, what are you talking about?'

'I'm on my way to see you.'

I drove back to Queen Street calling Lydia and yelling instructions for her to meet Hannah.

In my haste I double-parked alongside one of the

old pool cars next to the police station and then raced up to the Incident Room. Lydia was already waiting for me. 'She's in one of the conference rooms.'

We made our way down through the building. I stopped before the door, and drew a hand over my hair. I could feel the sweat around my temples.

Hannah sat hunched over the table, a weary look in her eyes. Her elbows pressed onto a buff folder that she scooped up and clutched firmly.

I smiled. Then I stared at the folder in her hands. I pulled up a chair and Lydia did the same. 'Hannah. You have something that you want to show us?'

She nodded a tentative confirmation. 'Alan gave me a file with some original papers.' She put the folder on the desk. 'He had been working with Matthew Dolman on plans to have the bank sold. Mr Dolman had signed a power of attorney in his favour in the week before he died.'

Hannah composed herself, drew the chair nearer the table and then pushed the folder over towards me. 'The power of attorney is in the papers as are the details of the people Matthew and Alan were dealing with.'

I read the papers as Lydia asked her some more questions. 'Why did you only mention this now?'

'After the break-in I thought that something wasn't right and that it must have been this power of attorney that the burglar wanted.'

I sensed Lydia looking over at me as I flicked through the documents. It looked to be in standard legal language and then I found a sheet with contact details.

'How much did you know about the sale of the bank?' Lydia said.

Hannah shrugged. 'Troy Dolman was dead against it.'

A frightened look reappeared on her face.

'What had Alan and Matthew Dolman been doing?'

'It's all in there. Matthew had been negotiating with another bank to take them over. But Troy wasn't happy. There was one meeting when I heard him shouting at his father.' She shivered. 'He had a hell of a temper.'

Hannah sipped some water from a beaker that Lydia had pushed in her direction.

'They were hoping to get the sale finalised quickly.'

I scanned the papers. 'There's mention of a man called Fairbrother.'

She nodded. 'He was the agent acting for the other bank. It was all very confidential.'

Then she said slowly, 'I don't feel safe any more, Inspector.'

I looked up and saw the fear in her face.

'I'm going away for a few days.'

'Is there enough to arrest him, boss?'

Lydia sat in my office; the only piece of paper on my desk was the power of attorney and the papers that Hannah had given us. Contemplating the arrest of Troy Dolman needed careful thought. I could imagine the reaction from Cornock if I suggested it.

'We know he has temper. And that there were blazing rows about the future of the bank. And he has a relationship with Youlden and he's got free access to Turner's office which accounts for there being no forced entry. He must have been searching for the power of attorney, hoping he could destroy it and prevent the sale of the bank.'

'And when he cannot find it he kills Alan Turner?' I sensed the scepticism in her voice.

After the last meeting with the Dolman family,

which had been stage-managed with such precision, it was clear that every future decision about the family was to be signed off by Cornock, the assistant chief constable, and then double-checked by the lawyers of the Crown Prosecution Service.

I reached for the telephone. 'We need to talk to Fairbrother first.' I found the sheet with the details and then I dialled the number and waited. 'I want to speak to Richard Fairbrother.'

'Just a moment.' The voice was silky.

'Fairbrother.'

'My name is Detective Inspector John Marco of the Wales Police Service. I'm investigating the deaths of Matthew Dolman and Alan Turner.'

'How can I help?'

I was expecting some surprise, not a business-like response.

'I understand that you were involved in discussions over the sale of the bank?'

'Yes. That's correct.'

'I was hoping that you might be able to give me some details.'

'Of course.'

Fairbrother took half an hour to outline the negotiations for the sale of the NBW to a German bank. I had been scribbling notes as he spoke and then when he had finished I asked. 'What happens now?'

'The discussions are ongoing with Tony Harper.'

'Tony Harper?' I could not hide the surprise in my voice.

'He is acting as Mr Dolman's executor.'

Chapter 35

By Wednesday Wyn and Jane had made little progress with assembling any meaningful evidence. A gentle despair had descended on the Incident Room. The French authorities had confirmed that a limited company registered in the Cayman Islands owned the flat in Nice and there was an annoying silence from the Australian authorities about Turner's apartment.

I returned to the Incident Room after a fractious meeting with Cornock where he point-blank refused to contemplate making any resources available for surveillance on Henson, Cleaver and Youlden.

'I still think we should be keeping an eye on them,' Lydia said.

I nodded before pacing in front of the board.

'They might meet together,' she continued.

It was frustrating knowing that without a full surveillance team there was nothing we could do. 'The super won't contemplate any surveillance. It's not a "justifiable use" of resources.'

Lydia frowned. 'We could do it ourselves.'

I looked over at her. I had seen that serious dedicated side to her before. Wyn and Jane had stopped working and they were waiting for me to reply. I looked back at the board and wondered if spending hours undertaking surveillance would give us anything valuable, but on the other hand we might, just might …

'We could do the two nights before the demonstration,' Jane said.

Wyn was nodding as she continued.

'There won't be any overtime,' I said, cursing myself as I sounded like an accountant. I glanced around the room, saw the acceptance of the position in their faces, and felt pleased that I could really rely on them.

I sat down heavily and after an hour we had mapped out who was going where and when.

'We do tonight and Thursday night only.'

Lydia had been nodding her head appreciatively as I ran through the plans. 'And if there's nothing helpful coming from the surveillance then we go home.'

I was going to take Henson's place, Lydia Cleaver's terrace and Wyn and Jane would sit outside Youlden's home.

By late in the evening I was tired and regretting my enthusiasm in believing that surveillance of this sort would be valuable. But sitting in the office trying to think strategically hadn't worked. I found a place to park a little way down the street from Henson's and conveniently there was a street light just outside that cast a weak shadow all over the small front patios of the houses nearby. It was quiet; a woman took a small dog for a brisk walk, talking to it continuously until it shat on the pavement. She looked down and then around and seeing no one in sight walked smartly away. I texted Jackie and she replied instantly telling me that Dean was much better. Then I sent a message to my mother and she replied too. I was getting to catch up on my family duties. Being with Dean in hospital reminded me that I had missed being a father. And Jackie was treating me like a human being again and I wondered if that meant she might want to rekindle our relationship. In truth I really did not know how I felt about such a prospect.

There was a shooting pain in the base of my back. Shifting my position didn't help and a dull ache developed. I drank some lukewarm tea from a flask, chewed on a chocolate bar and smoked another cigarette. By midnight nothing had happened and lights in the various houses went off as the residents all went off to bed. I messaged the others who reported the same absence of activity so I texted them all to go home.

The following night I had even less enthusiasm for the surveillance. The ache in the small of my back had moved to a spot at the top of my leg and no amount of moving my position was going to help. Lydia was the first to message me that evening. *Nobody moving tonight.L* And then Wyn sent a similar message from the car he was sharing with Jane. *Youlden dead quiet.* By ten o'clock there had been no visitors to any of the houses we were watching and, more than that, the streets were quieter than the night before. I was expecting a meeting in one of the houses to prepare, share plans for the destruction of Western civilisation.

Half an hour later, I sent a message to them all to leave.

Lydia was the last to reply – *Might stay for half an hour.*

I replied. *Don't bother. Get home. Busy morning.*

Cornock had been right: it had been a waste of time but at least no additional resources had been wasted. Frustration dominated my thoughts as I pondered whether Henson was responsible. He was linked to Youlden who knew Troy Dolman, whose belligerence made him a natural suspect, and Mrs Dolman, from his time in the hostel. I still hadn't dismissed the possibility that she was involved. I passed one of the delivery vans from Pizza House on the way home and I realised that having obvious suspects like George Stanway didn't mean the case would be straightforward. I parked the car before walking over to the flat, ticking off my to-do list for tomorrow and hoping that I'd sleep.

Chapter 36

I looked out of my kitchen window. The city looked fresh and sanitised by the early-morning spring sunshine. It was early and I hadn't slept well. I reached a hand to the small of my back where I could still feel a dull ache.

Behind me, the toaster on the worktop popped out its contents. I found butter in the fridge and scraped a covering onto the evenly browned toast before piling on some jam just as the final drops of my espresso emerged from the coffee machine.

I stepped back towards the window, eating my breakfast. There were blocks of flats everywhere. After the banking crisis when property prices collapsed many of the apartments had been left empty. And then the buy-to-let landlords stepped in and the properties were gradually snapped up. Blaming the bankers was simple, especially as the country had bailed them out and every week there was a headline about bankers' bonuses.

I reached for my mobile and tapped out a message to Jackie. *How's Dean?* It was taking me some time to become accustomed to the domestic routine of thinking about my son every day. But the regular messaging was becoming natural and something that I looked forward to. I pulled on a brown jacket that complemented the dark jeans. I had checked first thing that the black brogues I had chosen were clean. After dragging a comb through my hair I left the flat. Jackie's reply arrived when I pulled the door closed behind me. I smiled to myself as I read the text. *Good night's sleep. Much better.Jx.*

I drove into town and found a parking slot in a side street a little way down from the bank.

Morning commuters snaked over the concrete, talking on mobiles and tapping on screens as I arrived in the square. I noticed Wyn walking up to me.

'Good morning, sir. All quiet so far.'

'Have you seen Jane or Lydia?'

He shook his head. 'I came straight here. I thought that would be best.'

I nodded. Wyn could be too serious for his own good. We walked around the square, occasionally standing to let an office worker brush past us.

Talking to Wyn while we paced around the concrete square waiting for something to happen made me feel old, older than I wanted to be. He was young and inexperienced. I could remember the detective inspector that I had worked with as a young constable. He was an ancient chain-smoking relic who had a deep cynicism about human nature and little patience with junior officers who made mistakes.

I stopped and tapped out a text to Lydia. We carried on towards the entrance of the bank. I wasn't certain what my strategy would be. Would we wait around all morning? Cornock would have questions about the proper use of resources if we did. The same security guards were standing in the foyer of the main bank building. They gave us a brief nod when we entered and made for the main reception.

We waited as the staff spoke in hushed tones on the telephone. Moments later the same personal assistant emerged from the lift and glided towards us.

'Has there been any unusual activity this morning?' I asked.

'Nothing unusual at all, Inspector. Both Troy and Rex have been in since first thing.'

A message reached my mobile and I dipped into my jacket pocket hoping it would be from Lydia. Jane's name appeared apologising that she would be late. Then I tapped out another impatient message to Lydia. There was nothing further we could achieve so we headed towards the lawyers' offices. Jane caught up with us as we approached their building.

I still had no message from Lydia. I turned to Jane. 'Have you seen Lydia this morning?'

Jane shook her head. I wondered if she was unwell, but her lack of communication unsettled me. She could have been in contact somehow. I found my mobile and dialled her number but it went straight to voicemail.

Then I heard a voice behind me and saw the familiar face of Tony Harper talking to a man dressed in an expensive-looking pinstripe suit. He was tall, six foot two at least, with broad shoulders and the build of a man who spent hours in the gym.

'This is Ian Lewis, our Chief Executive,' Harper said.

Ian thrust a hand in my direction. 'Good morning.'

'Detective Inspector Marco.' I extracted my fingers from a crushing handshake.

'There's been nothing unusual happening as yet,' Ian added, looking out and through the expanse of glass at the front of the building.

Harper glanced at his watch. 'It's early yet.'

He was right. We exchanged small talk for a few minutes but I kept looking away, hoping to spot Lydia. I couldn't stand still so I made my excuses and walked back outside with Jane and Wyn.

I surveyed the office blocks surrounding the square, pondering what Henson might have planned.

'Let's get back to Queen Street,' I said, making for my car. I had wasted enough time already and I needed to contact Lydia. None of the previous sergeants I had worked with had made themselves as indispensable as her. I cursed when I saw the parking penalty notice stuck to the windscreen and I tore it away and thrust it at Wyn. 'Sort that out, for Christ sake.'

Minutes later we were pulling up at the car park behind Queen Street. I stabbed the code into the security pad before taking the stairs two at a time to the second floor. My mobile was pinned to my ear as I dialled Lydia's mobile again. Her voicemail message started so I finished the call and threw my mobile onto the desk. From my computer I found Lydia's home telephone number, alongside an address in Pontypridd. If she had slept late I was going to give her a dressing down but it was so unlike her and her home telephone just rang out.

I realised that I'd not heard from her since last night. A knot of anxiety developed as I scanned through the emails in my inbox.

I should have welcomed my mobile ringing, but I snarled at the caller. 'DI Marco.'

'It's Ian Lewis, Inspector. We met this morning—'

'What is it?'

'There are streams of people crossing the concourse in front of our building. They've got placards and they're shouting—'

I stood up abruptly. 'We'll be there as soon as we can.'

I shouted at Wyn and Jane and then we galloped out of Queen Street and found a pool car that Wyn hammered down Churchill Way towards the Bay.

'Any news about Lydia?' Jane asked.

I was peering out of the front windscreen. I turned and looked over at her. 'No answer from her mobile. And I tried her home number before we left.'

Jane frowned. Wyn mounted the pavement with the nearside wheels. We ran over towards the offices. There must have been two hundred people congregated outside. And there were more streaming in from each corner of the square in a coordinated approach. They gathered outside the bank. I saw Henson opening a small stepladder. Then someone passed him a megaphone and he began a tirade about the redistribution of wealth, demanded the introduction of a Robin Hood tax, all to the cheers and encouragement from the swelling crowd. Wyn tugged at my jacket sleeve. 'The TV crews have arrived, sir.'

I looked over to the far end of the square where Wyn was pointing. 'For Christ sake. That's all we need.'

I reached my hand into a pocket and stared at my mobile hoping that in the middle of all the activity around me I had missed the sound of Lydia's call, but the screen was blank. Her lack of contact was entirely out of character and the irritation it caused had now developed into real concern.

The television crew walked over towards the assembled crowd. It all seemed stage-managed as though Henson had choreographed everything to the finest detail. He finished and cheers erupted from his audience just as a journalist stuck a microphone under his face. I kept looking around hoping to spot Lydia.

Then I rang area control who put me through to the desk sergeant in Pontypridd. He was reluctant at first but eventually he agreed to send someone to Lydia's home. As soon as the television cameras left the mood in the crowd changed. A section peeled away towards the lawyers' offices. The same number headed for the front door of the bank. The security officers didn't have time to lock the doors and the group flooded in, shouting abuse.

'What do we do, boss?' Wyn said.

I was thinking the same thing. But there was no breach of the peace, yet. The first group had been swelled by more protesters and they were flooding into the foyer of the law firm. Then my mobile rang and I heard Ian Lewis' ragged voice. 'These people have gone through our entire building. They are everywhere. Surely you can do something about it.'

I turned to Wyn. And then Jane. 'One of you call the sergeant in the Bay and the other the sergeant on duty in Queen Street. We need some uniformed lads down here. Now.' I jogged over towards the main entrance.

A deafening scream made me stop in my tracks. I stared around, and then from the side of the building I heard a woman shrieking.

Chapter 37

I raced over to where I'd heard the scream and noticed a crowd had gathered. I heard someone shout for an ambulance. A woman pushed past me and promptly spewed up on the pavement. I elbowed my way through the throng. There were snippets of conversations that barely registered. Then I heard my voice shouting. 'Police. Move to one side.'

Jane had raised her voice too as we struggled through the mix of protesters and onlookers. A gap opened abruptly and I stood looking down at a mangled body.

Harper must have died instantly. The cord of a lanyard hung around his neck and tied to the end was a plastic envelope. *One More Greedy Bastard* was typed on the paper in the same large font as before.

I shot a glance up at the top of the building.

I turned to Jane and Wyn. 'Wyn, you secure the scene until we get a full CSI team here. And get the names of witnesses. Jane, you come with me.' I turned and barged my way back to the square through the thinning crowd.

I called Ian Lewis who answered immediately. 'Get the front door closed. Now.'

I finished the call without waiting for a reply. Then I called area control and gave clear instructions about the CSI teams needed. A siren sounded and I saw an ambulance mount the pavement and then travel down the square towards us, quickly followed by a paramedic car covered in the bright-yellow livery. The siren died but then another screeched as two police cars neared.

I reached the main entrance: two security guards stood inside looking helpless alongside the noisy protesters. I hammered a fist on the door until I caught the attention of one of them. He squeezed open the door and a bank of sound escaped. Discarded placards littered the floor, demonstrators milled around, and the staff all looked uneasy and frightened.

I headed for reception, Jane close behind me.

'I need to see Ian Lewis,' I said to a terrified receptionist. 'Now!'

She nodded to the lifts. 'Third floor.'

I jabbed at the button calling the lift and it lit up at the third attempt. The lift indicator told me it was at the first floor. But it had been there for ages. The seconds dragged, I couldn't delay. I looked around for the stairs just as the doors opened. I had to find how Harper fell to his death. I had to find out from where. And I had to find out if Henson was in the building. Ian was waiting for us when the lift doors opened. 'Is it true?' His face was three shades paler than when I had seen him that morning.

'Where did it happen?' I said.

Lewis jerked his head down the corridor and we followed him. 'There's a small balcony area on the next floor. It has views over the city and sometimes we use it to impress clients and have drinks parties in the summer.'

He led us through various offices with staff huddled together in groups. I noticed a group of the younger girls wiping away tears.

'Do you have CCTV in the building?' I said.

'In the public areas only and there's a system in the lifts. But not in the offices.'

It had been too much to hope that CCTV would give us a nice clean image of the killer grabbing Harper, dragging him to the fourth-floor balcony and then hurling him over to his death. We reached a door to a staircase and Ian led us up towards the balcony area.

My mobile rang. It was Alvine. 'Where are you Marco?'

'On the fourth-floor balcony. I need a team by the body.'

'Done.'

'And another team up here. And Alvine,' I hesitated. 'Is ...?'

'No. Tracy's on her rest day.'

Part of me was relieved, another annoyed that I had wanted to see her again.

A gentle breeze warmed my face once Ian opened the door. He stepped over the threshold and let Jane and I walk out onto the balcony. I stopped for a moment, listening to the faint chatter of voices from the square below. I didn't have any latex gloves with me, nor covers for my shoes. So I stepped around the perimeter of the balcony and, careful not to touch it, peered over the handrail. I could just about make out Wyn, various paramedics and the CSI team that were busy establishing a perimeter. There were only a few spectators dawdling on the square near Harper's body.

I stepped back, turning to Ian. 'Who has access to this balcony?'

His shoulders sank. 'Anybody really. It's not restricted.'

'Did Harper have any personal problems?' I had to eliminate every possibility.

Ian snorted. 'Don't be absurd. He was the most well-adjusted person I have ever met.'

'Any financial problems?'

Ian stared at me, scarcely believing my question. 'He was one of the senior partners of this firm. He has made a fortune over the years from banking and commercial work.'

The door behind us opened and Alvine stepped onto the balcony. She scanned our shoes and hands.

'I haven't touched anything and we haven't walked over the main part of the balcony.'

She nodded. 'It's chaos downstairs.'

Another investigator carrying bags of equipment joined her in the doorway.

'We'll need to get started.' Alvine was already reaching for plastic covers for shoes and snapping on latex gloves.

We retraced our steps to the third floor and Ian led us into his office. I had telephone calls to make, officers I needed to organise. There were dozens, maybe more, of demonstrators in the building, all of whom needed to be spoken to, and their details taken before we started on staff and visiting clients. Among them somewhere was a killer with a motive for the deaths of Dolman and Turner and now Harper. My excitement was raw at the certainty of being within touching distance of the murderer.

'I need a list of all your staff. Everyone that was here this morning.'

Ian nodded.

'Were there any clients visiting the building?'

'The visitors' log should give us that information.'

'And I want CCTV tapes from every part of the building sent over to Queen Street immediately.'

Charlotte Parkinson appeared at the door of his office with two men in their mid-thirties wearing expensive-looking suits, crisp white shirts with equally expensive-looking ties.

'Is it true?' she said.

Ian stumbled over something to say. One of the men standing with Charlotte put a hand over her shoulder. 'Mr Harper was fine this morning. He was looking forward to his meeting today,' he said.

Ian nodded. 'The police,' he glanced over at me, 'are

treating it as suspicious.'

'What!' Charlotte gasped.

The second man – I had assumed they were all lawyers from their clipped measured tones, almost as bad as accountants – chipped in. 'You mean somebody killed him?'

'We'll need to speak to you all in due course.'

Then I remembered that Lydia had still not been in touch. I reached into my jacket pocket, fumbled and almost dropped my mobile. Then I dialled her number – straight to voicemail again. I rang Queen Street – she hadn't called in either. Then I tried her landline number but as it rang out it only increased my anxiety.

Then my mobile rang and I noticed Cornock's name. 'We found Lydia's car.'

After hammering along the A470 towards Merthyr Tydfil and then taking the junction towards Quaker's Yard I jolted my car to a standstill on the pavement outside an old dilapidated industrial unit. A bad feeling developed in the pit of my stomach when I realised we were nowhere near the property where she had been last night. A patrol car was parked diagonally across the entrance and after carding the uniformed officer I strode past him.

There were six units with electrical sectional doors, each firmly closed. One of the units was occupied by a double-glazing company, a second by a business selling solar heating panels, where two brightly coloured vans had been parked outside. The other units were all securely locked and barred. I saw Cornock looking through the driver's side window of Lydia's Ford and I walked over towards him.

'I understand that she was on surveillance last

night.' Cornock used a measured tone.

'All the team did a few hours.' I should have known the surveillance would be pointless. What could we have possibly learnt?

'I'm going to see if anybody saw anything.' I glanced over towards the units behind me.

'Bring me up to date as soon as you're back in Queen Street,' Cornock said before walking towards his car.

I paced over to the double-glazing company. The door was a PVCu variety that squeaked when it opened. A well-endowed woman with startling blond hair sat behind a desk. Her make-up cracked as she smiled. 'What do you want, love?'

The accent reminded me of my childhood in Aberdare.

'Have you seen anybody with the Fiesta that's parked in the corner?'

She gave me a blank look. 'What car is that then?'

'The silver Ford. You must have seen it.'

'Sorry, love. Does it belong to somebody you know?'

'Who owns this place?'

'You'd have to ask the boss. I just do the paperwork. He doesn't own it, mind. Some property company or other. But they don't look after the place. I've got a bucket by here: the rain pours in through a hole in the roof.'

I didn't need a summary of the property's condition so I turned my back and left, hoping that the carpentry business next door would be more helpful. I was disappointed. The woman behind the counter could barely string a few words together. She gave me the contact number for her boss. Some instinct made me check the front doors of the three other units. They were all safely secured and then I scrambled around the back hoping there might be an open window or a broken door. But there was nothing to suggest recent activity.

I walked over to Lydia's Fiesta and stared in. Nothing had changed since I'd done the same thing a few minutes earlier but repeating the exercise was reassuring. A small Scientific Support Vehicle drew up on the main road. A single crime scene investigator emerged and exchanged a few words with the uniformed officer before walking over towards me, bag in hand.

I stood and watched him unlock the Fiesta. I snapped on a pair of latex gloves and then rifled through the papers Lydia had stuffed into the storage compartment in the doors. In the glove compartment there was a CD of a Bizet opera and another of *Nabucco*. Satisfied that I could leave the investigator to his work I told him to contact me soon as he'd finished.

I drove back to Queen Street, my mind a complete haze. I thumped the steering wheel as I cursed myself. There had been texts every few minutes from Wyn and Jane bringing me up to date with the activities at the lawyers' offices in the centre of the city. My frustration caused me to miss a red traffic light and I narrowly avoided an accident with a BMW whose young driver raised his middle finger at me.

I don't recall parking or punching in my security code or taking the stairs to the second floor of Queen Street. But when I arrived Wyn and Jane were speaking in animated tones on the telephone. There was a pile of paperwork strewn all over the desks and the telephone in my office rang off the hook.

And then my mobile rang. It was Cornock, chasing no doubt for an update even though he knew full well I'd report progress as soon as I could. I curbed the irritation, hoping it wouldn't show in my voice.

'Just got back, sir.'

'This is even more serious than we thought, John. You need to get over here.'

Chapter 38

Watching the video in Superintendent Cornock's office curled a taut knot in my stomach. I was convinced I would never eat anything again. The lighting was the same, the voices were the same but I couldn't take it in. I watched the screen a second time, staring at Lydia's face. Her hair was a mess, her mascara had blotched the skin around her eyes and she looked as though she hadn't eaten for days.

'It was posted on YouTube in the last hour.'

I nodded. 'Play it again.'

I watched, mesmerised.

'The ordinary people will not stand for the banking system causing harm to millions. If the government won't punish the bankers then we the people will. And anybody protecting the bankers and their associates will be punished. Ordinary working class people will not stand idly by and see their lives destroyed and homes lost, just to pay bonuses for sick greedy bankers. Anyone working with the bankers to protect their interests is a legitimate target.'

The message was the same as the previous videos. But this time a police officer had been abducted. Lydia had been taken: her life was being threatened.

Cornock stood by my side; a hard, determined look on his face. A muscle twitched on his jaw. 'This changes everything.'

He pointed the remote at the television again and replayed the video.

My mouth dried; there was no saliva to run my tongue over my lips. The two people standing either side of Lydia resembled both men from the previous videos. So it was impossible to describe them. They wore a one-piece dark suit and had their faces covered in black balaclava masks – even their mouths had been covered. Only their eyes were visible. I squinted at the camera hoping for a glimmer of recognition. Then I listened again to the monologue – it was the same as before. A voice fed through some electronic machine.

As it ended the telephone on Cornock's desk rang. He paused the screen.

'Yes, sir,' he said. 'He's with me now.'

There was silence. Cornock nodded, still clenching his jaw. I guessed the chief constable was on the telephone. 'I don't have that information, sir.'

He glanced at me, narrowed his eyes.

'We'll do what we can.'

Cornock finished the conversation. 'The press are all over this like a rash. The first minister in the Welsh Assembly has been in contact. And the chief constable wants a full report into what happened.'

'I'll get onto it.'

'Forget the report for now. Just find her, John.'

In the Incident Room Jane and Wyn stood up as soon as I walked in. They seemed to have aged since first thing that morning. Both opened their mouths to speak but the right words failed them. I knew what I wanted to establish – whether Henson was in the building at the time of Harper's death. My excitement mounted as I read his name on the list of demonstrators.

'The results of the voice analysis of the video we found on Youlden's laptop came through this morning, boss,' Jane added, looking pleased. 'They say it's a match to Henson and one other. They can't tell who, but it's not Youlden because they could eliminate him after your interview with him. But—'

'Cleaver.' I spat out his name. Lydia had been outside his home last night. I stood up and shouted at Jane.

A line of traffic slowed our progress and increased my anger tenfold as we drove towards the Corporation Street Working Men's Club. I swore at various cars and vans and one driver earned a vigorous gesticulation of my right hand. Jane drove but said nothing. She parked next to an old blue Land Rover, its wheel arches rusted with age.

'There was nothing you could have done, sir.' Jane switched off the ignition and leant forward against the steering wheel. It didn't feel that way but I appreciated what she was trying to do.

'Let's go and talk to Henson.'

'Is that his Land Rover?'

'We'll soon find out.' I sat for a moment, pondering, before turning to Jane. 'You wait here. I won't be long.' She protested but I was out of the car before she could say anything. I was breaking protocols of course. There should have been two of us going into the premises that morning. But I had Lydia to find and protocols could go and fuck themselves. I tensed as the front door appeared locked but it gave way after a heavy jolt and a gentle tap with my shoulder. Someone was whistling in the rear of the building and then I heard the sound of a vacuum. I reached the hallway and stopped, looking up the stairs. I took small deep breaths and kept my footsteps soft on the risers although my heartbeat raced. At the top, I paused and listened for any sound. It was ridiculous to think that Lydia might have been kept here but desperation can play terrible tricks on the mind.

I heard the sound of fingers racing across a keyboard and then the clicking of a mouse. My heart moved sideways in my chest. I pushed open the door and saw Henson and Cleaver sitting at their desks, eyes staring intently at their computer screens. Henson jolted backwards in his chair when he saw me.

'How the fuck did you get in?'

'The cleaner opened up.'

The printer purred into life and a few sheets popped out. At least the printer hadn't changed. I walked over to the desks and stood over Henson. 'We've got some catching up to do.'

'Fuck off.'

'Where is she, Jamie?'

Henson sniggered. 'I don't know who you mean, *policeman*.'

'Let's make this easy for you. Detective Sergeant Flint is missing. You and your friend here are the number one suspects.'

'Was she the one outside my place last night?' Cleaver managed a thin-lipped grin.

Mistake. Big mistake.

'Did you know that the sentence for kidnap is at least eight years in prison?'

Henson sneered at me. His best sneer yet and it made my blood simmer.

'And cons don't like people like you in prison.'

'What they hell do you mean?'

'Word will get around about your background with young kids.'

Henson stood up and kicked the chair behind him and it flew back, crashing against a filing cabinet. I stepped closer to Henson. I could see a brown mole on his cheek. His sweater was thin with age, the collar of his shirt frayed.

Cleaver was on his feet now. 'He's winding you up Jamie. Don't let him get to you.'

Henson stepped back.

'Cons don't like paedos,' I said. 'How old were they Jamie? Ten, wasn't it? A young girl and boy. News travels fast inside prison. And even on remand, awaiting trial, you're not safe.'

Jamie stiffened as I stepped closer to him. I could smell the cider on his breath. 'And then there's the cons who don't like wife beaters.'

I had to hope that would have been enough. Time stood still for a moment before he launched himself into me with his shoulder. We crashed backwards. Somehow, I pulled a pile of papers off the desk and they covered the floor by my side. I could sense Henson struggling to overpower me. I fisted my right hand and smacked him hard on the side of the face. He grunted in pain and loosened his grip, obviously weaker than I'd expected, flabby from planning the revolution.

'You fucking knobhead,' Cleaver shouted.

He was right but Henson was beyond caring. He thrashed around, kicking my shins and then I turned him over and pushed his face into the floor. I yanked his arms behind his back and snapped on a pair of handcuffs. There was a trickle of blood on my hands and I touched my nose and realised I was bleeding. Between breaths, I recited the standard warning and then I found my mobile and called Jane.

Moments later, I heard her footfall on the stairs.

Jane looked at my face. 'Are you all right, boss?'

I stood and dabbed the back of my hand to my face. Then I dragged a handkerchief from my pocket and thrust it against my nose. 'Get some uniformed lads here. I've just arrested Jamie Henson for assaulting a police officer. Once we've taken him to the station we'll search the premises.'

Henson squirmed on the floor. 'You can't be serious.'

Cleaver frantically gathered all his papers together. 'You've got no lawful reason to search our place.'

I showed him my blood-soaked handkerchief. 'Your friend has just been arrested. That makes any search lawful. And you're under arrest for obstruction.'

He gaped over at me, hesitated, and then threw the papers on the table.

Alvine gave my nose a suspicious glare. Then she looked past me at Jane who had said very little on the way back to Queen Street. 'So this printer needs to be checked to establish whether the messages found on Dolman and Turner were printed on it?'

I glanced over at Jane. She opened her eyes wide but decided against saying anything.

'It was very lucky that Detective Constable Thorne was with me. Henson just launched himself at me. Totally unprovoked attack. He must have been hiding something,' I said.

'So you searched the premises,' Alvine said.

'Failing in my public duty if I didn't.'

Alvine narrowed her eyes and gave me a troubled look. I trooped back to the Incident Room with Jane. My nose was aching and it felt three times its normal size. Wyn was poring over his computer. We needed to know who had been in Harper's offices that morning. I stood with my back to the board and caught Wyn looking in my direction. I nodded over at him. 'Any progress?'

'There was a total of one hundred and fifty-seven demonstrators in the building this morning, including Henson , Cleaver and Youlden.'

I raised my eyebrows as I calculated how long it would take to interview that number of people.

'And over two hundred members of staff.'

This could take days.

Fear gripped me that we'd find Lydia floating in Cardiff Bay, her face swollen and disfigured, her hair a sodden mess. The update from Wyn was interrupted by my mobile ringing on the desk in my office. I had already left Terry a message as, if any of my regular informers might know where Lydia was being held, it would be Terry.

'Meet me in Frank's in half an hour.'

Chapter 39

Terry had a propensity for melodrama but he hadn't suggested meeting at Frank's for, well, it must have been two years. I should have been back in Queen Street preparing for an interview with Henson but something in Terry's tone had made me decide I should see him.

I parked the car and headed towards the gate into the cemetery. I saw a man in the distance being dragged by a Labrador and then a jogger raced past me. After a couple of minutes on the narrow tarmacked road I took a left along a narrow footpath, its surface rutted with age. Shrubbery had grown wild on one side, choking the gravestones. I reached another path and knew that I was near the obelisk for Frank Baselow. And I knew that Terry wasn't far away. I slowed my pace and stopped by the memorial. A sign told me it was number twenty-nine on the Cathays Cemetery heritage trail. But there weren't any cemetery-tourists that evening and I looked up at the image of the woman and child knowing that Terry was probably looking at me. He had checked that I was on my own by now. I turned and looked around but saw no one.

I heard a sound in the trees to my left and turned sharply. A cat, thin and ragged with age scurried past me. I glanced at my watch.

'In a hurry?' Terry's voice said, emerging from a nearby path. He must have been crouching behind one of the memorial stones nearby.

'Isn't this a bit cloak and dagger?'

'Sorry to hear about your sergeant.' He glanced along the path in both directions and then jerked his head for me to follow him.

'Have you heard anything about her?'

'Someone you need to see.'

'I hope this is going to be important.'

Terry stopped and turned to look at me sharply. 'All I wanted was your help with Doreen's case. Make it go away. Disappear.'

'You know—'

'You can fucking fix it if you really want. And now I've got something that'll make your head spin. I've been asking all about your friend Jamie Henson and all them fucking kids that want to change the world.'

He turned and paced away.

I caught up with him as we reached a small well-cultivated area where a man sat on a wooden bench. He stood up as soon as he saw us approaching.

'This is Bert Goodway.' Terry sounded matter-of-fact.

Bert darted a glance up and down the footpath. Terry tried a reassuring tone. 'There's no one else here. You need to tell Marco what you know.'

'You're after them terrorists?'

I stepped towards him, wanting to look him in the eye, get the measure of the man. He had long greasy hair and an old navy T-shirt under a half-zip sweater.

'Are you involved with them?'

He shook his head. 'But I met Neil a while back.'

'Cleaver?' I said.

He nodded.

'And?' I thought that I should be back in Queen Street and that this man and Terry were wasting my time.

'Tell him what you fucking saw.' Terry raised his voice.

'I used to hang out with one of his mates. And he got me to go with him to some of his meetings with that bloke Henson.'

'Jamie Henson?'

'Yeah. I pushed leaflets through doors and stuck them onto car windscreens. And then there was a demonstration through Pontypridd one Saturday. Waste of fucking time.'

Terry again. 'For Christ's sake tell him.' He turned to me. 'And remember Doreen.'

'I was in one of them pubs in Womanby Street by the clock tower. It was last week and the place was dead quiet but I saw Neil walking up the street so I left the pub. He was with Henson and I spotted them going into one of them old properties at the end of the street.'

I stared at Bert, wanting to believe him and wondering if he had just told me where Lydia might be kept. Terry had always been reliable with information in the past but now the impending case against Doreen was giving him an ulterior motive. There was only one way to find out.

I reached for my mobile and called the Incident Room.

Wyn answered.

'Get an armed response unit and a full team down to the entrance of Womanby Street.'

'What—'

'Now.'

I turned to Bert. 'You're coming with me.'

We raced down towards the middle of town. Cars pulled to one side as I flashed the car headlights. Bert had adopted a running commentary on why he wasn't getting out of the car and that I couldn't make him and that if anyone realised he was a 'grass' he'd end up as fish bait in the Bay.

'Shut up,' I shouted. 'You've got more to worry about from me if your information is no fucking good.'

That did the trick and he kept quiet until I braked

hard near the entrance to Womanby Street. Then I had to wait. The streets were choked with people enjoying their evening. I answered my mobile in monosyllabic tones. The ARU would be another five minutes and just as I finished the call I saw Wyn and Jane running up behind my car. Both jumped in and gave Bert a suspicious glare.

'What's the score?' Jane asked, breathless from jogging over from Queen Street.

'Bert has intelligence on Henson and Cleaver. They may have been using a property at the bottom of the street.'

Wyn's breathing was returning to normal. 'When was that?'

'I can't remember dates. I don't even have a fucking watch.'

Then I noticed the flashing lights of the approaching police cars that drew to a halt in front of me. Now passers-by stopped and gawped as officers with semi-automatic carbines emerged onto the street. I dragged Bert behind me as we followed the team. He pointed to a dilapidated door and then I nodded to the ARU sergeant who gave the order for it to be broken down. Seconds later we streamed into the building. Bert disappeared up Womanby Street away into the night.

Four officers went up to the first and second floor of the building as Jane and Wyn accompanied me through the ground floor. At least the absence of clouds of dust suggested recent use. Swiftly we went from one room to another hoping that we'd find Lydia.

Then there was a shout and I raced up the stairs.

On the second floor, one of the uniformed officers waved me towards a room at the rear. I stepped inside, heart pounding.

Inside a large blank cloth had been pinned against

one wall. A rigid plastic seat placed before it. And a few metres in front of me was an empty tripod.

I stood for a moment gathering my breath. Lydia might have been here and I cursed silently at the possibility that we had missed her. I surveyed the room knowing we would need the place examined, taken apart. I turned to Wyn and Jane. 'We'll need a full search team.'

Chapter 40

I woke the following morning convinced that I had not moved a muscle all night. Immediately I thought of Lydia and then checked my mobile before swinging my legs off the bed. I was out of the flat having showered and dressed quicker than normal. I pushed the handset into the cradle on the dashboard, switched on the hands-free connection and made some calls. Search teams had been working all night on Henson's house, another in Womanby Street and a third at Cleaver's place. It was still early and the streets were quiet. I reached the motorway soon enough and powered my way towards Henson's property.

I stopped at a small café and bought a bacon sandwich in a soft floury roll and a black watery coffee. I had finished eating by the time I parked near the various police vehicles in the street outside Henson's house. I grabbed the plastic mug and walked over to the front door. The sound of a car engine drew my attention and I noticed Wyn and Jane emerge from one of the pool cars.

It should have been Lydia meeting me that morning. Where was she? I wondered whether her captors had given her anything to eat or drink.

'Good morning, boss,' Wyn said.

Jane mumbled a greeting. I nodded. They both looked tired but they'd probably be looking a lot worse by tonight.

A sergeant emerged from the house. He yawned energetically before putting his hands to the small of his back and stretching his body backwards. Then he gave my coffee a long stare.

'There's a café round the corner,' I said.

'The place is all yours. There's a dozen T-shirts with Che Guevara's face on them and countless hippy beanie caps and more cider than you could drink in a month. I'm off to see how the other team are getting on. Must be a hard life being a revolutionary.'

'We'll be over there shortly.'

The sergeant shouted for the team to leave and then dropped a set of keys in my opened palm.

A poster with the impassive face of Chairman Mao greeted us in the hallway. Over the fireplace in the sitting room was the image of Lenin reaching out his hand against a background of industrial buildings and troops in armoured vehicles.

'Bloody hell,' Wyn said, looking at Lenin. 'Henson must be a real nutter. Has he got no idea about the millions who died under these two? People like him would have been the first for the gulags.' Wyn sounded irate.

An old sofa had been pushed against the wall and a large television had pride of place on a small table – connected to it was a games console. In the room at the back an ancient computer and a laptop sat on an office table, a filing cabinet in the far corner. The kitchen had crockery and cutlery piled into boxes and the place smelt of decaying food. It clung to my clothes and tickled my nostrils so I headed back to the hallway and then upstairs. The toilet had a brown stain smearing the edge of the basin and the grouting of the tiles surrounding the shower in the bath had turned a uniform black.

I retraced my steps back downstairs, none the wiser having tramped around Henson's home. It struck me then that he was an unlikely killer. He may have been a devoted convert to the anti-capitalist cause who wanted to change the world. But would he kill someone? The evidence from the printer he owned was convenient but now we had a link to the video on Youlden's laptop. But I knew that none of it would prove murder. So I had to hope that the search team in Womanby Street would turn something up.

The sat-nav directed me to Cleaver's address where I walked around the house with Wyn and Jane. Again it had an old hippy stripped-down feel. Even the fridge looked lonely and for some reason I looked in at packets of cheap ham and eggs and margarine. Cans of lager crammed the door – at least we could tell what his priorities were. Cleaver's house left me with the same frustrating impression that we were looking in the wrong place. I glanced at my watch. I knew that by mid-morning, the computers and exhibits would be in Queen Street and we could get to work.

Before returning to Queen Street I called the sergeant leading the search in Womanby Street. 'There's a shed load of stuff that'll need forensics to go through. But otherwise there's no link to anyone.'

'Are CSIs there?'

'Been here since early morning.'

I walked back to my car and returned to Queen Street wondering how my interview with Jamie Henson would pan out.

Glanville Tront had taken years to develop the perfect head of manicured hair that was drawn back over his head in long strands. He wore a bright pink shirt with a pair of Welsh dragon cufflinks. I made do with a jacket from Marks & Spencer every couple of years but a lawyer of Glanville's reputation probably had a new suit every season.

'Inspector Marco.' He emphasised my name as though my involvement had come as a complete bombshell to him.

'Glanville,' I said.

We were standing in front of the sergeant's desk in

the custody suite.

'I understand that Jamie Henson has suffered injuries while in custody.'

'Really?' I turned to look at the custody sergeant who unfolded his arms and arched his eyebrows. 'He slipped on the threshold. Banged his nose.' He kept a completely deadpan expression.

The entrance door was well away from the CCTV cameras that covered the custody suite.

Glanville continued. 'You'll have no objection if we have an independent doctor examine him.'

'As soon as we've finished the interview.'

He gave me another wary look. The custody sergeant shouted for one of the constables to collect Henson from his cell. I headed towards an interview room and sat down, waiting for Henson to arrive and I suddenly realised how odd it felt without Lydia. I was still thinking about her when Tront entered with Henson.

I pressed my lips together and narrowed my eyes. He had a round, almost chubby face but it couldn't disguise the contempt in his eyes. His ginger hair fell over his forehead in unruly waves and he brushed it back as he sat down. He stared at me over his long nose. The bruise under his left eye would be a vibrant colour later today. Once I'd got the formalities for the interview finished I rearranged the papers on my desk and then looked over at Henson.

'Tell me about what you do in your protest group?'

He sat forward, pleased with the chance to convince me of his cause. 'We're doing everything we can to get people to see that there is an alternative to the way our economy is run. It doesn't have to be about paying bankers huge bonuses. Things can be different.'

'Did you know Matthew Dolman?'

He turned his face into a contemptuous grin.

'You know full well that he was on the television programme with me.'

'That interview didn't go too well, did it?'

He averted his gaze. Glanville scribbled something in his notepad.

'The establishment was against me of course. The television company had planned it that way. Everyone could see that they conspired with Dolman.'

Looking into his eyes I tried to fathom out whether he really believed that.

'How did that make you feel?'

'Everyone could see that I was right. Dolman was a typical capitalist: only interested in making profit.'

'Did you meet him at any other time?'

'No. Never wanted to either.'

I shuffled my papers. There had been no time to prepare an interview plan. I had to find Lydia, and I was convinced that Henson knew where she was.

'Then tell me about the morning Matthew Dolman was killed.'

Henson crossed his arms and gloated. 'Is this part of the plot to silence me?'

'A note was left at the scene.'

Henson shrugged.

I shifted through my papers even though I knew exactly where I had left the relevant message. I pulled it out and then pushed it over at him.

'Take a look at this.'

He gave it a cursory glance before throwing it back over the table at me.

'Do you agree with what was written – Greedy Bastard?'

Henson couldn't help himself. 'Of course I do. He was exactly that: a Greedy Bastard who made millions on

271

the back of ordinary working class people—'

'Where were you that morning, Jamie?' I had had enough anti-capitalist rants to last a lifetime.

'In bed.'

'Anyone vouch for that?'

He slowly shook his head. 'I didn't kill him. There's no way you can prove that. You're just part of the establishment attempt to smother our protest.'

'And Alan Turner. Did you know him?'

Henson leant forward – even he could see how the questioning was going. 'I had never heard of him until after his death.'

He rested his elbows on the table, his face in his hands. All I needed to do was reach over the table, grab him by his shirt and then smash his head against the wall until he confessed and told me where he had hidden Lydia. Bad idea. So I went back to the script.

'There was another message left with Turner's body.'

Henson started picking his nails.

I found the second message and gripped it between two fingers. 'Read this,' I managed.

He gave it another cursory look and threw it back at me.

Bad move. The tension just moved up a notch and I breathed out slowly, hoping Henson and Tront wouldn't notice.

'It was found on Turner's body.'

Tront picked up the plastic envelope from the desk. 'Is this all the evidence you've got?' He curled up one eyebrow and gave me a patronising smile at the same time.

'Where were you on the Sunday night that Alan Turner was murdered?'

'At home drinking pink gins and watching Downton

Abbey.'

I gazed over at Henson. I didn't think he was capable of humour.

'Do you recognise the message left by his body?'

'Why the fuck should I?'

I found the message delivered to Queen Street police station. 'We received this over a week ago.'

He didn't bother to pick it up this time. 'So what?'

'Do you recognise it?'

'Of course not.'

'Detective Sergeant Lydia Flint has been missing since last night. She's been abducted. She was conducting surveillance outside the home of one of your friends. He's a member of the group that you lead.'

Henson leant back, folded his arms severely and stared at me. 'And what has that got to do with me?'

'Kidnap and assault are serious charges.'

'We know that Inspector,' Tront said with a tired tone to his voice.

'And you're certain you know nothing about these messages or the abduction of Lydia Flint. A video has been released and it's just like the previous ones that condemn the bankers.'

He shook his head repeatedly.

'Did you know where Matthew Dolman lived?'

'Some fancy place in the Vale, no doubt.'

'Did you know Paul Youlden?'

He gave me a supercilious glare. I reached for the laptop on the desk. I opened the cover and switched it on.

'I'll ask you again. Do you know where Matthew Dolman lived?'

He avoided eye contact.

The screen flickered to life. 'I'm going to show you some footage we recovered from a laptop seized at the home of Paul Youlden.' I clicked the play button and we watched in silence. 'The recording is taken outside Matthew Dolman's home. Forensic analysis has confirmed that it's your voice we've just heard.'

Henson shook his head again.

Glanville had a neutral look on his face. Then he scribbled furiously in his pad.

'And one of the videos was posted to the internet from a café in Pontypridd. We're waiting to speak to one of the staff there who's been on holiday. But if you have been there now is the time to tell us.'

'You have no idea. No idea at all.'

'And on the morning of Matthew Dolman's death we have CCTV coverage of someone leaving the scene. Forensics are trying to establish the identity of the individual involved. If it was you, Jamie, then cooperation now will help.'

I tilted my head towards him and managed the barest of smiles. I lingered over the papers, saving the best until last. I scanned the CSI report from Alvine that confirmed the link to Henson's printer.

'The messages left on the body of Matthew Dolman and Alan Turner were produced on the printer we discovered in your premises.'

'You cannot be serious.' Henson straightened in his chair and glanced at Tront. 'This is a fucking set-up.'

I looked over at him, directly in the eyes. 'And we searched a property last night in Womanby Street. Our information is that you used that property to make your propaganda videos. If there is any forensics to link that property to the three deaths so far or the abduction of Lydia the CSIs will find it.'

He folded his arms and stared back at me. I tried one more question.

'Jamie Henson. This is your opportunity to tell me what you've done with Sergeant Flint.'

Chapter 41

The wrinkles of worry deepened on Cornock's forehead with every explanation I offered him about the justification for charging Henson. He shook his head before sighing when I answered his question about the complete absence of any eyewitness evidence. Then he stared over at the tropical fish hurtling around the tank.

'I hope the search of his home and premises will be more productive.' He spoke so slowly that even I had doubts. 'Was there any forensics in Lydia's car?'

'None, sir.'

'So if Henson isn't responsible for abducting her, who is? Have you thought about that?'

I nodded.

'And what has Cleaver said?'

'He knows nothing about Dolman or Turner and we can't put him in Harper's office building at the time he was killed.'

'So he's a dead end.'

It took me an hour to explain our suspicions about Troy Dolman. Increasingly his eyes narrowed until they had almost disappeared into small dark nuggets. When I had suggested we interview Troy he shook his head. So I stopped.

I returned to my office; desperation and exhaustion were beginning to have a numbing effect on my body. I couldn't remember whether I had eaten but I knew from the wheezing in my chest that I had smoked far more than I should have done.

It was late when I left the office. The journey back to my apartment passed in a blur. Cornock had spoken with Lydia's parents that afternoon and they had reacted badly, wanting to point the finger of blame and demanding to know everything that had happened and why their daughter had been on unsanctioned surveillance in the first place.

I tried to imagine how my mother would have reacted in the same situation. I knew she would have been distraught. I had to have a clear head for the morning and I knew I had to sleep. But instead of parking outside the flat I drove on the short distance to the Bay and then down a side street towards The Captain Scott. The public house was still there and light poured out of the window. The front door opened and three men in their early twenties streamed out; laughter and the faint sound of a television followed them onto the pavement. Years ago, the events of the day would have justified a long stay in the pub until well after closing time. The landlord at the time would have protested but I'd flash my warrant card and he'd roll his eyes and close the curtains.

One of the men bumped into my car as they walked past and he raised a hand as an apology. I pondered what a pint of Brains might taste like and how it would help to soothe my guilt. I got out, crossed over to the pub and breezed in like a regular. None of the bar staff were familiar and I guessed that I would not have been welcome had I been recognised.

I walked up to the bar and stood waiting to be served. I should have known that the surveillance was an idiotic idea and I should have dismissed it as soon as Lydia had made the suggestion. Suddenly the urge to down a large vodka in one mouthful was overpowering.

A barman stood in front of me. 'What can I get you?'

I stared at the bar.

He cleared his throat. 'What's your poison?'

I jerked my head towards him. 'Vodka and tonic.' It was my voice but I didn't recognise it.

Henson knew more than he was telling me. I had been doing this job too long to ignore that annoying gut feeling that senior management scoffed at. What the hell did that mean? I hadn't done too well organising the surveillance and now I had a thin case against Henson and no more than a 'gut' feeling to propel the case forward.

A glass arrived with three lumps of ice and a slice of lemon draped over them, its bottom edge licking the vodka. A small bottle was dumped alongside it. Wordlessly I paid and the barman left. I moved a shaking hand to the glass and grasped it. Tomorrow I would make progress. Tomorrow we'd find Lydia and that extra piece of evidence. Tomorrow I would be sober and clear-headed.

I stood, killing time, the glass cold against my fingers.

Then I drove home.

Chapter 42

Most Sundays I would have been sitting at home reading the sports pages in the supplements calculating if it was mathematically possible for Cardiff City to make certain of a place in the Championship promotion play-offs. And then it would be a matter of deciding which teams Cardiff might be better off playing for that third promotion spot. Instead, I had arrived early at Queen Street and was busy going back to the start of the investigation and cursing myself for not having done that sooner.

I was staring at the board when Wyn arrived, Jane following seconds later.

'Good morning, boss.' They both said, almost in unison.

'We've missed something,' I said, my gaze drifting to the image of Matthew Dolman on the board. I thought about everything we knew about his life. His wife and Troy and Rex and mistress and then Charlie. They had holidays in the South of France that were now irreplaceable. At least I could see Dean whenever I wanted even though until now it had been sporadic. 'Did we get the full details of that flat in Nice that Dolman owned?'

'It was in the name of an offshore company,' Jane said.

'Of course. Did we ever get the details of the apartment that Turner owned in Sydney?'

Wyn replied now. 'Sure thing, boss. It came in yesterday. I emailed you the details.'

Minutes later the printer spewed out the details from the New South Wales police. The flat was in Turner's sole name. Then I double-checked the name of the company on the French land registry. Something about an offshore company rang a bell. I scrambled through all the records until I found it: an offshore company was involved in the electrification contract.

I reached for the telephone and rang Harding.

'I'm just tying up some loose ends. Do you have the name of the offshore company that won the electrification contract?'

'Somewhere. I'll need to call you back.'

The line went dead and I recalled my conversation with Harding. I dragged a shred of recollection about Frost's first wife but it had been something I had ignored so I resolved to ask more about Malcolm Frost.

Harding rang back sooner than I had expected. I listened as he gave me the name. I didn't need to write it down: it matched the name on the French land registry. The electrification contract linked Dolman and Turner, and the investigation into Malcolm Frost's company had drawn a blank. Until now.

'Thank you,' I said, hoping he wouldn't notice the tension in my voice. 'Did Malcolm Frost have any children from his first marriage?'

'A daughter. A real pretty girl who doted on him apparently.'

'Do you know her name and address?'

'I think his first wife was called Daphne and I seem to recall that she was older than the average mother. In her forties, maybe. I think she went to live in London. But other than that I can't help.'

I was already on my feet before he finished. I called Jane and Wyn through and barked orders for them to get digging into Frost and his company and family.

'Is this going to help us find Lydia?' Jane said.

'Just do it,' I said through lips that were fast losing their colour.

I requisitioned all the usual searches to find Daphne

Frost but having a name and the vague knowledge that she was living in London wasn't a great place to start. A Google search had produced 411,000 results and I knew that the WPS budget would not stretch to having an officer search each one.

I didn't know if she was alive or dead. Or emigrated. There was nothing in the Police National Computer and I had no national insurance number to use. She could have changed her name so I was beginning to think it was a loose end.

It didn't help that there was computer maintenance ongoing in the office of the registrar of births, deaths and marriages so it would be Monday before I could instigate a search for their marriage certificate. If she had remained unmarried she might have reverted to her maiden name and I had no idea what it was.

I requisitioned uniformed officers from Pontypridd to track down some of the old employees of Frost's business and see if they could help. I spent the rest of the morning clicking through as many press reports about Frost as I could find. *Prominent Businessman Kills Himself* was the least colourful. And the press printed everything they wanted: it made sordid reading. How much of it was true was probably irrelevant.

I read again about the electrification of the railway from London to Cardiff and then the Valleys line. The money involved was staggering and it was probably borrowed by the government from banks. No wonder they needed the banks. And the banks needed them. Nothing changes really.

I blanked out the activity in the Incident Room, beyond my firmly shut door. Lydia would have interrupted me. She would have barged straight in if she needed something. I kept thinking about her and it hardened my resolve to find her.

I stopped for a moment and thought about the look on Henson's face when I showed him the messages found with the bodies. It had been genuine surprise. There hadn't been any of the pouting bravado of the zealous extremist. I tapped a ballpoint on the desk; the noise helped me think. I had to think.

Maybe Henson wasn't the killer and someone else was responsible. I sat back in my chair and read the names of the people in the offices. There were legal assistants and paralegals and lawyers with different titles and then the administration staff. There were clients of the firm attending meetings but there wasn't a name that I recognised apart from Charlotte Parkinson and Troy Dolman. And then I thought about Harding's remark – *pretty girl.*

Charlotte ticked that box.

And so, I decided, did Tracy. And she had been right at the heart of the case from the start. A sick, hollow feeling crept through my body.

The professional community in Cardiff was more claustrophobic than I had expected. I stepped out into the Incident Room; my thoughts were emerging from yesterday's fog.

Wyn and Jane looked up at me.

'Have we had details of any of Harper's clients? And more importantly, anyone common to Dolman and Turner.'

'Ian Lewis has just sent the details over,' Wyn said, clicking into his inbox.

The list was of current cases, which didn't interest me.

Pretty girl Harding had said.

A lump developed in my throat. And it got much bigger and more uncomfortable the more I thought about Tracy. Then I thought how much I actually knew about her

... And ... it got worse.

I stood up and pulled a hand over my mouth.

I felt sick to the pit of my stomach.

When I realised that I knew someone who might help I had a momentary sensation of relief. Margo Smith had been named after an opera star but she'd not been rewarded with a singing voice. A career in the human resources department of the Wales Police Service meant she had seen every possible new policy and protocol and that she had a jaded attitude to match. She owed me a favour but, even so, I scrambled to think of a reasonable excuse, one that might sound vaguely plausible. I found my mobile and made the call. It went to voicemail and I cursed. Ordinary people had Sunday with their families away from work. I left a message and rang off.

By lunchtime, the only progress I had made was to suspect every attractive woman that had been involved on the strength of a remark Harding had made. My confidence that I was making progress was evaporating. I left Queen Street, passing a van belonging to one of the television channels. I skirted round it and carried on walking towards the castle. I pressed onwards towards the river before dropping down onto the opposite side of the Taff and walking down Riverside. The Millennium Stadium towered above me, large hoardings fluttering from its balconies advertising the Wales v Belgium soccer match the next weekend. All Wales had to do was draw and we would be through to the European finals.

I crossed back over the bridge, hoping the walk was doing me some good. My mobile rang and I pulled it from my back pocket.

'How are you, John?' Margo said. 'Long time no-contact.'

'Hi Margo, how are you?'

'It's Sunday, John. You must want something?'

'I need a favour.'

After arranging to meet her I drove over to headquarters. An audit was starting the following week and it meant that her department was working all weekend. I had decided that honesty would have to be the only option. Margo raised her eyebrows and kept them high as though some invisible thread had pulled them when I explained about Tracy. Chivalry got the better of me and I kept it simple.

'I need background to eliminate her from the inquiry.'

Margo sat back in her chair. 'I've heard that before.'

'It's just that with Lydia missing and the cases of Matthew Dolman still open—'

'Is that the banker?'

I nodded. 'I need to untangle everything. You know what it's like ...'

Margo wasn't impressed. She narrowed her eyes and stared at me. I smiled back.

'Give me a minute,' she said.

She perched a pair of reading glasses on her nose and squinted at her monitor before the printer churned out various sheets. She quickly checked the pages and thrust them over the desk. 'I hope it helps.'

I left clutching the paper securely. Back in my car I uncurled them and let out a long breath.

Chapter 43

'Where the hell are you?' Cornock shouted down the telephone.

I slowed the car and pulled up in front of a newsagent. 'On my back to Queen Street.'

'We'll bloody well start without you then.'

I thumped my hand on the steering wheel having forgotten about the Major Incident Team meeting. Slamming the car into gear, I careered off towards the station. I parked clumsily and then ran over to the rear door. By the time I reached the conference room perspiration prickled my brow.

The ACC glowered at me; Cornock gave me the briefest of nods. None of the others looked in my direction. I fumbled a gasping apology as I sat down.

The tone of the meeting had changed from yesterday. The atmosphere had altered imperceptibly too. Darkness had descended. The ACC made clear that all available resources should be focused on using intelligence to trace Lydia.

'I've got every intelligence analyst working on the case.' She looked over at me, her eyes hooded and severe now.

'Have you got anything to report on the Harper case, Inspector Marco?'

Full rank and surname, bad sign. I took a deep breath and hoped my breathing would get back to normal.

'I've allocated a small team to build a picture of his family and background. I'm waiting for forensics and the post mortem report.' Even I was impressed with how important it sounded.

The ACC nodded and carried on with the briefing. I listened to the other officers but they had nothing to report and the tone of their voices was solemn. After half an hour she finished the meeting and I got back to my office.

In common with most detective inspectors I had built up a large bank of people who owed me favours over the years and the sergeant in Pontypridd was one of them. I'd covered his back in a nasty complaint a few years back but now I needed the help of his officers.

I called the police station in Pontypridd. 'Anything on the Frost business?' I said.

'Sorry, Ian. They found nothing on the Frost bloke. The former employees only remember all that bad publicity. They couldn't remember anything else.'

'Thanks.' I hesitated. Then I reached for Tracy's personal details. 'I need another favour.'

The Harper family home was a sumptuous detached property in Cyncoed, one of the wealthier suburbs to the north of Cardiff. It was the sort of neighbourhood where every house had an alarm screwed to the outside wall, windows with secure locks and households with substantial home insurance premiums. I pulled into the drive and parked just behind a rental car. A light came on as I approached the front door. It was opened by a woman in her thirties who looked pale and drawn. She held out a hand. 'Dawn Harper. My mother is in the conservatory.'

We shook hands. 'Detective Inspector John Marco.'

We walked through into a sitting room at the rear that led out into a large conservatory. I could see down to the bottom of a well-kept garden, where a small summerhouse sat underneath the branches of a carefully pruned sycamore. Mrs Harper sat at the end of a sofa looking drained of life, dark shadows under her eyes. She wore a baggy fleece over an old T-shirt, a pair of fifties-style glasses perched on her nose.

'I'm very sorry for your loss, Mrs Harper. My condolences.'

These situations were the hardest part of being a police officer. Offering condolences, trying to sound sincere about the loss of somebody who was a complete stranger.

Dawn Harper gestured at the sofa opposite her mother and I sat down.

'I need some background. I was hoping that you might be able to help. Did your husband seem worried about any anything?'

Mrs Harper shook her head. 'Nothing, nothing out of the ordinary.'

'Was he complaining about work at all?'

She pulled a face at me. 'That's all he did. He'd leave before seven o'clock in the morning and wouldn't be back until seven in the evening.'

Dawn Harper interrupted. 'My father was very dedicated to his work. The business came first for him.' Her tone was matter-of-fact.

Jean Harper gazed over my shoulder. 'We didn't have much of a social life. He would even have files and papers to work on during the weekend. He always said that he might retire sometime. But I really don't know what we would have done...'

I cleared my throat and adjusted my position before asking Mrs Harper about her personal life and wondering how she might react. 'I know you've spoken to some of my colleagues,' I said. 'But how were things between you and your husband?'

She gave me a blank look. I couldn't read any expression in her eyes. She glanced at her daughter. Then she settled back into looking down the garden. The door from the hallway opened and a man, wearing a heavily striped blue shirt and well-pressed denims, came in and sat down without introducing himself.

'Geoff,' Dawn Harper said. 'This is Detective Inspector Marco. My brother, Inspector.'

Geoff Harper gave me a vague grin and flipped an ankle over one knee. No grieving son here I concluded.

'Any financial problems, Mrs Harper?'

She shook her head. 'He worked very hard...'

Geoff Harper made a brief grunt. 'Not since those problems with the company.'

I turned towards him and sharpened my gaze. 'What were those problems?' I tried to make the enquiry sound conversational.

'It was nothing,' Geoff said, waving a hand in the air. 'Dad sorted the whole business out.'

'It might be relevant. Do you remember the details?'

Geoff sighed as though assisting me with the inquiry was a massive chore. Disliking Geoff Harper was becoming very easy.

'Mum had this production company. They had *great* plans. But things never got off the ground. Expensive offices in the Bay and they had a handful of documentaries commissioned by the BBC.'

Jean Harper took on a sharp tone as she reprimanded her son. 'We did six documentaries altogether. And they were all sold successfully to the BBC.'

'But it was the other programmes that were a *complete* flop.'

Jean Harper shook her head.

'Come on, mum. The business was a disaster.'

I raised my voice. 'When did the business close down?'

Geoff waved a hand in the air again. 'A year ago.

Dad sorted it all out with the bank.'

'Which bank would that have been?' I sounded hoarse as I spoke.

'National Bank of Wales, of course.'

The thump of my heart threatened to drown out my words. 'How much money was involved?'

Geoff glanced at Dawn and then over at his mother. 'It was over £250,000. All gone on fancy offices and grand plans.'

Now he had all of my attention. 'And what happened?'

'Dad did a deal with the bank somehow.'

Chapter 44

It was nine-thirty am when I returned from the Major Incident Team meeting. Both Wyn and Jane were chained to their desks, staring at the flickering monitors.

'Anything new, boss?' Wyn said.

In truth I had sat through the meeting, unable to concentrate as the assistant chief constable had gone round all the participants asking for an update. A detective inspector and two sergeants at the first meeting, whose names I couldn't remember, gave summaries of all the ongoing activity in the search to find Lydia. 'Nothing.'

Jane stood up from her desk. 'There's something I wanted to ask you about these messages, sir.' She moved over towards the Incident Room board.

I joined her as she pointed at the sheets. 'We know that the third message was produced on a different printer.' She must have seen the confusion on my face. 'You know, the one that was delivered here?'

I nodded.

'The first two messages accompanied the first two deaths. What was the motive for sending us the third message?'

Wyn butted in. 'These guys are just deranged. They believe in all this anti-capitalist crap.'

'What's your point?' I said to Jane.

'It might be nothing. But we know that the message found with Harper was printed on the same machine as the first two.'

I could see where Jane was taking this argument. 'So why was the third message printed on a different machine?'

Jane tapped a ballpoint on the relevant message on the board. 'It's out of sequence. And then I thought about the timing. You had a meeting at the NBW on the Thursday before the message was delivered on that Saturday.'

Unease gathered as I scoured my memory trying to recall exactly what had been said at the National Bank of Wales. I had spoken to the Dolmans about Matthew Dolman's financial position. I had told them about the discovery of the flat in Nice and I could remember the surprise on their faces. Although only Troy Dolman had known about it beforehand.

Astonishment: had been Lydia's description of Charlotte's reaction. An invisible strap drew itself closer and closer around my chest.

'Of course,' I mumbled, before clearing my throat. 'We told them about the flat in Nice. I wanted to establish if they knew about it.'

'And did anything happen on Friday, the day after you were in the bank?'

'I saw David Turner. And ...' Suddenly, I remembered my Friday evening with Tracy. And that green dress. I rubbed a hand over the hair on the back of my neck, and tried not to look self-conscious. I had talked about work over dinner but I always talk about work. Tracy had been inquisitive and working in forensics meant I didn't worry about confidentiality.

I thought about my conversations with Tracy over dinner that Friday, in bed Friday evening, over breakfast the following morning. I wanted to kick something, really hard. If either Tracy or Charlotte was Malcolm Frost's daughter and they were on a campaign of revenge I had to find out which one and fast. There was no credible evidence and I had no basis for taking my suspicions to Cornock.

As soon as I got back to my office, I dialled the number of the sergeant in Pontypridd.

'Sorry, I've got nothing to report just yet.'

I stood, momentarily uncertain where to turn next. Then I noticed two boxes on the floor in one corner. A brief examination told me they contained the personnel records from Harper's law firm. I found Charlotte Parkinson's file halfway through the second box.

There was an address in Penarth, a certificate from the University of Bristol confirming her first class honours degree. She had been qualified for ten years and there was a summary of her experience at the firm where she had trained. I even found the website where the firm described itself as 'highly specialist' in the niche 'international banking sector'. Most of the work that she had done made little sense to me.

I found the details of her next of kin as an aunt – Mary Lloyd – who lived in Kidderminster. I made a call to central operations requesting a search against the name.

'I need a standard financial search against Charlotte Parkinson as well.'

I could hear the groan down the telephone. 'That's going to take time.'

'I need it urgently. And I need a search on a Tracy Jones.'

Another groan. I scrambled through my papers for Tracy's personal details.

'All I want is the standard preliminary financial enquiries. Bank statements. And I need it today.'

'You've got to be joking. I'll do what I can by first thing in the morning.'

I glared at the phone once the call had finished.

By mid-morning, I was standing outside the rear door of Queen Street, smoking. It gave me time to think, not that it was doing any good. One of the reception staff came out to stand by my side. She gave me a self-conscious smile as she lit up, as though we were sharing a dirty secret.

She had a sweet, overpowering perfume that I decided was quite repulsive. It was one of those cheap versions of expensive perfume you bought in a discount shop.

Then I realised that throughout the inquiry my senses had been assaulted by various perfumes. Charlotte Parkinson's was expensive, drilling its way deep into my senses, setting off all sorts of alarms, bells and urges. I thought again about the Friday night with Tracy. I closed my eyes, tilted my head upwards, recalling the sensation of her hair brushing my face as she sat astride me.

And then for some inexplicable reason I thought about Alvine Dix. Perfume. I threw the butt onto the tarmac and bolted back upstairs.

'You said something about a smell, a perfume in the Royal Bell that first morning,' I said as soon as she had answered the telephone.

'What the hell are you talking about?'

'You mentioned something about a perfume. You must remember. For Christ's sake, Alvine. You mentioned it.'

'What's all this about, Marco? You're in some blind panic about a smell.'

'Don't be bloody difficult. Can you remember anything?' I slowed down. 'It's important Alvine. Important for the case and probably about finding Lydia.'

She hesitated. 'Well, there was smell in the air and it was in the plastic pouch that held the message. Expensive I would say. I can't explain it really, there was nothing on the paper, it's just that ... Well, some perfumes can linger.'

'Would you recognise the perfume again?'

'I don't know ... What do you think I am? A perfume expert?'

I didn't reply. I spent the next few hours drinking coffee, eating biscuits and the occasional sandwich that

Jane and Wyn took turns in supplying from the kitchen. Occasionally I walked out into the Incident Room and stood staring at the board and then thinking aloud. I could sense Wyn and Jane staring at me. I spoke to the search team supervisor who had taken the property in Womanby Street apart, finding nothing of value. An email from forensics confirmed it was the setting for the videos but they were still working on the old clothes we had recovered.

I tried to unscramble the connections between everyone involved in the failed bid for the electrification contract. It had been Frost Enterprises advised by Dolman and Harper and on the sidelines, Turner, who made things happen. Then I read again about Stanway. The memorandum from Charlotte Parkinson made Stanway and his family a convenient scapegoat. Frost Enterprises and Stanway Engineering had even shared the same liquidator. I spent a mind-chilling ten minutes speaking to an accountant who confirmed that the NBW had 'sorted out' a charge they had over a property owned by Frost's first wife. When Boyd rang soon afterwards it was a pleasure to speak to someone who varied the tone of his voice.

'I've got the details of the shareholdings of Silverwood you wanted. A majority is owned by Silverwood but twenty-six per cent is owned by an offshore company in the Cayman Islands. Just enough to give them effective control.'

When he gave me the name, I fell back in my chair.

Then I reached for the details of the ownership of the flat in Nice where I had read the same name.

Another large piece of the puzzle fell into place.

Chapter.45

A puddle of fluid on the floor of the custody suite near the sergeant's desk had a very peculiar consistency. An odd smell hung in the air and the light from the fluorescent tubes was grey and depressing. One of them throbbed and it had the hypnotic effect of casting faint shadows across the walls.

'One of the cleaners is coming to see to that,' the sergeant told me without explaining what it was.

He flashed his fingers across the keyboard. 'Henson was due for transfer this afternoon.'

He wasn't expecting me to reply.

'I hope this is worth it, John. You won't believe the paperwork I have to complete if we have a prisoner here longer than we need to.' The sergeant managed a surly look.

'For Christ's sake. *He* asked to see *me*.' This was my investigation and it was my partner that was missing. Henson's request to talk to me was a surprise after the initial interview.

'You can use interview room ten down the corridor. Is this on tape?'

'It's not an interview under caution.'

He sat back in his chair. 'So it's off the record. And what if things go tits-up and you get the flak for not recording the interview. On my shift and then I'm in the shit.'

'That's about right.'

He waved me away and returned to the screen.

I walked down to interview room ten and waited. The room hummed from the sound of the air-conditioning unit somewhere nearby. A table in the corner had a cassette machine and underneath it was a small bin full of the discarded plastic wrappings of cassette tapes used to record interviews. I sat down.

I never liked these windowless rooms. They could get stuffy and hot and if the prisoner smelt the odour could stick in my nose for hours. Henson had refused to tell us where he had hidden Lydia. A team was unpicking his background as we sat there. Every friend and every acquaintance established and considered; every house and bedsit where he'd ever lived called at.

The door opened and a young officer entered with Henson. He looked gaunt and needed a shave. The officer left, pulling the door firmly closed behind him.

Silence fell on the room like a damp towel.

'I didn't kill Dolman or Turner or—'

'I haven't got time to listen to this.' I straightened my position in the uncomfortable plastic chair. 'Where is Lydia Flint?'

Henson put his hands behind his head. 'How many times have I got to tell you? I didn't take her.'

I stood up.

'Sit down, Marco.'

'It's Detective Inspector Marco to you.'

He eased his body into a relaxed seating position and crossed one foot over the other knee once I had sat down.

'The messages weren't sent by me. I didn't do any of them.'

'Then how do you account for them matching your printer?'

'We've been fucking set up. It's a bloody trap ...'

He ran out of steam when he realised I wasn't paying any attention.

'The printer was a gift from a benefactor.'

He must have read the incredulity in my face.

'Honestly. We'd made an appeal on the website for office equipment and supplies so that we could continue with the struggle. We got loads of people donating old filing cabinets and shelves. And then one morning the printer arrived. In the box. I thought it had been stolen.'

'You didn't report it, of course.'

He bowed his head. 'No.'

'What have you done with Lydia?'

He looked over at me. There was real desperation in his eyes. 'If someone is trying to set me up and destroy the work my group is doing then they'd stop at nothing to implicate me in her death.'

I smarted and moved my chair nearer to his. 'If you tell me now where she is then it'll go in your favour in front of the judge.'

'I didn't take her. But there are places that they might use to hide her, keep her captive.'

'Who?'

'The enemies of the people.'

I snorted my disbelief.

'We met in a pub in the docks – The Anchor – a few years ago. And I ran a small business for a year from a unit in the industrial park in the old airfield between Cowbridge and Llantwit Major.'

'What makes you think we don't know about these already?'

There was a plaintive look in his eye. 'I haven't killed anyone. And I haven't taken Lydia Flint.'

I peered at Henson. Gone was the contempt for authority, replaced by the barest hint of vulnerability, and I wondered for the first time that he might be telling me the truth.

Chapter 46

It was twilight when I parked opposite the boarded-up public house in the docks. Large sheets of plywood had been screwed to every window and door. Some of the creative locals had been spray-painting faces and small scenes from horror movies all over them until they looked like grotesque gargoyles. I imagined the pub alive with customers decades ago when the docks had thrived.

I left the car and walked over to the building. A padlock and a thick chain secured the main door. There was no sign of any recent use so I walked around the back. A gate creaked open as I rammed my shoulder against it. Beyond it was a car park and some outbuildings. Crossing potholed tarmac I stood by the window of the outbuildings and gazed in. Some old metal shelving racks had been discarded on the floor. But there was no sign of recent activity. I turned and walked towards the pub and by the rear entrance noticed old-fashioned outside toilets. I walked over and ventured in, half-expecting the smell of urine to be overpowering. But it was just cold and decrepit.

I left and then walked around the area, gazed into some derelict shops, and spoke to locals about any activity around the public house that met with shaking heads and reminisces about how things were not the same.

I decided there was nothing more that I could achieve so I called Queen Street. Wyn answered.

'Any messages?' I said.

'Nothing, sir.'

Traffic was light as I drove over to Culverhouse Cross before taking the A48 towards Cowbridge. I passed through the villages surrounded by the lush agricultural land of the Vale of Glamorgan. I'd found the postcode for the site before leaving Queen Street and the sat-nav led me off the dual carriageway into Cowbridge and then on through the town and then left towards Llantwit Major and the coast. Another ten minutes passed until I saw the sign for the Vale Enterprise Zone. It was a fancy name for a dozen or more cheap units that had been created from redundant buildings along the perimeter of an old airfield.

The lights from my car swirled along the tall shutters of a unit advertising prefabricated garden sheds and summerhouses. I parked and scrambled in the glove compartment for my torch. It was cooler now so I dragged a thick fleece from the rear seat of the car and walked over to the first unit. It was two storeys high and I put the torch to the window. The beam caught the grinning face of a garden gnome and I caught my breath. I stepped back and ran the torch over the second-floor windows. The place was secure so I moved on.

I turned the corner and ahead of me were three rows of Nissen-style huts like props from a Second World War film. They looked like small workshops and offices. Suddenly the sky cleared and moonlight lit up the uneven track leading down between the huts. I switched off the torch and walked down the first row, already having decided that I would return with Wyn and Jane.

A fox crossed the path a few metres ahead of me, its tail catching faint wisps of light.

At the end of the first row, I turned and walked to my left. The ground was soft underfoot and my shoes sank into the mud. I stopped and examined the ground ahead. The squawking of a bird of prey broke the silence but then I heard something else. The sound of a door opening, a window being forced ajar. I tightened my grip on the torch and headed along the second row. This time I kept to the shadows along the walls and entrances of each unit, stopping occasionally, straining to hear something.

Anything.

I reached the end of the row and stepped into the doorway of the final unit. It was quiet. The heavy pungent smell of creosote hung in the air. I glanced around and then stepped out to make my way towards the final row of Nissen-style units.

I paused by the corner of the gable of the end property and slowly peered down the final row. Nothing. Every door firmly shut and every window closed. I ventured slowly over the path and then over to the gable of the third and final row. It was identical to the other two apart from the faint shard of light coming from the corner of one window in a unit halfway down the row. I could hear nothing.

Looking down the row, I could spot that one of the units had a porch. On impulse I retraced my steps down the second row of buildings . I took small steps, judging every footfall, making certain I was quiet until I arrived at the bottom unit of the second row.

I slowly popped my head around the gable and saw the light more clearly this time.

I darted over the ground, praying that it wasn't wet and that the sound of my feet on mud wouldn't be noticed. Breathing heavily now I reached the porch. I was standing one unit away from the open window. I stepped nearer. Only a few feet away.

Suddenly the door was yanked open and it squeaked against the floor.

I almost fell over myself getting back to the nearby porch. I started breathing out slowly, hoping I wouldn't be heard. Then I heard the spark of a lighter and the bleeping sound of a mobile being used.

Then I heard a voice I recognised. 'She's fine.'

A pause. 'I really don't know.'

Another pause. It felt like minutes.

'Okay. Okay. I understand. I'll call you later.'

Then the call was finished and I heard a sound, a toe grinding a cigarette butt into the soil, and then the door closing again. I had to think. I needed to call operational support and get back-up. It had to be Lydia inside, no question.

Then the door opened again. I heard a fiddling with the lock and then a padlock being snapped into place and the sound of footsteps walking away. Thankfully, my car was tucked away to one side so there was a good chance it wouldn't be spotted. I tried to estimate how long the walk to the road might take. I heard a car engine start up and drive away.

I rang Wyn and gave him the postcode. Then I waited. But I was never any good at waiting. And I had a strong suspicion that Lydia was inside.

I needed to free her. Now.

I stepped out of the porch and over to the door. I gave the padlock and chain a cursory look.

I stepped back and kicked the door with my right foot. It hurt, really hurt. I tried repeatedly until I could hear the door hinges straining. I walked out into the path and ran at the door with my shoulder. It shook this time and I could see the fastening of the padlock loosen. I tried my foot again. Then my shoulder until the door gave away and I kicked the padlock to one side.

I rushed in, torchlight cutting through the darkness.

I scrambled to find a light switch.

The first room nearest the door was empty apart from a table and some old wooden chairs. I darted through the hallway and into the back room.

I flicked on the switch and a low-wattage bulb came to life.

Lydia was tied to a bed, her eyes wide open. She started crying as I ran over to her. I undid the rope and pulled her close to me.

Chapter 47

'It was good old-fashioned policing, ma'am.' Cornock drank heavily from the tumbler full of whisky. The assistant chief constable nodded and gave me a broad smile. 'I'll leave you to plan an arrest.'

'Ah ... Yes, ma'am,' I said.

She left the conference room having finished her whisky in one gulp.

I sipped the plastic water bottle someone had shoved in my hand. 'I need twenty-four hours.'

Cornock stared at me. 'What the hell do you mean?'

'I need time. We've got direct evidence against Greg Jones. I recognised his voice after all. He won't know about us finding Lydia unless he goes back there and I suggest we have two officers there if they do.'

'And you expect me to agree that Greg Jones has free rein until then? You must be mad.'

'I know it's unusual, sir, but—'

'Unusual!'

'He's got an accomplice. And I need to work out who that was.'

'It's obviously Youlden or one of the other extremists. Greg Jones has been leading you a merry dance. Go and arrest him. Tonight. I'll get a full team organised within an hour. An armed response team – the works. Then we'll see what they think about policing in Wales.'

I sat down by the table and Cornock gave me a wary, uncertain look.

'It's not that simple, sir.'

Cornock sat open-mouthed as I explained about Tracy and Charlotte. He leant forward unblinking as I confirmed that the same limited company owned the flat in Nice and the shares in Silverwood Limited. And that they shared the same registered office in the Cayman Islands as the company that won the electrification contract.

'So you think that Dolman, Turner and Harper plotted together to make certain that Frost Enterprises failed in its bid to win the railway electrification contract.'

'Looks that way.'

'And Frost's daughter is implicated but you're not certain if it's Tracy Jones or Charlotte Parkinson?'

I nodded. Occasionally he challenged some of my logic but he had always been supportive enough to hear me out and that evening, despite the aching tiredness in my body, I managed a clear, detailed explanation. I hadn't kept track of time but once I'd finished Cornock grasped the whisky bottle again and poured himself two fingers.

He savoured a mouthful and replaced the glass carefully in front of him.

He drummed two fingers on the table. 'Twenty-four hours, John. No more.'

Lydia looked peaceful as I sat by her bedside in a small private room at the end of a ward in the hospital. I reached out and let my fingertips brush her arm. I recalled the night at Dean's bedside when I turned his fingers through mine and I realised that it had been over a week since I had seen him. An intravenous drip led into her arm as she slept. My chair was one of those upright varieties with a plastic covering and a high back. I kept recalling the decision to press ahead with the surveillance and I knew that it had been unwise, stupid even, and looking at Lydia's face I blinked away tears of relief.

A nurse came in so I averted my eyes. She made to say something but I'd found my mobile and pretended to send some message. After she left I glanced at my watch wondering if the surveillance teams had made any progress finding Greg – three teams of three men meant an enormous hole in the budget. It was six am when I woke up; my neck was stiff and I was twisted into an uncomfortable shape in the chair. I had been dreaming about Tracy and our nights together. I wanted to believe that she wasn't involved.

Then a nurse came into the room and glowered at me. 'You have to leave now.'

Lydia was still sleeping, her head rolled to one side.

'You'll call me once she's awake.'

She nodded unconvincingly.

Back at my flat I showered and found clean clothes. I decided on a pair of black moleskin trousers with a pale denim shirt and then I left the flat. The car park was quiet but as I strode over to the Mondeo I noticed someone emerge from a nearby car. I slowed and then realised that it was Terry.

'What do you want?'

'You could at least thank me for putting you onto Bert. Was your sergeant at that property then? I thought it would have been all over the newspapers by now.'

'I need to get to work.'

Terry didn't move. From a pocket he extracted a small sheet of paper that he held in the air. 'Last chance, Marco. I need Doreen's case to go away.'

I said nothing. He thrust the paper in my direction.

'Cardiff City are playing in Bristol this Saturday and the Soul Crew are planning to trash a pub. Here are some names and the address.'

I read the details.

'Just see me right, Marco.' For the first time since I knew him Terry managed a simple pleading tone to his voice.

On the drive into Queen Street I pondered whether I should really bother telling Hobbs. He'd probably ignore the information. After punching in the security code, I headed straight for Hobbs' office. He was on the telephone when I entered. I stared at him until he realised the urgency and finished the call.

'I've got some intelligence for you.'

'It's not from—'

'Yes. And you can do with it what you like. But if you ignore it and it turns out to be accurate then you're in the shit. If it's wrong then you've not lost anything. And you can blame my source. Win-win for you, Dave.'

He scribbled down the details as I left.

Wyn and Jane scrambled to their feet when I strode into the Incident Room. The atmosphere was different from the day before. Now we were making progress and there was excitement in their eyes.

'How's Lydia?' Jane said.

'She'll be all right,' I said. 'My office, both of you.'

Wyn closed the door behind them and they both sat down in front of my desk.

'Not a word of this gets out to anyone else.'

They nodded their understanding.

'Greg Jones hasn't been arrested and the super has authorised a full surveillance team from Swansea. I want you both checking his past. Family, schooling, but start with Bristol University. I want to know everything about him.' I turned to Jane. 'And I need you to visit the perfume department of the House of Fraser department store.'

A narrow grin soon replaced her puzzled look when I explained what I wanted her to do.

'Do we leave the inquiry into Dolman and Turner?' Wyn said.

I nodded. 'And if anyone asks we still have an

ongoing inquiry into tracing Lydia.'

'There's another email about the flat in Nice,' Wyn said. 'I've copied it you.'

I scanned the PDF attached to the email, stopping at the details of the lawyers in London that had registered the ownership. The name was familiar and I knew immediately where I had read the name before. I stood up and pushed back my chair, crashing it against the radiator behind me.

In seconds I was on my knees scouring through the employee records of Harper's law firm. It didn't take me long to find Charlotte's CV and read the confirmation I needed.

She must have seen that Dolman's reward for ensuring that Frost lost the tender was a handsome flat in Nice. Another email arrived and I clicked it open. The result of the standard financial search on Charlotte Parkinson opened on the screen. I read through her latest bank statements. There were subscriptions to a gym, one of the more expensive in the city, payments to various restaurants, supermarkets, local council tax and petrol. The regular payments to the Sundown Nursing Home made me sweaty-palmed and I let out a slow breath. I had to hope that I'd found Malcolm Frost's first wife. I Googled the Sundown Nursing Home and found an address in Chepstow. There was a nice website with pictures of the communal areas and a menu card and the latest reports from the care inspectorate.

I picked up the handset and punched in the telephone number.

'Sundown Nursing Home.'

I paused.

'Hello. Is there anyone there?'

I replaced the handset. I couldn't risk Charlotte finding out. I memorised the postcode and headed for my car.

Chapter 48

The Sundown Nursing Home was perched on the top of a hill on the outskirts of Chepstow. It looked like an old rectory that had various extensions added to it over the years. After parking I strode up to the front door, rehearsing my lines. I glanced at the camera high up on the wall, pressed the bell and a crackly voice said something through the intercom.

'I'm visiting Mrs Parkinson.' It was a guess but it worked.

'Just a minute.'

A woman in her sixties opened the door, wearing a light-blue uniform, the name of the home sewn into the left-hand side of her blouse. She had a severe haircut and two small earrings in both lobes. I held out a hand and smiled. 'Good morning. I do hope this isn't inconvenient. I've just arrived back from South Africa. I've been catching up with some old relatives. You know how it is with us in the colonies. We have to visit every relative when we're back in the old country.'

She managed a narrow smile.

'This is a lovely place. Wonderful location. The residents must love it. Charlotte told me her mother was here and I'm going over to visit my cousin later but I thought I'd drop in and see her mother first.'

'We are preparing for lunch you know. It's our busiest time.'

'I shan't stay long.' I smiled again.

'You'd better come with me.'

She led me through a long corridor towards the front of the building. 'You do know that she's had a stroke?'

'Terrible isn't it. How many of your residents need regular care? I'm sure your staff do a wonderful job.'

'Ever since the stroke she's been very poorly. I'm surprised that Charlotte hadn't told you.'

'She's very busy. What with her new job and everything.'

The woman nodded. 'I know she had a lot of problems when her mother lost the house. Poor thing. That was all she had.'

'There was nothing I could do out in Cape Town. How *did* she manage?'

'Charlotte thought all the stress when her father's business went bust made the early onset dementia much worse. Before the stroke that was all she talked about. It was quite sad.'

'I know, Charlotte did email.' I nodded sagely.

'She was forced to sell her home. Last thing you want at her time of life.'

We reached the end of the corridor and a door with the number fourteen hanging from it – it said Mary Parkinson.

She knocked softly and we entered. The woman sitting in the chair gazing out of the window had thin wispy hair and the left side of her face had slipped. A drizzle of food still lay on her cheek. She had no life left in her eyes but her breathing sounded forced as her chest heaved.

'I'll have to leave you alone. I have to get back to work.'

I gave her another warm compassionate smile. 'Of course. I shan't stay long.'

She closed the door behind me. I surveyed the room, thinking that the cupboards might hold something of value. I fingered the drawer handle of a storage cabinet and glanced over at Mrs Parkinson. She hadn't moved and was oblivious to me. But I had the information I needed so I left.

Outside in my car I switched my mobile back on.

There was message for me to contact Cornock so I dialled his direct number.

'The surveillance team can't find Greg.'

My optimism with progress suddenly vanished.

'He wasn't at home and they're trying the various addresses we have for him.'

I slammed my hand against the steering wheel. I hammered the car back along the motorway to Cardiff, flashing the occasional motorist dawdling in the outside lane.

A black BMW cut across me and then braked suddenly. I flashed my lights, pressed the horn and then raised my middle finger and glared through the windscreen. The driver indicated left and shot off the motorway. A few minutes later, my mobile rang as my temper subsided.

'Good morning, John.' It was the sergeant from Pontypridd.

'Have you got any news for me?' I held my breath.

I was overtaking a line of articulated lorries and as I passed each one a gust of wind rattled the car.

'We managed to trace that Jones family you are after. They moved away a few years ago to live in Bournemouth. Apparently the old man has bad asthma and he was told to have a change of climate.'

'Any other children?'

'There's one brother like you said. One of my lads spoke to the head teacher from the school he attended. Apparently, Greg Jones was really bright. He went to Bristol University. He thought Jones may have had a breakdown and dropped out.'

Now we had a connection between Charlotte and Greg and I still hoped that Tracy wasn't involved.

Back at Queen Street I pushed the door of the Incident Room too strongly and it crashed open against the wall behind. Wyn turned towards me, a pleased look on his face.

'Good news, Sir.' Wyn stood up. 'I've traced Charlotte Parkinson when she was at Bristol University. She took a first class honours degree in law and then trained as a lawyer. I got hold of one of the tutors who was still on the academic staff. And he mentioned that she had a relationship with one of the other students: a certain Greg Jones.'

I had pins and needles in my hand and I was still breathless from scaling the stairs to the second floor of Queen Street. I sat down and let the tension slip away. The door behind me opened and Jane breezed in. Seeing fellow police officers with a pleased look on their face was getting to be habit I welcomed.

'You were right of course, boss,' Jane said, dropping a plastic bag carefully onto the desk and then shrugging off a light-green fleece. 'I've just spent an hour in the perfume department of House of Fraser.' She tilted her head towards the bag.

She opened it and drew out a small container emblazoned with the logo of a perfume company. It looked expensive and she held the cords to the bag delicately before putting it down on the table and then dipping her fingers inside to pull out a bottle of perfume.

'This is her favourite brand,' Jane said.

Wyn stared at the bottle. I had to hope that perfume really had been Charlotte Parkinson's Achilles heel.

Jane continued. 'You know the old saying – if you ask how much it is you can't afford it. It's almost as much as I earn in a week.'

Wyn let out a whistle of surprise.

I was even more surprised when I heard Lydia's voice behind me. 'Is that her perfume?'

I almost fell off my chair. Then I gave her a big hug that almost knocked her over. 'I thought you were going to be in hospital?'

'I didn't want to miss the action.'

Lydia sat down heavily and let out a sigh that said she was both tired and pleased to be back.

I walked over towards the board and stared at the various names.

'So what now, boss?' Lydia said.

'Charlotte Parkinson was Frost's daughter from his first marriage. The failure by his company to win the electrification contract meant that her mother lost everything. We know that Matthew Dolman has a flat in Nice owned by some offshore company, Alan Turner acquires a flat in Sydney at about the same time. Harper's wife has a big debt written off. Charlotte works in the law firm in London that handled the registration of the flat in Nice, owned by the same offshore company that owns the shares of Silverwood Limited.'

'The same company that won the electrification contract?'

I nodded. 'My guess is that Charlotte finds out that the three of them conspired against her father.'

'And now it's payback time?' Lydia said.

'Exactly.'

Chapter 49

Lydia reached over to the perfume bottle and removed the top. She held it up to her nose and then grazed her wrist with enough of the perfume to fill the air. It was like walking through a field of lavender and lemon groves and then there were strawberries and that same sensuous cream again. She rubbed one wrist against another and then breathed in deeply.

Then Lydia nodded. 'I was blindfolded for most of the time but when I came to in the back of Greg's van he was talking to someone sitting in the passenger seat. I didn't hear a voice but I'd recognise this perfume ...'

She replaced the top. 'How did you find it?' Lydia said.

'Charlotte spent a fortune in the perfume department. Jane went along and pretended to be her friend – you know, the usual trick. "Charlotte is a friend and I'm very embarrassed but I've forgotten the name of the perfume she recommended".'

Lydia nodded. 'When do we go and arrest her?'

I smiled. It was good to have a full team back.

I stepped towards the board. It was less then twelve hours left before Cornock was going to arrest Greg Jones, assuming that he could be located. The regular reports messaged to my mobile during the morning had confirmed that Greg hadn't returned to the unit where he'd kept Lydia prisoner. Good news, I supposed, unless he knew that we had found her already.

'There is just one problem in all of this. Wasn't Charlotte at work on the morning Dolman was killed?'

'I don't think we've checked ...'

I found my mobile and called Ian Lewis. 'It's no more than routine. I need your records for when your employees sign in each morning for the past two months.'

It was an hour before we had the information from Lewis. I was only interested in one person on one day. I scrambled through the paperwork until I found the day of Dolman's death. The others were standing at my desk staring as I thumbed to Charlotte's name.

'Five past ten. She arrived at five past ten.'

Lydia leant against my desk. 'It's her.'

'We'll take two cars and start at her offices.'

Jane and Wyn rushed for their coats. I turned to Lydia. 'You should rest.'

'I wouldn't miss this for the world.'

I picked up the telephone and dialled the lawyer firm's number.

'DI Marco, WPS. Is Miss Parkinson available?'

'She isn't in today. She called in this morning telling us she was working from home today.'

We ran down to the cars. I leapt into my Mondeo and screamed along the narrow street to the main road and then onto the link road for the Bay. We headed out for Penarth. Soon we were on the elevated dual carriageway. We left the apartments and expensive hotels and restaurants behind us and hammered along to the Penarth junction. Her flat was in one of the modern developments and I guessed that Charlotte had exquisite leather sofas and valuable modern art lit by discreet hidden lighting. And a fantastic view over the Bay. There would be a coffee machine that made authentic espresso.

We pulled into a slot near the main entrance and streamed over to the main door just as one of the residents left. He mumbled a complaint but when he saw the two uniformed officers wearing stab jackets, cradling batons with cuffs hanging from their belts he cowered to one side.

I stabbed at the lift call button but there was no sign

of it so we took the stairs. Flat 316 was at the front of the building and at the end of the corridor. I ran ahead of the uniformed officers and then hammered on the door.

'Charlotte Parkinson. Police, open up.'

There was no reply.

I nodded at one of the uniformed officers.

He swung at the lock with the 'big key', a piece of equipment designed for opening locked doors, and the noise reverberated around the passageway. A resident looked down the landing at the commotion. Wyn raised an arm and ushered him away. Within seconds it was over and the door gave way under the sound of splintering wood. I followed the uniformed officer into the flat, Lydia immediately behind me.

My footsteps reverberated over the wooden laminate flooring.

I was right about the view. The sun streamed through the windows and the Bay looked peaceful. I was wrong about the flat. The furniture looked old and tired and there was definitely no coffee machine.

Chapter 50

Wyn and Jane opened every kitchen cupboard and then searched each bedroom before returning to the living room where I was standing with Lydia, staring out over the Bristol Channel. Wyn had a sheaf of papers that he thrust in my direction. I read the details of the job offer from a law firm in New York.

'Looks like she's doing a runner,' Wyn said.

I found my mobile immediately and organised a full alert, airports, seaports and formal notification to all other police forces in the country. Jane stood by Wyn's side clutching a pair of Doc Marten lace-up boots. It looked a perfect match to the boots I'd seen on the CCTV coverage of the anonymous hooded pedestrian hurrying away from the Royal Bell.

Frantically I tried to think where Charlotte Parkinson might be.

I rang Cornock. The telephone rang out a couple of times before he answered and the delay didn't help my impatience. 'She's gone, sir.'

There was a sound like a fist colliding with a desktop. 'For Christ's sake. And we still haven't been able to find Greg Jones. We'll need to question Tracy.'

I fell over the right words. 'I don't know that that will help ... It might just ...'

'Get back to Queen Street. We need to work out where Charlotte has gone.'

I finished the call and turned to look out over the balcony. It was a clear warm late spring day. People don't just disappear; you need travel documents, and a passport.

Lydia had been uncharacteristically quiet by my side as we drove back into the city. She looked pale but I could guess that she wanted to see this through to the end as much as I did. Superintendent Cornock was waiting for us in the Incident Room. He stood, hands folded and a dark intense look in his eyes.

'We've still not been able to trace Greg Jones.'

Lydia relaxed into a chair and heaved a sigh. She was looking more tired by the minute.

'Tracy Jones is in one of the conference rooms,' Cornock said.

I blinked and then sensed several pairs of eyes all staring at me. I wanted to smooth down the hairs standing to attention on the back of my neck. Clearing my throat didn't break the awkward silence so I turned to Lydia. 'Let's go and talk to her.'

Tracy looked at me through dejected and confused eyes when we entered. The uniformed officer assigned to sit with her left to organise coffees.

'Why am I here, John?'

I pulled a chair from beneath the table and sat down alongside Lydia who spoke first.

'We need to find Greg.' Underneath the sincerity was a steely determination.

Tracy glanced over at me. Then back to Lydia. 'I haven't seen him for a few days.'

'Do you know where he is staying?'

'Isn't he at his flat?'

Lydia shook her head. Although I was pleased that Lydia had spoken first I had to say something. 'We've been there to look for him and his neighbours haven't seen him.'

Tracy frowned and gave me another confused stare.

I continued. 'It is really important that we find him. Do you know where he might be? Do you know any of his friends? People he might stay with?'

'I really don't … I didn't talk much about …'

I leant forward over the table. 'Did he talk about any

girlfriends?'

The officer returned with mugs of coffee. Tracy stared down at the steaming liquid. 'He never mentioned anyone.'

I glanced at Lydia who nodded an encouragement for me to ask about Charlotte.

'We've had some information that he had a relationship with a Charlotte Parkinson when he was at Bristol University. Have you ever heard of her?'

Tracy let her head droop. 'I knew there was somebody in university but he never spoke about ... He could be odd like that.'

Tracy looked up at me. I wanted so much for this not to be happening to her. We spent an hour asking her about her brother and her frustration only heightened my anger that he had dragged her into the case. The excitement of our relationship had been lost somehow and I doubted we would ever get it back.

I left Tracy sipping on her coffee, her eyes distant.

I walked back to the Incident Room with Lydia. We said nothing.

'Do we still need officers at those huts in the Vale?' Lydia said as we stood by the board.

It was dusk now and from outside the windows I could see the evening drawing in. I had to accept that Greg wasn't going back to the Vale. It was a waste of valuable resources having officers there who could be out looking for Greg and Charlotte.

'Greg must have spotted the cars as he left and realised what had happened. It ruined their final plans.'

I turned to her. 'Final plans?'

'Yes. If you're right then Greg and Charlotte were going to implicate Henson in my death.'

The murder of Dolman and Turner and Harper had

been arranged like a military campaign. And they were all linked to the electrification contract. Plans. Final plans. It meant that all the loose ends needed to be tied up. All those responsible for Frost Enterprises collapsing being punished. I stepped towards the board. There was some other part of Charlotte's plans I hadn't seen.

'Harding,' I said aloud.

I turned to look at the team. It earned me puzzled looks.

'No, of course,' I said, turning to stare at the faces on the board. 'There was Dolman and Turner, who made things happen, and Harper who coordinated all the legal work.' It had been three weeks since I had read the preliminary reports about the publicity surrounding the contract. After the Welsh government had settled its differences with the United Kingdom government things had proceeded smoothly. Then I remembered that the award of the contract had been coordinated in Cardiff. I had spoken with the civil servant involved but I couldn't remember his name.

'Call him, call him now!' I shouted at Lydia.

She gave me a puzzled frown. 'What are you talking about?'

'That civil servant I spoke to right at the beginning – Dr something.' I bellowed in frustration. 'Dr fucking … something … Owen … Vincent Owen. He was involved in awarding the contract.'

I reached for the mobile in my jacket and wasted valuable seconds searching for the number. Eventually a receptionist in the government offices answered.

'The offices are closed. I'm sorry.'

'I need the contact details for Dr Vincent Owen.' I slowed my voice. 'His life may depend on it.'

'I don't think—'

'Now!'

The voice dictated the name of another member of staff and then the line went dead. I tapped in the number and waited. This time, trying to calm my nerves. The civil servant at the end of the second telephone call listened courteously as I explained what I needed.

'This is all a bit unusual,' he said.

'Do you have the number?'

I held my breath as I heard the clicking of a mouse.

'Do you have a pen?'

I reached for some paper and jotted down the number.

A woman's voice answered after half a dozen rings. She sounded breathless.

'Mrs Owen?'

'Who is this?'

I let out a long slow breath. 'I want to speak to your husband Dr Vincent Owen.'

'I was expecting him home several hours ago. I don't know where he is. We were supposed to be going out this evening. He was playing golf this afternoon and he should have finished by now.' Now there was a worried edge to her voice. 'Is there anything wrong? Why do you need to speak to Vincent?'

'Stay where you are. We'll be there as soon as we can.'

An hour later we left a family liaison officer with an increasingly hysterical Barbara Owen. Uniformed officers had already tracked down Vincent Owen's playing partners who confirmed that he had left the golf course mid-afternoon.

We sat in the car outside the Owen home watching

cars pass us in the small village near Caerphilly. If Charlotte and Greg were holding Vincent Owen they'd be trying to pin the blame on Henson. And if Greg hadn't seen the cars it was possible they still believed Lydia was a captive. I rang the officers sitting in the Nissen huts but there had been no sign of anyone. I wondered whether Greg would be taking Owen back there, unless he had been killed already.

Killed already.

I drove while dictating instructions for Lydia and then turned the car towards the units in the Vale. She called Wyn and Jane and we reached the units at the same time and parked our cars in a secluded spot.

The workshops had closed for the day and the few staff that milled around barely gave us a second glance. I walked round casually to the unit at the back. One of the officers opened the door wide enough for me to enter. I explained the position and then I got back to my car and waited.

Time dragged. I looked at my watch regularly. The prospect that Owen was dead, a stiletto through the heart, became more acute with every passing minute. And my backside was numb and the bottom of my back sore.

Moonlight broke through the clouds and splattered the surrounding trees with a pale cream light. I spoke to Wyn and Jane and the two officers inside.

'What makes you think he'll be back?' Lydia said.

'He'll come back to check if you're still there.'

'And if he doesn't?'

'Then … I'm wrong and Owen is dead. And …'

A transit van slowed by the entrance to the units and my body tensed. Lydia moved in her seat. I leant forward trying to make out the driver but he drove away.

An hour passed before another white transit drew up outside the entrance and stopped. The engine was left running.

'Is that him?' Lydia whispered.

'Can't tell.'

I prayed that it was Greg and that Owen was alive.

The van reversed and I reached a hand for the door handle, ready to yank it open and then run. Slowly I put my hand back on the wheel and gripped it gently, my knuckles tense. Gradually the van reversed backwards towards the huts at the back.

Quietly I got out of the car with Lydia, and crept to the edge of the nearest building. It was still too dark to see the driver. Carefully he guided the van out of sight towards the unit where Lydia had been held. We ran down and then stopped abruptly when the engine was switched off. A door opened and I heard footsteps.

I heard the squeaking of the rear doors opening.

Jane joined us. Wyn covering the exit near the road.

'Let's go,' I said.

I rushed forward. Greg was inside the van. He looked surprised to see us and then he dived at me, knocking me off my feet before careering down the muddy track. Jane was only a few feet behind him; she launched herself into a rugby tackle, and they both fell onto the soft earth.

Chapter 51

I splashed water all over my face in the bathroom at Queen Street before staring at the tired face in the mirror. It was nearly midnight and I had already delayed the interview with Greg Jones longer than I should have done. Greg had nothing on him to suggest where he had been and forensics were taking the van apart for any trace of Vincent Owen. All I had to do was extract a confession from Greg with information that would lead us to Charlotte and Vincent Owen.

I walked back to the Incident Room and nodded at Lydia. 'Ready.'

She managed a smile and we found our way to the custody suite. The night shift was well under way. A drunk banged on the door of his cell and another was singing 'A Bridge Over Troubled Waters' loudly. The custody sergeant, a bluff man with a wide jaw and a narrow mouth, glanced over at me as I reached his desk.

'Howdy, John. You here to interview Greg Jones? His lawyer has just arrived.'

We had only sat down in the interview room for a few seconds when Greg entered with his lawyer. Lydia recognised him. 'Hi, Stuart.'

'Lydia.'

I held out a hand. 'DI Marco.'

We shook. He nodded an acknowledgement. 'I'm sure you're familiar with the PACE regulations about allowing a suspect to be interviewed after proper rest.' He made an exaggerated gesture of looking at his watch. 'And it is now—'

I was ready for this sort of lame excuse to delay the investigation. 'As the senior investigating officer I have decided to conduct this interview now. And depending on your client's replies I may hold further interviews during the night. If you don't like that, *Stuart*, then you can complain or you can leave. But we'll carry on with the interviews.'

Stuart pouted and sat down next to Greg and we got started.

'You're under arrest for the abduction of Detective Sergeant Flint.'

Stuart piped up. 'Look, you cannot interview Greg about the abduction of Sergeant Flint with her present.'

Mentally I should have counted to ten. But I didn't. 'Shut up, Stuart. This is my interview.'

'What's your association with Charlotte Parkinson?'

Greg grinned.

'We know that you were at Bristol University together. We believe that she was responsible for the deaths of Matthew Dolman, Alan Turner and Tony Harper. You were responsible for the abduction of Detective Sergeant Flint.' Stuart groaned. 'And at the moment your van is being taken apart by forensics. So if there is any link to either of these three men we will charge you with their murders too.'

I saw Greg blink and then he tipped his head and leant towards me.

'Are you going to make any reply?'

He just blinked some more.

'We have reason to believe that Charlotte and you abducted a Dr Vincent Owen earlier today.'

'Who the hell is that?' Stuart said.

I ignored him.

I glanced over at Lydia and she saw the prompt in my eyes. 'Greg, this is important. Do you realise that being involved with Charlotte in the abduction and death of Dr Owen would make you jointly responsible with her?'

He frowned now. My blood pressure rose. He knew

where they were. I interjected. 'He's an innocent man and you're going to condemn him to die.'

'None of them were innocent.' He snapped so suddenly it caught me and Lydia unawares and we stopped and gazed at him for a few seconds.

'What do you mean?' Lydia said.

Greg settled back into an emotionless grin.

'Where is Charlotte?'

This time he didn't even move in his chair.

And for the next hour Lydia and I alternated asking the same question in different ways. Whenever Stuart tried to interrupt, I ignored him or told him that the interests of justice demanded that I conduct the interview exactly how I pleased.

Occasionally Greg raised an eyebrow and then he played with his fingers and sometimes he would give us a quizzical look as though we were poor pathetic people that had to be pitied. I wanted to grab him and shake him.

I had sent Lydia home at two o'clock in the morning when her yawning became so frequent she could barely speak and her complexion was the colour of ten-year-old magnolia paint. I sat with Wyn and Jane in the Incident Room wondering what I had overlooked. There had to be something. Then just before three, when my eyelids felt heavy, I left with Wyn and Jane trailing gratefully behind me.

I fell exhausted onto my bed without taking off my clothes. I was in exactly the same position three hours later when the telephone rang. I was convinced that I was back in the Incident Room staring at Greg's mobile, deliberating whether I should answer the number.

I turned over, grabbed the mobile from my trouser

pocket, and fumbled to find the right button. It was area control. 'There's a report of your suspect being seen driving north on the A470 half an hour ago. Small black Ford Focus.'

'Half an hour ago! Why the bloody hell wasn't I called.'

'I've just had the call, sir. An unmarked patrol car spotted a woman answering her description but he couldn't follow because he was called to a fatality on the motorway.' She rang off and I hurried out of the apartment.

Why the hell was Charlotte going north on the A470? There had to be something significant we were missing. And then, with a sudden blinding clarity, I knew exactly what it was.

Chapter 52

I reached the M4 at the outskirts of Cardiff as I finished dictating instructions for the armed response unit. I powered the car along the curving sections of the dual carriageway as it followed the contours of the A470 north. Traffic was light, the occasional white van and some early commuters. Soon I hurtled past the sign for Pontypridd. My mobile rang on the passenger seat and I reached for it, keeping one hand on the wheel.

'Sergeant Pearson. ARU. We are just leaving headquarters now. We'll be five minutes behind you. Maybe less.'

I could imagine the speed the ARU's specially adapted BMW Series 5 vehicles could make on the clear open road. At eighty miles an hour my Mondeo was rattling its disapproval.

'Are you certain about the location?'

I hesitated. It was a guess to assume that Charlotte's final act of revenge would be to take Owen to the Cefn Coed Viaduct. He was the last of the men responsible for her father's death, her mother losing her home and her stroke. I could see how Charlotte might blame them all. I recalled the press articles when Malcolm Frost had thrown himself off the viaduct so it made sense to think that a sad mind would want her final act of vengeance to have some significance for her father.

'Trust me. It makes sense.'

'Okay. When you get there keep your earpiece on all the time.'

Abruptly the call ended. I flattened the accelerator and swung the car through the long bends of the road. Soon I was approaching the roundabout where the Heads of The Valleys road meets the A470 and I glanced over to my right.

The viaduct snaked over the valley in a majestic curve. I craned to see if there was any sign of Charlotte. But I had to brake and the tyres squealed; I almost lost control of the car as it lurched through the roundabout.

I negotiated the side streets of Merthyr Tydfil by flashing my lights and sounding the horn until I pulled up near a rugby club where I discarded the car. My pulse quickened as I saw a black Focus parked near the Station Hotel. Quickly I scanned the surroundings hoping I might spot Charlotte. Then I ran. At the same time I fumbled for the earpiece for my mobile and rang Pearson.

'We should be there in two minutes. Any sign?'

'Her car is here. She can't be far ...'

I was onto the viaduct now and gasping for breath. It was deserted – no early-morning joggers or dog-walkers. I kept to the right hoping it would give me more of an outlook over the curve. I stumbled over the gravel realising that the wall at the edge was low enough to climb over easily.

I was almost onto the middle when I saw them.

Charlotte and Vincent Owen. His hands had been tied behind his back and she dragged him along until she pushed him against the sidewall. He collapsed onto his knees but she pulled him back onto his feet.

I got closer and shouted. 'Charlotte!'

Suddenly she turned and glared at me.

'How ...?'

I could read her face now and saw the surprise.

'Don't get any closer.' She pulled Owen nearer to her. He looked tired, his clothes dishevelled.

'Don't do this, Charlotte.'

'What? Do you think you can talk me out of this? Don't insult my intelligence Detective Inspector Marco. We both know how this will end.'

A voice crackled in my earphone. 'My team is in place.'

'Don't be absurd, Charlotte. There is no need to harm Vincent Owen.'

Now she spat out her reply. 'No need?! No need?! This man is a murderer. He killed my whole family while you did nothing about it.' She pulled Owen nearer to her and then cast a glance over the side. She shuffled backwards, grasping her hand around his neck. Then she produced a knife that glinted in the early-morning sunshine.

'Target has knife, Inspector. That puts an innocent life in danger.' The voice crackled in my ear. 'As soon as we have a clear shot I shall give the order.'

'Charlotte. Stop this. Killing another person won't help.'

'Justice. That's what it means. For everyone. Vincent Owen will have atoned for his sins and there will justice for my father and mother.'

'Step two paces to your right, Inspector.' The voice was calm and measured in my ear. I did as I was told.

'Don't get any nearer, Marco. Stay right there.' Charlotte scrambled to push Owen to the top of the retaining wall. She fumbled with his legs, pushed him until he was half lying on the wall.

'This isn't what your father would have wanted. And what about your mother? What will she think?'

She turned towards me. 'How dare you talk about my father. He was a good decent man. Not like this piece of shit. And my mother. Don't ever—'

Then a single shot rang out and I watched as Charlotte's body twisted itself into a curving motion. Her head tilted away and then her body fell onto the chippings and dirt.

I ran over and dragged Owen off the wall just as I

heard the screams and shouts hurrying towards me.

Chapter 53

The next few days passed in a blur of activity. A preliminary examination of a laptop we had recovered in Mrs Parkinson's room in the Sundown Nursing Home had discovered a powerful software application capable of producing high-quality videos. More importantly, Charlotte's fingerprints were all over the machine. A report from the Metropolitan Police had arrived in my inbox that clearly linked the firm where Charlotte had worked in London to all the companies that paid bribes to Dolman, Turner and Harper. And Vincent Owen's confession when he was interviewed completed the evidence we needed.

I spent Saturday with Dean and we watched the highlights of the Cardiff City game in Bristol. The trouble at one of the pubs earned a brief mention on the news and I saw Dave Hobbs preening himself alongside a superintendent from Bristol who boasted of an inter-force working relationship achieving major arrests and thwarting hooliganism.

Jackie and I finalised the plans for the impending Easter weekend break. She complained that I slept too much over the weekend but once I relaxed, my body had simply switched off. I noticed the occasional long glance and warm smile. But for now I was happy just to get back to being a dad again.

I sat at my desk looking at the pair of Doc Marten boots carefully deposited in the evidence bag. Lydia and I had just watched the CCTV coverage from the street behind the Royal Bell car park and the person on the screen wore a similar pair. It had to be Charlotte. We could see it now.

'Why do you think she kept them, boss?'

I shrugged. 'There were expensive.'

It had taken us hours of interviews with the lawyers

and staff at Harper's law firm to piece together Charlotte's movements on the morning that Harper was killed. By the end we realised she had opportunity enough to kill him. And we found the number she used to call Greg on Turner's mobile on the night he was killed. He had been expecting her, which explained the open bottle of wine.

I finished the last of my coffee and turned to Lydia. 'Ready?'

She nodded and we headed out of Queen Street.

At the university hospital we walked through to the ward where Charlotte had been kept in isolation from the day she was admitted. I entered the private room that operational support had adapted as a makeshift interview room. Charlotte was sitting in bed, her arm held in a sling. I looked over at her and recalled the ARU team leader assuring me in clinical terms that only Vincent Owen moving his position had meant that the intended head shot had been unsuccessful.

The make-up had gone. Her lips were rather thin without lipstick and her skin looked blotchy now. Her blond hair, pulled back behind her ears, needed brushing. But there was still that steely grit in her eyes.

I looked at Lydia who nodded back.

'Are you ready to start?' I said to Charlotte.

Her lawyer answered. 'Yes.'

I pressed the record button on the machine and the cassette spools started turning.

'Do you know why you have been arrested?'

Charlotte reached for the beaker of water and took a minuscule sip.

I waited.

She said nothing. And I continued with the interview for another hour and half, changing tapes when the first were full.

She said nothing. Absolutely nothing. By the end, I looked into her eyes.

Her mind was resolved.

There had been closure for her.

Chapter 54

I drew a finger over Tracy's shoulder and then down to the tattoo she had on the small of her back. She had another, a small butterfly directly opposite on the other side of her body that had taken my attention last night. She stirred. Her skin was warm and she adjusted her position. It was still early so I moved closer to her, shared the rhythm of her breathing.

Easter had been the previous weekend, which I had spent with Dean and my parents in their caravan in Tenby. My parents had filled the freezer with his favourite food. We had gone fishing and on boat trips and it made me realise that I didn't want to waste more time not being a proper dad. He had smiled broadly when I told him I had booked a holiday over the summer in Lucca for him to meet some of the Italian family.

Last night Tracy had told me of her parents' stoicism when she had broken the news about Greg. However, it had been something they had expected and in a sense were prepared for it. She had wanted to know what was going to happen to Greg and all I could tell her was that the Crown Prosecution Service would decide.

A child cried somewhere in the building, the morning sunshine streamed through the blinds and I had a court hearing to attend so I slipped out of bed and headed for the kitchen. The news on the television no longer had regular reports and analysis of the anti-banking videos. The financial crisis in Russia was making the headlines. And Cardiff City were likely to be in the Championship play-offs again, which lifted my spirits. After a shower, I went back into the bedroom and pulled my best suit from the wardrobe. I heard Tracy stirring behind me. I reached for a white shirt and a red striped tie.

'That navy tie would be more suitable for court,' Tracy said, propping herself up on two pillows.

I turned and smiled at her. 'Good morning.'

'Let me know what happens.'

'Of course.'

I ran a brush through my hair and leant over to kiss her on the lips. She curled a hand around my face; I pulled her close.

'I'll call you later.' I turned and left.

I went straight to my scheduled meeting with Superintendent Cornock. His door was open and I gave it a brief tap but I didn't wait for an invitation. His skin had that unhealthy pallor that men sitting behind a desk develop, together with folds around their jaw that sag into pouches. Not even the warm spring sunshine coming through the windows and the smell of air freshener could make him look healthy.

'Have you heard about the National Bank of Wales?'

He nudged a newspaper folded at the financial pages over the desk at me. I noticed the smiling faces of Mrs Dolman and the man I had seen in the Vale of Glamorgan Racquets Club. He was a senior vice president for a German bank that was buying the NBW.

'Apparently Troy Dolman is moving to New York. He's going to work for one of those fancy hedge funds although Rex is staying put.'

I mumbled an acknowledgement as I scanned the headlines.

'Ready for court, John?'

'Yes, sir. Have the prosecutors decided about Greg Jones?'

He sat back in his chair. 'They'll tell you at court but it's likely they'll drop the charges of conspiracy to murder and just continue with the abduction charge. They'll take account of his admission to being the second person in the videos.'

I wanted to call Tracy immediately but I knew I had to wait. Even so, I could feel the relief.

'He's still looking at a long stretch in jail but with his mental state and a lenient judge ... Well, he might get lucky.'

I nodded.

'And, John, well done.'

I left Cornock to turn his attention to the pile of paperwork on his desk. Outside I stuck a cigarette between my lips and then sparked my zippo into life. It was my first of the day – later than usual. Then I draped my jacket over one shoulder and headed for the Crown Court building.

It was one of the cluster of civic buildings erected over a hundred years ago in the middle of the city. The tiles glistened and the smell of floor polish hung in the air. Barristers in legal gowns and wigs thronged around the waiting area. Terry stood in one corner deep in conversation with three lawyers and he kept staring at the barrister who was clutching his wig in one hand and jabbing a finger excitedly at him. I had made two telephone calls before the weekend. The first was to the sergeant that I knew who was handling the prosecution of Terry's girlfriend. He had moaned that I was interfering with the cause of natural justice and that I really should know better and that even if he did get the charge watered down the judge could still send her to jail.

I stopped by a list pinned to the board and spotted the name of Terry's girlfriend – she was in Court 1 before Judge Patricks who had been the second person I'd called last week. I had to hope that natural justice would, indeed, prevail.

I looked through the window of the heavy wooden

doors and saw Lydia sitting on one of the benches. Her hair was clean and pulled back neatly behind her ears. There was colour in her cheeks. Inside the large vaulted courtroom, the air conditioning hummed in the background. I slipped into the bench and sat next to her.

'Inspector Hobbs was here earlier. He hoped he might catch up with you.'

The public gallery filled as did the benches reserved for the press. Even though it was a remand hearing when nothing much was going to happen, the press would give the case maximum coverage. Soon there was activity from the dock and Charlotte emerged from the cells below. She gave me a defiant look. Then a prison officer preceded Greg.

When the judge entered everyone stood and the hearing started. Journalists were scribbling frantically and some in the public gallery leant forward wanting to hear every word. When the judge asked if either defendant wanted to enter a plea the lawyers made various excuses that they hadn't had all the papers from the prosecution and that it was far too early. The hearing was over quickly and we trooped out into the lobby.

I heard a voice behind me calling my name and saw Terry sitting in a small alcove. He jerked his head as an invitation for me to join him. 'Thanks, Marco.'

'I didn't do anything.'

'Of course you didn't. Doreen got a suspended sentence. Bloody brilliant result. She'll be released in an hour. I owe you.'

I thought I saw a tear in his eye.

I made for the main lobby, collecting Lydia on the way. Dave Hobbs stood with Assistant Chief Constable Neary. She was in full uniform and her hair had a newly washed sheen. She wore the faintest hint of blusher but no lipstick. I knew nothing about her and wondered if there was a Mr Neary. She was deep in conversation with Hobbs who was nodding and giving her his most obsequious face.

'Good morning, John,' the ACC said. 'I was just talking about you with Dave.'

A pained expression creased Hobbs's face.

'Your use of intelligence sources was exemplary. Sometimes you need to go with your instinct and trust your gut.'

'Yes, of course, ma'am,' I said.

She grabbed my arm and led me away from Hobbs. I left Lydia talking to him but I could sense that he had one ear straining to hear our conversation.

'Have you thought about considering the possibility of seeking a chief inspector promotion?'

'Not really, ma'am.' I glanced over at Hobbs. From the shock on his face, I could tell he had heard.

'Then you *should* do so.'

And with that she trooped off.

I made for the entrance and found the cigarettes in my pocket. Dave Hobbs had caught up with the ACC but even from a distance, I could tell he was trying her patience.

Lydia stood by my side. We stood for a moment looking at the television cameras and journalists milling outside on the tarmac. It was a bright spring morning.

'Did you see that interview with Henson on the news last night?' Lydia said.

I shook my head.

'Apparently there's going to be a documentary.'

'Really?'

'Fancy a coffee, boss?'

We walked away from the Crown Court towards Queen Street and stopped by a stall in Gorsedd Gardens. I had double espresso and we sat talking in the morning sunshine.

Made in the USA
Las Vegas, NV
10 November 2020

10687285R00188